Moon Water

A Novel

Pam Webber

SHE WRITES PRESS

Published August 2019
Printed in the United States of America
Print ISBN: 978-1-63152-675-6
E-ISBN: 978-1-63152-676-3
Library of Congress Control Number: 2019938182

For information, address:
She Writes Press
1569 Solano Ave #546
Berkeley, CA 94707

Interior design by Tabitha Lahr

She Writes Press is a division of SparkPoint Studio, LLC.

Moon Water is dedicated to my family, past, present, and future. They are the inspiration and motivation for the storytelling.

Preface

Nibi pulled her shawl tight against the midnight chill. The unearthly call of the weathered dreamcatcher had beckoned her from a sound sleep. Studying the portal in the center of the web, she understood why. A human darkness lurked among the shadows, waiting patiently for a chance to hurt the woman-child she loved.

"Not this night." Eyes skyward, Nibi raised her hands and chanted an ancient Monacan prayer. High, swirling winds caught the plea and carried it toward the moonlit peaks to the south.

Gazing into the portal again, Nibi shivered, but not because of the cold. Another darkness loomed at the edge of her sight, lifeless yet more powerful than any she'd ever known. This darkness would not be stopped as easily, if at all. Either way, the price they'd pay would be dear.

Stepping to the edge of the porch, Nibi studied the sleeping valley below. She closed her eyes and appealed to the wisdom of those who had come before. In the wee hours of the morning, she had an answer. Some things must end for others to begin.

Chapter 1

Central Virginia, Summer 1969

Velvety moss cushioned Nettie's back as she enjoyed the soft, meandering sounds of the Piney River and the sweet smell of blooming honeysuckle. The small glade had been a perfect hideaway for her and Andy since grade school. The smooth, tangled roots of the old riverbank trees made comfortable benches, and their long, arching limbs provided a shady respite. Coupled with the eventide, the glade's thick forest walls and leafy canopy still offered them secrecy.

Andy's strong arm under her head and his hand on the curve of her hip were warm, comforting. Not long ago, Nettie would have punched any boy who tried to put his hands on her like this, but not now, and not Andy. They'd been exploring the rhythms of this almost-dance at River's Rest since the weather turned, enjoying togetherness yet managing to stop on the good side of bad. Tonight, things were different. She and Andy were touching but miles apart. Nettie knew why, but wasn't ready to have that conversation. Brushing her fingertips along his jawline, she opened her lips to kiss him just as the wind began to blow. The layered treetop canopy pitched back and forth, slowly at first, then harder and faster, whipping leaves and surrounding them with eerie shadows. Nettie couldn't tell her goose bumps from Andy's.

"Storm coming?" she asked.

Andy pushed to his knees and scanned the moon-colored riverbank. "Maybe. It doesn't feel like rain, but something's off." Sitting back on his heels, he pulled Nettie up. "Come on. We should go."

"But—"

"I know. We should go."

Nettie flushed as she tucked in her blouse.

Getting in the car, she slid to her usual position in the middle of the seat and lightly bumped Andy's shoulder. "You said you wanted to come here tonight."

"I thought I did." He hesitated, gold specks flickering in his warm but troubled eyes. "Do you love me?"

Nettie slumped. Ready or not, the conversation had started. Words—right, wrong, and in between—surged behind her eyes, but not one made it to her mouth.

"You know I love you, but you've never said it back to me. Not once."

Most of the time, it wasn't in Nettie to be anything other than straight-up, a trait that had cost her plenty in the past and most likely would again. She cared about Andy, enjoyed his company and his touch. She couldn't imagine life without him, but the idea of forever love unnerved her—what it was supposed to feel like, the commitments that came with it, what it would mean for both of them. "I don't know."

Andy tensed and leaned against the car door. "What about the guy you met last summer—Mitchell? Did you love him?"

The memory of Mitchell stung as badly as the pain and jealousy in Andy's voice. She and Andy had grown up best friends, but since they'd started high school he'd made no secret about wanting more; he'd even asked her to go steady the previous summer, before she'd left on vacation. Nettie hadn't been interested in a boyfriend then, much less a steady one; however, spending the summer in the Alabama Wiregrass had changed all that. She'd met Mitchell, a handsome, troubled teen who knew better than anyone what love was and was not. By the time she'd returned to Virginia, her perspective on love and relationships had changed.

"We've been through this, Andy. I cared about Mitchell. He helped me figure out a lot of things: growing up, some of the boy-girl stuff, and how to choose to be happy even when you have no reason to be. But that's not forever love. I don't know what that kind of love is. I want to know what it means before I say the words."

Andy's jaw tightened as he turned away.

Nettie didn't bother to hide the frustration in her voice. "How do you know—I mean, *really* know—you love me like that? Forever is a long damn time when we're barely thinking past tomorrow. You already know what you want to do and who you want to be. A year from now, you'll be off to West Point, just like your father, and I'll still be here, trying to figure out the rest of my life."

Andy found Nettie's hand in the dark. "Look, all I know is that I've loved you since the day we met in the sandbox. I can't imagine life without you. I don't want to imagine it without you."

"I'm not ready."

His voice softened as he let go of her hand. "You've always moved slower than me when it comes to us, but it's tough being with you when you don't know how you feel. I love you. I need to know you love me too. If you're not sure, maybe we need to take a break until you know one way or the other."

The tangerine sunset nested in the deepest draw of the rolling Blue Ridge as Nettie made her way to the center of Allen's Hill. The field always welcomed her, its soft, flitting sounds better than quiet. Tall grass and feathery Queen Anne's lace tickled her outstretched arms.

The hill's long slope and its distance from the Upper Road and Lower Road made it unlikely anyone would see her, and if they did, she'd just be a someone. That was, except for spooky old Alise Allen, the wispy silhouette in the Palladian window of the mansion at the top of the hill. Always watching, never acknowledging, she allowed Nettie to come and go on the hill as she pleased.

Reaching her favorite thinking spot, Nettie burrowed through the stalks to lie among the silky new shoots. A few timid stars sparked above her, leading the way for thousands of more robust ones. Their slow, kaleidoscopic slide across the sky helped settle her jumbled thoughts.

Except for glimpses at school, she hadn't seen Andy since their standoff at River's Rest the week before, and her world wasn't right. Word of their breakup had gotten around, giving the gossips reason to twitter a little more loudly when she passed. Thankfully, this troublesome scrutiny by the curious, the sad, and the happy would end with the start of summer vacation in a few days.

With barely a rustle, tawny, moon-tinted legs slid into the grass next to Nettie. "There you are."

Win, Nettie's best friend and neighbor, could move so quietly that birds and butterflies stayed put as she passed. Her ability to be in the world and not on it came from her grandmother Nibi, a full-blooded Monacan Indian.

"You were supposed to meet me at the Tastee Freez after school, remember?"

Nettie pushed up on her elbows. "Sorry, I forgot. I'm having a hard time keeping my head straight. All I think about is Andy. I haven't talked with him all week. He won't look at me at school. I don't know what to do. I know why he said he wanted to break up, but I'm beginning to wonder if there's someone else."

"You know that's not true, right? There's room for only one girl in Andrew Stephen Stockton's heart, and he set his sights on her a long time ago."

"I thought I did, but now I'm not so sure. You know Anne

Johnson started working at her grandfather's hardware store right after Andy did."

Nettie and Anne had barely tolerated each other since grade school. Nettie played shortstop, ran, jumped, climbed, and got as dirty and caused as much mischief as the boys. She had little tolerance for any girl who preferred hair bows, dressing up, and dolly tea parties.

"Working with her is not the same as dating her."

"True. But she's always stared at Andy like he's an ice cream cone she wants to lick. Plus, she's been smirking at me all week, as if she knows something."

"You sound jealous."

"Wouldn't you be?"

"Why don't you just ask him?"

"Because I don't know if I'm jealous for the right reason."

"Let me get this straight: You don't know if you want him, but you don't want anyone else to have him either, at least until you make up your mind?"

"Yes. No. Damn! I don't know. What if I'm making a mistake? What if I'm wrong about Anne? Worse yet, what if I'm right? What if I lose him before I figure it all out?"

"Then you'll deal with it."

"Right." Nettie sat up. "Like I don't already have enough to deal with. Mom and Dad are pushing me to make a decision about applying to colleges, especially Sweet Briar. Plus, I've got to meet with Pastor Williams about this baptism thing. I can't stall him much longer. Everyone else in the Girls' Auxiliary has already had their interview."

"Don't you want to be baptized?"

"Of course. But I've heard that some of the questions he's asking are not easy."

"Since when have you shied away from anything because it was hard? If the other GAs can answer his questions, you can."

"I know. But he and I have never gotten along very well."

"It's been over a year since you stopped pranking him. Maybe now is a good time to mend fences."

"And if it's not?"

"Remember what Nibi says: Trust fate. It will see you through the storm."

"Not if it drowns me first."

Win laughed and pulled Nettie to her feet. "Look, you need to think about something else for a while. Let's go to Oak's Landing tomorrow. Nibi has a project for us."

"What kind of project?"

"She didn't say, but it must be important."

"Why?"

"She wouldn't take no for an answer."

"Like we'd ever say no to her."

As they turned to leave, Win stepped sideways, pulling Nettie with her. "Don't move."

Nettie tensed as a long, slithery shadow glanced her foot, hell-bent on beating them to the bottom of the hill.

"Blast it, Win! You knew it was coming. You could've said something sooner!"

"What would you have done if I had? Gotten yourself bit?"

"Smart-ass."

"I only knew a few seconds before you did. Besides, it's just a black snake. If it had been one to worry about, I would have said so."

"You know I hate snakes," whined Nettie. "That's the first one I've seen on the hill in a long time. Wonder why the hawks and raccoons didn't run it off."

"Maybe one of them just did and we were in the way."

"Well, at least you knew it was coming. That's good."

"I don't know if it's a good thing or not. There's no rhyme or reason to what I see or know, or when, or why. I can't control it—the visions just come. It's scary."

"Have you talked with Nibi about it? I bet she went through the same thing when she was learning how to be a shaman."

"She said she felt the same way at my age and to be patient, that my ability to see and interpret the visions will improve over time."

"Well, if you happen to get a vision about Andy and me getting back together, let me know. On second thought, never mind. I'm confused enough."

"See, that's the hard part: knowing what to say when."

"I'm glad I'm not a shaman. Life's easier if you don't know what's coming."

"My point exactly."

"Look." Nettie nodded toward the far corner of the field, where the Lower Road intersected a long path leading to the back of the Allen mansion. A moonlit figure climbed steadily along the shadowed side. They'd seen the inky form before, always after dark and always from this vantage on the hill. At first, they'd been afraid; however, it hadn't taken long for fear to give way to curiosity. Over the years, they'd hidden at different spots along the path in hopes of discovering the nighttime visitor's identity, but whenever they got close enough to recognize a face, no one showed. "One of these days, we're going to find out who that is," Nettie whispered.

"Maybe it's good we don't know," Win said. "Sometimes it's best if shadow dwellers keep their secrets."

"But they have the best stories. We don't even know if it's a man or a woman."

"Either way, Mrs. Allen is getting company, which is good, since she's lived up there all by her lonesome for the last forty years. The only people around to keep her company are the housekeeper and the gardener."

"Why do you think he did it?" Nettie asked. "Her husband, I mean. Marry her, then leave her alone for a lifetime. Why do that to someone you promised to love forever?"

"I have no idea. Whatever the reason, all that aloneness is a high price to pay."

Nettie's thoughts turned to her last conversation with Andy. "Forever love gone bad."

"What?"

"Nothing. I'll meet you at the train station in the morning. A summer project with Nibi is just what I need."

Chapter 2

Climbing the steps to the traveler's platform of Amherst's turn-of-the-century train station, Nettie scanned the crowd for Piccolo, the station's custodian. "There he is, sweeping the other end."

She and Win threaded through the milling crowd of uniformed workers. "Hey, Pic."

"Mornin', girlies."

Giving them a contagious smile, Pic propped his broom in the corner. His clothes were clean but worn, shoes covered with work dust. Across his shoulder hung an ever-present leather bindle, a holdover from his rail-riding hobo days.

Nettie handed him a rolled-up brown grocery bag. "Momma sent you a picnic."

Pic settled on a bench and dug through the bag with his only hand. As the smell of fried chicken wafted up, a smile deepened his ruddy wrinkles and sparked his faded blue eyes. In days gone by, he would have been considered handsome. He devoured a drumstick, chewed off the ends, and put the remains in the bag. "I'll save the rest for lunch. Tell your momma I said thanks."

"Will do. She wanted to know if you'd check the kitchen faucet at the church after the potluck supper Wednesday night. It's got another slow drip. She put a bucket under it."

"Ever know me to miss one of those suppers? 'Course I will. You girls headed to Nibi's?"

Win pulled a couple of apples from her pockets and gave them to Pic. "Yes, sir. Any message?"

"Tell her I'm cleaning the station at Oak's Landing tomorrow, so I'll be up to see her after."

A short whistle blast from the station's oldest train, the *Weak and Weary*, announced its imminent departure for the thirty-minute ride north to the town of Oak's Landing in Nelson County. Regular as clockwork, that whistle kept folks moving better than a watch.

"Got to go, Pic. Maybe we'll see you on the way back."

Nettie and Win jumped from the platform and waved to the train's engineer, Mr. Roberts, who sat in the window of the idling locomotive. For as long as Nettie could remember, he'd made several trips a day carrying logs and shift workers to the pulp mill near Oak's Landing, returning to Amherst with thick fiber boards that other trains would deliver to paper mills up and down the East Coast.

"Hey, girls! We pull out in five. Tell Nibi I could use some more remedies when she has time."

Nibi kept Mr. Roberts supplied with ginger root for his arthritis, as well as feverfew for his wife's all-the-time headaches. Nettie and Win had couriered the cures back and forth for years, so he let them ride the train to see Nibi whenever they wanted.

"Yes, sir!"

Running past a couple of passenger coaches and flatcars stacked with tree trunks that smelled of old earth and sap, they climbed the steps of the cozy, washed-out red caboose and settled at the top, spring too present to sit inside.

Nettie and Win swayed with the *Weak and Weary* as it trundled up the peaks that divided Amherst and Nelson Counties. An artist's palette of pink dogwoods, white laurel, an bursts of cherry-colored somethings blurred against the new greens and old browns of the mountains as they rounded the summit and rolled down into Rockfish Valley.

As the train sloped onto the valley floor, the Tye River dominated the view, its water sparkling and lazy after its four-thousand-foot journey out of the mountains.

"River's up," said Win.

"It rained here. Look at the puddles."

One long whistle blast followed by a short burst announced the train's approach to the Oak's Landing station. On the left, rolling, asymmetrical foothills flanked the small town. On the right, dozens of majestic oaks separated the town from a wide bend in the Tye.

When the train stopped, Nettie and Win skirted the bustling railyard and headed to Main Street along the crushed-stone river walk the community had built decades earlier. Shaded by the oaks' interlaced canopies, they walked under the arched wrought-iron entrance to the town's park. Passing benches, Adirondack chairs, picnic tables, a playground, and ropes long enough to drop swimmers into the river, they stopped in front of the park's grand gazebo where ladies were scurrying up and down ladders, trying to measure, cut, and hang uncooperative streamers.

Win stood up on her toes and twirled. "Friday-night dances must be starting. We should come to a couple this summer."

Nettie reached for the missing necklace that used to hold Andy's class ring. He'd given it to her at a dance the previous fall. She'd given it back to him at River's Rest.

"Still haven't heard from him?"

"Not a word."

"Maybe you should call or, better yet, go see him."

"He broke up with me, remember?"

"He loves you, remember? You two started as friends. Maybe you could be again."

Nettie shook her head. "That walk doesn't go backward."

Bells jingled as Nettie and Win entered the Candy Store, one of the few businesses in town that had air-conditioning. Mrs. Loving eased around the counter; her size equaled her generosity. A childhood friend of Nibi's, she lived farther upriver, on the valley side.

"Hey, girls. It's good to see you. There's some fresh rock candy in the sample box. Cinnamon and apple today. Help yourself while I get Nibi's peppermints."

"Thanks, Mrs. L."

Nettie popped a piece of the red crystal candy into her mouth, rolled it around, and quickly spat it out. "Damn! That's hot." When repeated swallowing didn't stop the burn, she wiped her tongue on a napkin, then on the hem of her shirt, but the pain still escalated. Eyes watering, she gobbled a piece of fudge, which did little to relieve the scorching.

"Here you go, girls. Give my best to Nibi and tell her the echinacea worked great. My cold is all gone. Goodness, Nettie, what's wrong? Why's your face all red? Do you need a tissue?"

Without answering, Nettie flew out the door and across the street to Huffman's General Store. Stuffing a quarter into the Coca-Cola machine, she smacked the give-it-to-me button. "C'mon. C'mon." When the machine finally surrendered a bottle, she popped the cap and gulped. Blessing its coldness, she kept the last swallow in her puffed-out cheeks, hoping the carbonation would wash away the remaining embers. Sinking onto a nearby bench, she belched painful bubbles. "Holy hell! That stuff should be illegal."

A boy's laughter pierced the pulsing in her head. Perched on the same bicycle in front of the store were the two lookalike sons of Jim Warren, owner of the Farm Supply Store. They made deliveries for him all over the valley. Wade, the older of the two, had had a crush on Nettie for a while and stayed close whenever he saw her in town.

Skip, the younger, pointed and continued to laugh while Wade stared at Nettie, mouth wide open.

"If you two think this is funny, you should go see Mrs. Loving. She has some rock candy you should try."

Skip stuck out a bright red tongue. "We already did. Gotcha!"

Nettie looked at his brother. "Wade Warren, what did you do?"

Wade's face glowed as red as his brother's tongue. "Uh, we, uh—"

Skip piped in. "We got our candy before we put cayenne pepper on the rest."

"You did what?"

Wade rolled the bike closer. "Nettie, I'm really sorry. I didn't know you'd be here. We thought Albert Kenny and his buddies would get the candy."

Win came up behind him. "You two stay right here. I'm going to get Mrs. Loving."

With that, Wade took off down the street as Skip struggled to stay on the back, the bike chain rattling loudly.

"Can you believe that?" Win bought another Coke and handed it to Nettie. "We should tell their father."

Holding the icy bottle against her tortured tongue and flaming face, Nettie shook her head. "No, don't. They won't do it again."

"How do you know?"

"Didn't you see the look on Wade's face?"

Win opened Nibi's bag of peppermints and tasted one. "Well, at least they didn't pepper these. Mrs. L. will need to change out those samples of rock candy. I'll be right back."

Win returned from the candy store with an apology and a bag of chocolates. "Mrs. Loving said for us to stop by on the way home. She'll have some good rock candy for us by then. Those boys are going to get an earful the next time they're in her store."

Next, Nettie and Win headed to Carter's Drugstore, their last stop.

Two large ceiling fans kept the tepid air moving as they made their way down the center aisle toward the pharmacy counter. On one side were shelves lined with everyday products Nettie had seen advertised on television. On the other side were soaps, lotions, balms, and assorted remedies created and packaged by Mr. Dexter Carter and other folks living in the valley, including Nibi.

Nettie and Win waved to Alma Carter as she restocked the Beauty Corner with lipsticks, mascaras, eye shadows, and perfumes. "Hi, girls. Nice to see you." A naturally pretty woman, Mrs. Carter seemingly never wore makeup or used store-bought perfume. She always smelled fresh, like Nibi's lilac soap.

On the long pharmacy counter at the back of the store sat a turn-of-the-century cash register, a tap bell, and an open, three-ring notebook where folks could name their ailment and order custom remedies. Beyond the counter sat a marble-topped island with neatly placed measuring instruments, an old-fashioned balance scale, and different colored mortars and pestles. On the back wall were containers of different sizes, shapes, and colors. Some held liquids, others powders, and each had its own nameplate.

Win tapped the bell. Seconds later, Mr. Carter appeared, dressed in a light blue, raised-collared tunic, his round glasses perched precariously on the end of his nose. "Good morning, girls."

"Hey, Mr. Carter, do you have a list for Nibi?"

"As a matter of fact, I do." He rummaged behind the counter, found another notebook, and tore off the first page. "Tell her I'm out of foxglove and ginger, but she can take her time gathering the rest." Tucking the notebook back under the counter, he pulled $5 out of the cash register and handed it to Win. He did a double take at Nettie. "You're all flushed. What's wrong?"

After hearing the details of the red-pepper attack, Mr. Carter grabbed a tongue blade and peeked inside Nettie's mouth.

"I think we can put that fire out in short order."

Going to the island, he concocted a thick mouthwash that he had Nettie sip, swish, and swallow twice.

"Wow. The pain's gone. That stuff's magic."

"No," said Mr. Carter. "It's Nature. I made it from the same plant cayenne pepper comes from. One form of it causes pain; another relieves it."

Nettie grimaced. *Figures. Just like love.*

Chapter 3

Despite the early hour, shallow waves of heat radiated from the bright concrete as Nettie and Win crossed the new Route 56 bridge. Halfway across, they leaned over the railing to catch the coolness of the Tye's burbling water.

"Between the cayenne pepper and this heat, I may end up in the river before the day's over. And it's barely June."

"Nibi said this summer would be hot. The crickets have been chirping really fast."

"One of these days, you two will have to tell me how they know."

Win laughed. "I don't know how they know. They just do."

Nettie tossed a stick into the gliding current of the upriver side of the bridge, then ran to the downriver side to watch it tumble out in the foamy white water careening away from the support columns. "It's amazing how some things float no matter what."

"If it's lighter than water, it's going to float. Science, remember?"

"It's still amazing."

Farther downriver, tethered in the shade amid the reeds, lily pads, and flitting bugs, jostled a three-seat fishing boat. The old man in it waved and held up an almost full stringer.

"Save a few for the rest of us, Mr. Stevens."

Giving them a thumbs up, the mayor went back to tending his line. A decade earlier, in that same fishing hole, he'd hooked the largest catfish ever caught in the Tye. He'd been trying to beat his record ever since.

Just past the bridge, Nettie and Win turned right onto a worn footpath and wove among boulders and trees, before turning to climb the trail up Buffalo Ridge Mountain. Nibi's homestead sat in a clearing halfway up. Built by her father and husband as a wedding present, Nibi had lived, loved, lost, and learned to live again in the dovetailed log cabin.

The sweet scent of apple wood reached Nettie before she saw hints of white smoke whiffing from both of Nibi's fieldstone chimneys. "She's got her fireplace and woodstove going, as warm as it is. She did the same thing last summer."

"Old people are always cold. At least, that's what she says."

As they approached the clearing, the arrhythmic drumming of the wind chimes Nibi had hung in the woods around her house grew louder. Made of hollowed river cane, they were intended to deter evil spirits from coming too close. More fanciful chimes, made of shiny river glass, hung by the front and back doors, their knell meant to lull even the most determined menacing spirits into complacency.

Nettie and Win dodged thorny blackberry bushes to enter the clearing and carefully stepped over long strands of running cedar that crisscrossed in front of them. Commonly referred to as bear's paw, the rare plants provided the only green in the grassless yard.

"When can we start collecting this stuff for Nibi again?"

"As soon as folks stop using it for Christmas decorations and it comes off the endangered-plant list. Until then, Nibi says, we need to protect it."

"What's she using for ceremonial fires instead?"

"Juniper, sage, tobacco. She uses them all, but they don't sparkle as much as the cedar."

The four-room cabin, with its rusted roof and sagging porches, had never known a drop of paint inside or out, but its view of the valley provided a myriad of colors, including the meandering blue-gray of the Tye; the variegated whites, reds, and browns of Oak's Landing; and the pink and white blossoms of the orchards. Above the town's roofline glistened the silvery cross of the Baptist church Nibi's father had built at the turn of the century.

Nettie followed Win up the creaky steps to the porch. Stopping at the top, they watched Nibi's worn dreamcatcher lilt in front of her bedroom window, mesmerized by the parts moving together but not. Wrapped in grapevine, the two-foot-wide outer ring anchored a hand-tied, spider-like web. A pebble-size purple stone sat on one of the taut strands near the middle, its rough facets towing light when it moved. In the center of the web, small white feathers loosely covered a round opening. Suspended from the bottom of the ring, spaced equally, were thirteen strings of varying lengths. Each had a gold feather tied in the middle and a finely serrated arrowhead attached to the end.

"That is so beautiful," Nettie said.

"You say that every time."

"Well, it is."

Throaty humming drifted though the screen door as Win knocked. "Nibi, it's us."

"I'm in the sitting room."

Dressed in a long-sleeved, buttoned-up gray shirt and worn black pants, the Monacan elder rocked by the remnants of a fire, smoking a handmade clay pipe filled with tobacco she'd grown on her hillside. The room smelled sharp from the bearberry leaves she'd cured with tobacco to sweeten the taste. Around Nibi's neck hung a blue moonstone cross, and encircling her wrist was an intricately braided copper bracelet, both childhood gifts from her mother. Nettie had never seen her without them.

"Morning, girls."

Win kissed the old woman's weathered cheek. "Mom and Dad said to tell you hi and that they'll be up next Saturday. They're bringing a picnic lunch."

"Good. I like your momma's cooking better than my own." Even though Win's parents lived in Amherst, they nurtured her relationship with Nibi, especially after Win had begun demonstrating interest and skill in the ancient ways of the Monacans.

"Mr. Carter sent you a list. He's out of foxglove and ginger." Win set the list and the money on the table.

"I'll send some back with you all. I have ginger, and with luck we'll find some new growth of foxglove today."

Nettie poured the peppermints into a Mason jar, then hugged Nibi. "Mrs. Loving said to tell you the echinacea worked and sends her best."

"I'm glad she's better. She hates closing her shop." Nibi paused. "Nettie, are you feeling all right? You look a little flushed."

"Yes, ma'am. I'm okay now." She and Win took turns relaying what had happened with the Warren boys and the cayenne pepper.

"Those little scoundrels. They'll be bringing supplies up here the end of the week. I'll be sure to offer them some peppermints."

"Nibi, you wouldn't," Nettie said.

"Of course not." She chuckled. "But they'll know I know, and they won't be sure that I wouldn't. Even good boys need to know someone is watching. I'll send Dexter some extra foxglove to thank him for making the magic mouthwash. You'd still be on fire if he hadn't." Nibi emptied her pipe in the fireplace, then sat in a straight-back chair. "Win, would you braid my hair, please? Rheumatism is slow leaving my hands this morning. Rain's coming."

"Rain? So, we can't start the project today?" Nettie chafed at her own whining. She wanted to stay busy to keep her mind off Andy.

Nibi winked. "I said it's coming, not that it's here. First drops won't fall until dusk."

"Oh. Sorry."

Using her fingers as a comb, Win separated Nibi's long white hair into three thick strands and wove them into a soft rope that reached the old woman's waist. Picking a sprig from a bouquet of purple coneflowers on the table, Win wove the stem into the last knot of the braid.

"Nettie, I'm simmering some tea to help get my fingers moving. Would you pour for me, please?"

Nibi's kitchen also served as an apothecary. Shelves filled with colorful baskets, jars, and palm-size otter-skin bags full of this and that lined the walls. Drying herbs and other plants hung from dozens of hooks in the ceiling, and pieces of oak bark and earth-colored roots lined the windowsills. Sweet-smelling flowers and leaves lay in mounds on the mixing table near a worn stone mortar and pestle. Nestled among them sat Nibi's journal of medicinal recipes and a miniature cobalt-blue bottle with the words "Angel Water" on the side. Nettie popped the cork, closed her eyes, and sniffed. A delicious scent filled her head, crested, and flowed away like an ocean swell, leaving her unsteady. Leaning against the table, she replaced the cork. If heaven had a flower garden, she hoped it smelled like this.

Getting on with the business of pouring tea, she placed a piece of clean but stained bark cloth over Nibi's tin cup and strained the amber liquid from the pot of prickly leaves simmering on the woodstove. How could stinging nettles be so mean to the skin yet so soothing to the stomach? Using a tin saucer, she carried the warm cup to Nibi.

"What did you think of the Angel Water?"

"How'd you kn—. Never mind. Of course you know."

"A gift from my mother and hundreds of years of grandmothers."

Win's brow furrowed. "You made a love potion?"

"Think again," Nibi said. "What you know is only useful if it's correct."

"Oh, that's right. Angel Water isn't a love potion. It eases pain, like heartache."

"That's better."

Smelling the Angel Water hadn't eased Nettie's struggling thoughts about Andy. Maybe she needed another dose. "May I take some home?"

"One sniff should do. Give time and fate a chance to work. Is Andy struggling too?"

"I guess. I hope."

"Butterflies struggle to escape their cocoons, you know. It gives them the strength to fly."

"Or kills them."

Nibi's thin shoulders rose and fell with her soft laugh. "Patience, child. Patience."

Nibi had struggled with love. At eighteen, she'd fallen in love with Dell, a young man who'd settled in Oak's Landing. They'd married, moved to the mountain, and had a daughter. Dell died shortly after her birth, leaving Nibi to raise Win's mother by herself. Nibi never remarried. When asked why, she always gave the same response: "Love doesn't come and go just because people do."

"What's the project you want us to work on?" Win asked.

Nibi finished her tea. "Come with me." Leading them to the front porch, she nudged her dreamcatcher. The slight movement spun the purple stone and sent cascading waves of violet across the porch. "I want you two to make dreamcatchers just like this one."

Nettie and Win raised eyebrows at each other. They had asked to make dreamcatchers many times before, but Nibi had always been reluctant, citing their youth and the degree of difficulty.

"Is there a reason you want us to make them now?"

"There are things I want you to learn while I'm here to teach you."

"Are you sick?" Win asked.

"No. Just old." Something else flashed in Nibi's eyes and tinted her voice.

Nettie started to question her further but stopped when she caught Win's eye. When Nibi wanted them to know more, she'd tell them.

"This is not a typical dreamcatcher," Nibi continued. "Making ones like it will be the hardest work you've ever done."

Win didn't hesitate to answer, "Yes, ma'am."

Nettie agreed. "We have all summer."

"Not quite. They need to be finished by mid-August."

"Why then?"

Nibi hesitated. "You two will need to be getting ready for school about that time."

Win caught Nettie's eye again. What was Nibi not saying?

"If you're going to build dreamcatchers, you need to understand the legend." Nibi pointed to a fresh spiderweb in the corner of the porch, its creator busily bundling a wasp. "Centuries ago, an Ojibwe grandmother was doing the same thing, watching a spider build an intricate web. Her grandson became frightened by the spider and wanted to kill it. The grandmother stopped him, eased his fear, and taught him to how to appreciate the beauty of the web and the life creating it. Grateful for her protection, the spider gave the grandmother an extraordinary gift, a strong web spun between her and the moon to trap dark spirits and keep her from harm."

"Why put it between her and the moon?" Nettie asked.

"Because that's where darkness lives."

Hearing the legend made the dreamcatcher seem even more mystical, powerful.

"For some tribes, the dreamcatcher is a symbol of the human spirit. Each part represents a unique gift of Nature and brings with it special meaning." Nibi ran her hands along the rim. "The red willow ring represents the circle of life."

"Would any type of tree work?" Nettie asked.

"No. Red willow is not only strong but also flexible enough to bend in half and not break."

"Why is it wrapped in a vine?"

"This isn't just any vine. It's grapevine, which helps protect the ring and symbolizes life after death."

Nibi's fingers moved to the intricate latticework in the middle of the ring. "The web symbolizes protection. Dark spirits hide in bad dreams and enter our souls as we sleep. Just as a spider's web traps insects, the dreamcatcher's web traps bad dreams and the darkness they veil." Nibi pointed to the purple stone suspended in the web. "The amethyst symbolizes the spider. She protects us by devouring the bad dreams and allowing the good ones to reach us through the portal."

Nettie pulled back the small white feathers with black tips. "Why is it covered with these?"

"Those are the feathers of a snowy owl. Some tribes view them as the wisest of all birds, while others view them as omens of darkness."

"Which is it?"

"Both. Nature is never either-or. Covering the portal with their feathers symbolizes wisdom, our ability to choose between light and dark, good and evil."

Nettie shook her head. "Those are some powerful feathers."

"What about these?" Win pointed to the thirteen strings suspended at the bottom of the ring. The first seven strings grew progressively longer, while the last six grew shorter. Each string had a gold feather tied in the middle and an arrowhead attached to the end.

"The strings symbolize the thirteen phases of the moon. Waning moons get smaller, while waxing moons get bigger. A full moon appears in the middle of each cycle."

"Why are they part of the dreamcatcher?"

"Because they also symbolize the ability to discern light in the presence of darkness. Each phase of the moon balances the amount of light available, which in turn balances Nature."

Nettie touched the feathers tied in the middle of each string. "What type are these?"

"Those are the feathers of a golden eagle, the greatest of all birds. My grandmother said some eagles are so brave and fly so high that the sun turns their feathers gold. They can see farther than any other bird and are so strong they can fly for hours at a time, especially in an east wind."

"Why in an east wind?"

"Because they're heading toward dawn. Their feathers symbolize courage and hope."

Win balanced the tip of one of the arrowheads on her finger. "And these?"

"Arrowheads signify strength and commitment. Most important, they remind us to stay alert, always watchful. The stones used to make them arise from deep earth; they're hard and strong yet capable of being shaped to do the work necessary to survive."

A breeze spun the dreamcatcher. The varying lengths of the strings prevented the feathers and arrows from becoming tangled with one another. The weight of the arrowheads brought the ring to a gentle stop.

"Individually, these elements represent faith, wisdom, courage, hope, strength, and commitment. Together they make a whole that is greater than the sum of its parts." Nibi arched her right hand from her forehead toward her eye, Monacan hand talk for *Do you see? Do you understand?*

Win and Nettie responded yes by curling and tilting their right hands.

"You'll need the same qualities to build your dreamcatchers." Nibi arched her hand again.

Following Win's lead, Nettie slowly hand-signaled that she understood. What had started as a summer project seemed to be taking on a much bigger meaning. Faith she had, but the rest she'd never had to worry about before.

Nibi answered her unspoken question. "Time and patience, child. Time and patience."

Nettie nodded. Pushing the white feathers aside, she peeked through the portal at her distorted reflection in the wavy glass window. "Sometimes bad dreams make it through?"

"Yes. Some dark spirits are so powerful, dreamcatchers alone can't stop them."

"What more does it need?'

"You. And everything you learn during the journey to create it."

Nibi crossed the ties of her chest-to-knees apron behind her back, then knotted them in front. Made of thin leather, the apron had a dozen pockets that held everything from twine and scissors to salves. Empty ones were for whatever she found and needed during her treks around the mountains. A machete, small enough to be quick and sharp enough to slice paper, hung from a loop on the side of the apron. Nibi used it to harvest plants, clear brush, peel bark, and kill slant-eyed snakes foolish enough to refuse her one time offer to leave.

Nibi pulled a bottle from one of her shelves. "We're going off-trail today, and the bugs will be hungry. Cup your hands."

Nettie turned her nose from the tart-smelling liquid and rubbed it onto her exposed skin. By sunset, she'd be covered with red speckles anyway. "Bugs like me."

"It's the scent of your warm blood," Nibi said.

"Then I'd just as soon be cold-blooded."

"I thought you were afraid of snakes."

"That's right, snakes are cold-blooded, aren't they?"

"You remember how to tell the dangerous ones from the harmless ones, right?"

"Of course," Nettie said. "But both slither and bite."

Nibi laughed. "You two get some twine and another knife out of the barn while I pack us some lunch; then we'll get going."

Cool darkness and the scent of silage and fresh hay dominated the dimly lit barn as Nettie pulled a roll of twine from a stack in the corner and Win selected a knife from those hanging on the wall. Turning to leave, Nettie bumped into an old farm table, causing a balled-up burlap sack to flop open. Half a dozen tiny gray blobs with little tails scurried through the dust in all directions. Mouse babies.

Nettie jumped back. "Damnation! Nibi needs a cat."

"Or a couple of black snakes." Win said, giggling.

"Very funny."

Rejoining Nibi, they headed down the mountain.

While the Oak's Landing side of the river had a beautifully sculpted river walk, Nibi's side did not. Crossing Route 56, they waded through tall grass and prickly brush until they intersected a game trail. In single file, they zigzagged around trees, boulders, and clumps of Nature's debris. Along the way, they startled a doe, sent the squirrels into a panic, and surprised a fox breakfasting on an unlucky chipmunk.

Moving at a steady pace, Nibi talked over her shoulder. "There's a big stand of red willows about half a mile upriver. If we're lucky, we'll find some just the right size."

Nettie and Win struggled to keep up, having to stop over and over to remove the ropy briars that captured their clothes, skin, and hair.

"The stickers are awful this year," Nettie complained, wiping linear dots of blood from her arm.

"I feel like a pincushion," Win said.

"No whining, you two. Keep up," Nibi called.

The sun indicated midmorning before Nibi pointed to a cluster of young trees with reddish-brown bark. "There they are. Your saplings will need to be about a foot taller than you and half the width of your wrist. Less, and they're not strong enough. More, and they're harder to mold."

Nettie and Win body-measured dozens of saplings until they found two the right size. Under Nibi's supervision, they took them down at the base and angled the ends so they fit together.

"Pinch off the small sprouts and carefully cut off the larger stems. Preserve as much bark as you can. It helps keep the wood strong."

When the trees were pruned, rolled, and tied, Nettie and Win sat in a patch of moss to take a break.

Nibi waved them back to their feet. "There's no time to rest. You want to find the grapevines and get them down before the day heats up."

Nettie scanned the canopy. Unlike other vines, wild grapevines did not kill their host trees by strangling their trunks. Grapevines preferred to grow along sturdy branches and protect their host and themselves by dropping their bluish-purple trails high enough off the ground to avoid most damaging insects and animals, including the two-legged variety.

"I don't mind climbing, but the trees with the best vines don't have low branches. How are we supposed to get up there?"

"I'm sure you two will figure something out."

It took half an hour for Nettie and Win to find a vining tree with a limb close enough to the ground that one of them could reach it if they stood feet to shoulder. Drawing the long straw, Win braced her back against the tree and flexed her knees so Nettie could ladder up.

"You're heavier than you look."

"Keep that to yourself, please."

After multiple tries, Nettie pulled herself up and over the lowest limb. Lying belly down to catch her breath, she ignored the bark burns on her arms and legs. "We never had to do this in gym class."

"Nibi said it would take strength," Win massaged her shoulders.

"Knowing what she said and understanding this is how we're supposed to get it are two different things."

Nibi watched from a distance, her studied gaze not amused.

Limb by limb, Nettie made her way up the tree, dodging menacing moonseed and poison ivy to reach the branch hosting the desired vine. Again on her belly, she inched forward, grateful for the limb's sturdiness. Approaching a cluster of leaves, she froze.

"Oh, hell. There's a snake up here, a big one. It's a copperhead."

"What the heck is a copperhead doing up there?"

Nettie inched back. "Taking a damn vacation! What do you think it's doing? It's eating a baby bird."

"Take it easy. That fox must be getting most of the food down by the river."

"Win!"

"Okay. Don't panic. If it's eating, it's not worried about you. Keep backing up."

"Couldn't you have had one of your visions before I got up here?"

"Who said I didn't? Maybe that's why I ended up with the long straw."

"That's not funny."

"Just kidding. I didn't see anything. I told you the visions were unpredictable."

Intent on eating the remaining baby birds, the snake showed little interest in Nettie as she worked her way back to the trunk. Climbing higher, she broke a small branch to use as a deterrent in case the legless menace decided to go north instead of south when it left. "It's a shame about those babies."

"Snakes need to eat too. Nature's balance."

"What is it with you and snakes, anyway? Don't they scare you at all?"

"Only the ones I can't see."

"What's the difference? Big one, little ones, or sticks that look like them—they all scare the bajeebies out of me."

Nettie shivered as the copperhead lazily swallowed the last hapless tiddler, pausing afterward, as if enjoying the memory. With a lumpy middle and an ungainly wriggle, it exited the tree and headed toward the river.

Nettie inchwormed back out on the branch and past the now-empty nest. Spotting a downy feather among the twigs, she stuck it in her pocket. Someone needed to remember those tiny lives. She cut down the vine and backed out of the tree.

By the time they'd dropped the rest of the grapevines they needed, she and Win were tired, thirsty, hungry, itching, and bleeding.

Win braced her hands on her knees. "Nibi, can we go to the river for a drink?"

"Not yet. I want to show you something farther up." Nibi stripped some of the heart-shaped grape leaves from the harvested vines and passed them around. "Eat these. They'll hold you over until we get there."

Nettie puckered at the tangy taste. "That's awful."

Nibi stuffed extra leaves in an apron pocket. "Nature supplies what you need, not necessarily what you like."

"Well, it would have been nice if she'd supplied those vines a little closer to the ground and left that blasted snake down at the river."

"Stop whining. This is the easy part."

"Easy?"

"Yes. Easy."

Nettie started to question what could possibly be harder but stopped. Nibi's tone wasn't teasing. "Sorry, Nibi."

With the saplings and vines strapped to their backs, they made their way up the mountain and into a dense area of trees and brush. Using her machete, Nibi cut a long path to a hidden clearing that opened to blue sky. Along the uphill side sat a cove of tall boulders protecting a small clear-water spring.

"You girls get a drink and wash up."

Folks in Oak's Landing occasionally called Nibi a water witch because of her ability to find water when no one else could. Nettie had never seen her do it until today. "How did you know about this place?"

"My father used to bring us here when we were little. There were berry bushes everywhere. We'd pick baskets full."

Nettie searched the edges of the clearing, hoping the forest offered something other than leaves to silence her hunger. "What happened to them?"

"Evergreens blocked the sun, and the undergrowth crowded them out."

Nettie and Win drank their fill of fresh water, then washed the blood from their cuts, scrapes, and bites. On the far side of the clearing stood the largest oak tree Nettie had ever seen. Its branches towered upward while its thigh-size roots and knees curled under and around nearby boulders. Moving into its cool shade, Win broke off two pieces of bark and handed one to Nettie. They rubbed the smooth underside on their broken skin, hoping for pain relief and less swelling.

Nettie stretched her arms wide to measure the width of the tree's trunk. "How old do you suppose it is, Nibi?"

"Over two hundred, I'd guess. My father called it the Gospel Oak. Its roots run deep, and its spread is centered, which makes it strong." She cupped her hands around one of the layered minion plants growing on the tree's trunk and along the dips and curves of its branches. "Come look."

Win peeked between Nibi's thumbs. "It's glowing. Green."

Nettie followed, amazed. "You could light a room with this stuff."

"It's called fairy fire." Using her knife, Nibi chipped off clumps of bark hosting the glowing plant and placed them in her apron. "I'm going to see if it will grow on the oaks at home."

Nibi's fingers moved from the fairy fire to one of the oak's tightly closed buds. She turned to scan the small stand of ash trees near the edge of the clearing. The ash's leaves were already open and flush. "Win, how will the gardens do this summer?"

Win studied the oak's buds, then the ash leaves, and closed her eyes. "If oak trees leaf first, summer will be dry, but if ash trees leaf first, then there will be plenty of rain. So this summer will be hot, with lots of rain, and the gardens will do well."

Nibi nodded, pleased. "Let's eat." She pulled strips of dried venison and rounds of acorn bread from her apron and passed them to Nettie and Win. As they ate, the wind began swirling above them, tipping treetops in waves. Nibi's eyes narrowed as she studied the ridgeline, almost as if she were eavesdropping.

Win followed her gaze. "Is the storm coming earlier than you thought?"

"No. This wind carries no water. Listen, daughter. The mountains are restless."

"About what?"

"They're not saying. Yet." Nibi stayed deep in thought until the wind died down. Dusting crumbs from her hands, she went to the edge of the woods to gather a plant with long stalks and small leaves.

"What's she picking?" Nettie asked.

"Foxglove. It helps the heart."

"It hasn't flowered yet."

"It doesn't need to. The extract comes from the leaves."

Nibi called to them. "Let's head back. There's still work to do."

The hike down the rocky mountainside with the saplings and vines on their backs took as much energy as the hike up.

Nibi walked so far ahead of them, Nettie could barely see her. "For someone who's supposed to be old, she's hiking circles around us."

"She's up and down these mountains every day. We've been sitting at school desks for nine months. We'll get faster."

"I sure hope so."

They caught up with Nibi when she stopped along Route 56 to harvest some long seed pods from a Catawba tree. Nettie and Win settled in nearby shade to rest.

What's she going to do with those monkey cigars?" Nettie asked, pulling dozens of hitch-alongs off her jeans.

"Steep them to make a tea. It's good for breathing problems."

"Uh-oh." Nettie jumped to her feet and gave Win a hand up as the sheriff's car stopped near the Catawba.

"Afternoon, Nibi. Long time no see. How've you been?"

"Hey, Bill. Still kicking. How about you?"

"Can't complain, but I do."

Nibi waved them over. "Bill, you remember my granddaughter, Win, and our friend, Nettie?"

"I do indeed. Nice to see you both again."

"You too, sir."

"Nibi, I talked with Pic a few days back. We're going to have lunch at the diner tomorrow at noon. Want to join us? It's been a long time since the three of us had a chance to visit."

"I'd like that. I'll meet you there."

"Great. See you then." Sheriff Tanner waved and drove off.

"How long have you two known each other?" Win asked.

"Since we could walk. His family's farm wasn't far from ours."

"Pic grow up near you two?"

Nibi hesitated. "No. He grew up in South Carolina."

Nettie started to ask how the three of them had become friends, but Nibi crossed the road and headed home.

Back in the shade of her front porch, Nibi showed Win and Nettie how to mold their saplings into rings, intertwining the ends so each ring needed only itself to stay together. They stripped the tendrils and leaves from the grapevines, rubbed the stalks smooth with river sand, and coiled them around the sapling rings.

Testing the tightness of the coils, Nibi nodded. "Well done. As the vines dry, they'll support the rings and anchor the ends even more. Hang them in the elm out back. They can cure for a few weeks while you two gather the rest of what we need."

After hugging Nibi goodbye, Nettie and Win limped back toward Oak's Landing to catch the train home. Nettie didn't know what to do first, scratch the bites, rub her sore muscles, or check for ticks and chiggers. "If today was the easy part, I'm in trouble."

"Me too. I'm hurting," Win said. "I didn't realize I was so out of shape."

"If we hustle, we'll have time to get some aspirin and a drink before we get on the train."

"Hustle? Are you kidding? I can hardly put one foot in front of the other."

Nettie forced herself to move faster.

Dropping off the ginger and foxglove at the drugstore, they bought a tin of aspirin, then headed for Huffman's General Store to buy sodas.

"Hey, Nettie." Wade Warren balanced his bike with one foot on the store's first step.

"What did you do this time?" Nettie asked. "Spike the Coke?"

Wade's face glowed pink. "I didn't do anything. I just wanted to say I'm sorry for peppering you this morning."

"Did your daddy make you say that?"

"He doesn't know."

"Mrs. Loving?"

"No. I just wanted to say it."

Nettie's better angel won the silent debate. "Apology accepted."

Wade's smile dimpled both cheeks. "Would you like to go get some ice cream?"

"We have to catch the train home, but thanks for the offer."

"When are you coming back? Maybe we can do it then."

"I'm not sure. A few days, maybe."

"Okay. Mr. Roberts will let me know."

"Mr. Roberts?"

"I asked him to give an extra whistle if you were on the train. He said he would." Suddenly embarrassed, Wade pedaled to the end of the street, then stopped to wave.

"That little imp."

"Well, if you and Andy don't get back together and you want to date a younger man, he's your guy."

"Very funny." Nettie hadn't thought about Andy since morning. Her heart dropped.

Thunder boomed in the distance as Win tossed Nibi's package of remedies to Mr. Roberts through the engine's window. "Nibi was right. Here comes the rain."

They scurried toward the caboose.

"Have you ever known her to be wrong?"

"No."

The *Weak and Weary* pulled away from the station as the sky darkened and lightning flashed. Small fires glowed across the foothills; their low-hanging smoke smelled of hickory and birch.

Win grinned. "Moonshiners are at it again. Rain or shine, legal or not, homemade brandy flows like water in this valley."

"Some folks say it can blind you."

"If that were true, half the town would be walking around with white canes. Even Mrs. Loving makes rock candy with it. I saw her sell some to the mayor one day."

"One of these days, we'll have to try it," Nettie said.

As with most summer storms, this one came and went quickly. Steam radiated from the rails, and ozone sweetened the air as they stepped from the caboose in Amherst. Tree rain fell in big plops and little splashes on the gravel. Dodging puddles, they waved goodbye to Mr. Roberts and headed for the Lower Road.

"You're likely to see Andy at church tomorrow."

"I know. I still don't know what to do."

"Nibi said to give time and fate a chance to work."

"So far, they haven't been much help. Maybe I should go talk with him now, when we're not surrounded by a bunch of church people. He should be getting off work anytime."

Win winked. "Angel Water must be working."

"I don't know if it's that or not. I just want to talk with him."

"Are you ready for the discussion to go either way?"

"No. But not knowing what's going on is driving me nuts. Knowing can't be any worse."

"You sure?"

"I miss him."

At the intersection with the Upper Road, Win headed home and Nettie turned toward town and the hardware store. Her body ached, her clothes and hair were a mess, but she felt better than she had in days at the prospect of seeing Andy.

As she rounded the corner onto Main, the streetlights flickered on in front of the hardware store. Nettie's heart jumped as Andy came out the door. Waving, she started to call out but stopped. Anne Johnson followed him outside. She slid her arm through his, and they disappeared into the shadows of the parking lot.

Nettie's chest tightened as she forced herself to breathe. Turning for home, she bumped into Win.

"I was wrong. Knowing is worse."

Chapter 4

Nettie fidgeted. The pew felt like granite, the heavy choir robe made her sweat, the sermon droned, and she couldn't find Andy in the crowd. To make matters worse, Pastor Williams had asked to meet with her after the service.

She leaned toward Win as the organist pounded out the pass-the-plate music. "The old Bible-thumper has never forgiven us—me—for putting that bullfrog in the baptismal pool."

"Do you blame him? He almost drowned that woman when it croaked."

"No. But—"

"You also glued his Bible shut right before that big revival, and you put white vinegar in his water glass on Pentecost. Then there was the feral black cat that got loose in the sanctuary on Halloween. And they still haven't found the original clapper for the bell."

"It was a long time ago, and not all of those pranks were mine."

"That doesn't mean, he doesn't know. Like Mrs. Mac says, some Baptists are like cats, you know they're up to something, you just can't catch them."

"He's never said a word about any of it."

"Just because he turned the other cheek doesn't mean he's forgotten."

"Obviously. His lips go straight every time he sees me."

Sweat trickled down the curve of Nettie's back as the choir stood to sing the last hymn. By the time the benediction ended and they returned to the choir room to hang up their robes, Nettie's anxiety peaked. "Go with me, Win. Please."

"Not on a bet. I might get singed in the flames. Besides, he'd never allow it."

"You're just lucky your great-grandfather baptized you before he died, or you'd be in this with me."

Win detoured to a nearby bench as Nettie continued down the hall. *This must be what the damned feel like on Judgment Day.* She tapped lightly on the open door of the intimidating office, made more so by overflowing bookshelves, stacks of important-looking papers, and dust deep enough to write in. She dawdled.

"Come. Come, Nettie."

"You wanted to see me, Pastor?"

"Most assuredly." Moving to the front of his desk, he sat on the corner and motioned to the chair nearest him. "Have a seat."

Nettie sank so low in the worn cushion of the wing chair that the unsmiling face of the hard-shell pastor towered over her.

"The baptism for the Girls' Auxiliary is next Sunday."

"Yes, sir."

"As senior pastor, I'm responsible for determining the readiness of anyone who wants to be baptized."

"Yes, sir."

"Mrs. McDermott says you're a good student. You do all of the readings, stimulate good discussion, and rarely miss a GA meeting."

"Yes, sir. Mrs. Mac is a good teacher."

"The question is, what do you think? Are you ready to be baptized?"

"Don't you think it's about time? I've been sitting in this stuffy old church for a lot of years."

The hint of a grin twitched the pastor's straight-line lips. "Sitting in church every Sunday doesn't mean you believe."

"Just saying it doesn't mean you believe either. Sir."

"That's true. However—"

"I mean, I could tell you I believe, but how would you know it's the truth?"

"I realize that. But—"

"So, how do you know the other GAs believe?"

"Well, I—"

"How do you know they're not pulling your leg?"

"It's poss—"

"'Cause I know those girls, and some of them lie like a dirty rug."

"Uh—"

"Why, Anne Johnson said—"

"Enough." Pastor Williams rose quickly and paced back and forth beside his desk, opening and closing his hands. "We're not here to talk about the other girls. We're here to talk about you. Now, please, answer the question. Are you ready to accept Jesus Christ as your Lord and Savior and affirm your belief in the doctrines of the Christian church?"

"I think so, at least most of them."

"That's not good enough. You have to be sure."

"But some of the stuff we discussed in Sunday school and GAs doesn't make sense."

Pastor Williams's voice softened. "Being baptized doesn't mean you understand everything."

"But how can you believe what you don't understand?"

"Give me an example."

"Like, why bad things happen to good people."

"Well—"

"And why God allows evil to exist. Mrs. Mac said it has to do with the need for free will, but I still don't understand."

Pastor Williams returned to his chair and loosened his tie. "Those are complex questions that require time and study to answer. Fortunately, you do not need that level of understanding to be baptized. Now, let's get back to the issue at hand. In your heart, do you believe?"

"I think so. I'll be sure when I figure out how it all fits together."

"Baptism doesn't precede belief, Nettie. It follows it."

Leaning back, he propped his arms in a tepee and tapped his fingers. His chair squeaked like a mouse in a trap.

"You're not ready. We need to delay your baptism until you have time to figure out what you believe and what you don't."

Nettie locked her jaw. "Mrs. Mac says belief is a lifelong journey and that baptism is just the beginning."

"She is correct."

"But I can't be baptized with everyone else?"

"Not at this time."

"That's BS, Pastor. A lot of the other girls have doubts just like me. They said so. They're just willing to lie about it so you'll baptize them."

As soon as the almost cuss words were out of her mouth, Nettie knew she'd crossed the line that separated okay from stupid.

Red-faced and sputtering, Pastor Williams sprang to his feet and stepped left, then right, then left again. Leaning against the desk, he took a deep breath, then escorted Nettie to the hall with instructions to stay put.

Win's eyes bugged. "Good Lord. What did you do?"

"I told the truth."

"Then why is he so mad?"

"Because I did it with a dirty word. Or, rather, the initials of a dirty word."

Nettie sneaked back to listen outside Pastor Williams's door while he phoned her parents. Her heart sank as he suggested that lessons in respect, humility, and the evils of profanity were in order. Any hope of being rescued by her mom and dad disappeared when the pastor's voice relaxed and he thanked them for their support.

Nettie scurried back to the bench. "Heaven help me."

Pastor Williams called her back to the sunken chair. Pacing behind his desk, he mumbled to himself, then spoke out loud. "James 1:26. If anyone thinks himself to be religious and yet does not bridle his tongue he deceives his own heart . . ."

Nettie lost count of the Bible verses he recited during her dressing-down, but she felt the burn of the doomed-to-hell portions for the better part of an hour.

Returning to his chair, Pastor Williams pronounced her sentence. "Young lady, in light of the accusations you've made toward your peers, I think a lesson in humility is in order. In preparation for their baptism this Sunday, I'd like for you to scrub the church's baptismal pool until it sparkles." His eyes dared Nettie to speak.

"In addition, Mr. Danes, our new associate pastor, has volunteered to work with you over the summer to help you prepare for baptism. That is, if you are willing."

"You've discussed this with him already? You knew you weren't going to baptize me?"

Pastor Williams hesitated, then leaned forward in his chair. "Well, I wasn't sure about your level of maturity, Christian and otherwise. Mr. Danes will be able to help with this and whatever else is giving you pause. He can also help you understand the importance of respect, obedience, and vocabulary."

"No, sir. I don't think I need his help right now." Nettie dug her fingernails into her palm. The pain checked her tongue until Pastor Williams turned her loose.

Once outside the church, Nettie wilted. "It's so unfair."

Win put an arm around her. "It would have been easy to lie like the others, but you didn't. I'm proud of you."

"Anne Johnson and her posse are going to love this."

Cicadas began their treetop staccato as Nettie and Win turned onto the paved, circular driveway in front of the distinguished, two-story brick house. Tall boxwoods guided them to a brick sidewalk, which ended at matching splayed-out steps leading to a brick stoop and two Georgian-style doors belonging to Mrs. Graydon Smith.

Win stopped at the bottom of the steps. "So, why do you have to babysit her grandsons?"

"Because Momma said so. Ever since the cussing-in-front-of-the-preacher nightmare, the only thing I'm allowed to say these days is 'yes, ma'am.' Apparently, the boys' parents are getting a divorce and don't want them in the middle of the fray, so they're spending the summer here."

"Where are they from?"

"California, I think. Mrs. Smith told Momma they needed playmates."

"Playmates? Are you kidding? How old are they?"

"I don't know."

"Why you? Why not someone who likes to babysit?"

"Because Mrs. Smith knows me. Remember? I helped her reshelve library books until ninth grade, when we moved to the high school. She was too old to be climbing that rickety rolling ladder."

"I remember. But that doesn't explain why I need to help you babysit."

"Because I'd help you."

"You owe me. Big."

"For sure." Nettie went up the steps reluctantly. "We'll take them downtown, stop at the playground, buy them an ice cream cone, and with a little luck be done by noon."

"Dreamer. They're here for the whole summer."

"We'll figure something out."

"I hope so. We're busy enough without having to babysit."

"Maybe they won't like us."

"We're not that lucky."

Nettie raised and dropped the heavy door knocker; the sharp strike of metal on metal echoed through the house and back at them through open windows. Underneath the knocker hung a brass plaque: We See the Invisible, Believe the Unbelievable, and Receive the Impossible.

"Mrs. Smith had that same saying on her desk in the library. Hope she doesn't quiz me on the Dewey decimal system again."

"Don't complain. You got a lot of free books."

The familiar, quick clunk of wide, lace-up heels grew louder, then stopped as the doors swung inward, revealing an older yet still stately Mrs. Smith.

"Nettie, Win, how nice to see you again. Come in. Thank you for helping us out."

Nettie couldn't decide whether Mrs. Smith sounded hopeful or desperate as she led them around a wide staircase, past fancy, old-fashioned rooms, through glass doors, and outside to an elegant patio. "The boys have been with me only a few days, but they're already bored silly. I'm sure they'll be thrilled to spend time with children their own age."

Win made a little throaty sound and whispered, "She thinks we're children?"

Mrs. Smith stepped to the side as they approached a concrete game table at the edge of the patio. "Ethan, Cal, say hello to Nettie and Win. They've come to play." She tittered as Nettie and Win sucked air at the sight of her grandsons.

Ethan, the taller, light-haired one, slid over to make room for Nettie on the concrete bench, as dark-haired Cal did the same for Win.

Ethan winked at Nettie. "Thanks, Grams. We love playmates."

Nettie studied Ethan's face-up cards: all hearts—a four, an eight, a jack, and an ace. His eyes hinted at a win. She had a ten, a jack, a queen, and a king showing. Peeking at her last card, she knew she had him. "I'll call and raise you." She tossed two twigs in the center of the table.

She'd already lost to him at croquet and monopoly, but, thanks to her father, Andy, and the neighborhood boys, she could win at seven-card stud.

Ethan tossed in two twigs, followed by two more. "Call. And I'll raise you two."

"Call. Show me what you've got."

Ethan laid down a flush. "Sorry. Straights lose."

Nettie turned over two kings and a jack. "What straight? Try a full house."

"Damn! I thought you were bluffing."

"Gotcha." Nettie counted twigs and converted them to money. "You owe me four dollars and sixty cents, which will just about buy us all lunch."

"Want to go again?" Ethan asked. "Double or nothing?"

"I'll win again. You have a terrible poker face."

"I never had a girl beat me at poker before."

"How many times have you played poker with a girl?"

"Well, never."

"That's what I thought. Let's go. Win and I are hungry."

Nettie ignored the nosy looks from the locals as she led the way through Howell's Five-and-Dime to the orange swivel stools at the lunch counter. Everything was news in Amherst. No doubt Andy would hear about the new boys in town before close of business at the hardware store. Maybe that would be a good thing.

Win and Cal stopped talking to each other just long enough to order lunch. Summer might not be too bad if she and Ethan hit it off as well.

"I'm surprised we haven't met before now. Your grandmother lives so close."

"She usually spends summers in California with us."

"I'm sorry to hear about your mom and dad."

Ethan cringed. "I didn't realize you knew. Grams strikes again."

"Win and I don't blab."

"It's not that. I'm just tired of thinking about it and not knowing what's going to happen." Ethan's cockiness faded. "My dad had an affair."

"Oh."

"At least Cal and I are away from the arguing."

"Maybe things will get better over the summer."

"Maybe."

"Being here might help take your mind off it."

"Definitely. Things started looking brighter when you and Win showed up this morning." Ethan slid toward Nettie, his arm and leg touching hers.

She slid away. He followed.

"You want to move over?" Nettie asked. "You have a whole stool to yourself, you know."

"You smell good."

"So, you like the smell of Zest. Big deal." She pushed against his shoulder. "Move over."

"Okay, okay."

She didn't appreciate the pushiness, but his skin felt nice.

"Do you have a boyfriend?"

"Used to."

"What hap—"

"Do you have a girlfriend?"

"I did. She didn't want to be alone all summer, so she moved on to someone else."

"Sounds like she's a good one to lose." Nettie thought of Andy and Anne.

"I didn't think so at the time."

The waitress set their drinks on the counter, smiled at Ethan, and winked at Nettie.

Ethan noticed. "Nettie, close your eyes."

"Why?"

"It's a surprise."

"Huh-uh."

"Come on, trust me. Close your eyes."

"All right, but no funny stuff." Nettie blinked a couple of times, then did as he'd asked.

Ethan wrapped his hand around the nape of her neck and pulled her in, putting his lips on hers. Nettie hesitated, before turning her head. She missed kissing. Her stomach flip-flopped when she opened her eyes. Andy stood at the far end of the counter, watching.

Nettie jumped up, her thoughts scrambled. As quickly as Andy had come in, he turned and left. Nettie started after him, but Ethan grabbed her arm, oblivious to what had taken place over his shoulder.

"Let me go."

"Let's do that again."

"No. Let me go."

When Ethan didn't move his hand, Nettie pushed him off the stool. He landed with a plop as Nettie headed for the door.

"Try that again, you twit, and I'll tell your grandmother."

Andy's tires squealed out of the parking lot just as Nettie reached the sidewalk.

Nettie and Ethan didn't speak until they reached the Upper Road. Win and Cal walked well ahead.

"You said you didn't have a boyfriend."

"I don't. Not anymore. But, boyfriend or not, you stepped way over the line back there. Who gave you permission to kiss me? I sure didn't."

"I—"

"And when someone tells you to let go, you damn sight better do it."

"Right. Not my finest moment."

"To make matters worse, you did it in front of everyone in the store. The whole town will be buzzing by dinnertime."

"I surrender. I screwed up. I apologize."

Nettie let her anger beat itself out, unsure about what bothered her more, Ethan kissing her or Andy seeing it. "Don't do it again."

"Deal. Friends?"

"Maybe."

Nettie ran to catch up with Win and Cal, who were talking about going swimming.

"Good idea," Nettie said. "We can go to the Daily's pool if you all don't mind swimming with their three Saint Bernards."

Ethan stopped in the middle of the road. "What?"

"On really hot days, their horse gets in, too. You can water-ride all of them if you want."

"You're kidding, right?"

"It's no worse than swimming in a river or a lake."

"But—"

"Chicken?"

"No. Just surprised. You're full of them. Surprises, I mean."

Ethan's shoulders relaxed, as if he were seeing the Upper Road for the first time. "You know, I didn't want to come here this summer, but I'm glad I did."

"Isn't it too early to tell?"

"I don't think so. It feels right." His smile widened to a teasing grin. "Don't take this the wrong way, but one of these days, I'm going to ask you to let me kiss you, and you're going to say yes."

"Dammit, Ethan."

He threw up his hands. "Just sayin'."

Chapter 5

Camouflaged by thick brush, Nettie strained to see movement along the distant tree line. They'd arrived at the popular grazing spot before daybreak, hoping to spot a feeder. She and Win needed deer tendons to make the webs for their dreamcatchers, and the only way to get them was to kill a deer. She'd eaten venison many times but had never been on the killing side of getting it. Anticipatory guilt squeezed her insides.

The sapphire glaze blanketing the ridge faded as peachy light crested and flowed down the mountains, covering the swells faster than it filled the dips. The wave of light gave a roan glow to a big buck grazing his way into the clearing. The numerous points on his rack spoke to lineage, and his long neck, thick chest, and broad rump indicated a plentiful food supply. With no wind to give them away, Nibi dropped him with a single shot behind his shoulder. One moment, the handsome animal moved gracefully in his world; the next, he lay motionless in theirs.

Shooting the buck was the only thing Nibi had not wanted Win and Nettie to do by themselves. "Learning to kill humanely takes more than a summer," she'd said.

Nettie hung back as they approached the dead animal, the gunshot still ringing in her ears. His lifeless eyes were wide open, and frothy blood stained his furry chest. She'd never watched life leave before.

Nibi's arm closed around Nettie's waist, moving her gently toward the buck. "There are different kinds of killing. God put animals on the earth to feed and support us. Killing them is wrong only if it does neither. In return, we help keep the herds thinned so they don't starve in winter. Everything has purpose. Everything takes. Everything gives back."

"It doesn't seem right."

"Nature doesn't seek right. It seeks balance."

Nibi knelt by the buck to stroke its fur. "Proud brother, I weep but do not hunger." Opening a pouch of tobacco, she sprinkled the small flakes around the animal, then looked skyward. "Father God, please return his spirit to us in the spring, when all creatures are born again." She handed Nettie and Win skinning knives with whetstone edges so sharp they were barely visible. "If you are going to take this animal's gifts, it is important to respect the process of harvesting them. Do what I say, and be careful. These knives can slice you to the bone, and you'd never feel it."

Nettie retched repeatedly as they gutted the buck, finally losing her breakfast as they spread his smelly entrails around for scavengers. She sank to her knees in the scratchy field, her stomach pressed against her spine.

Nibi pulled several small leaves from an apron pocket and handed them to Nettie. "Win, what kind of plant is this?"

"Peppermint."

"How should Nettie use it?"

"Crush the leaves and sniff them."

Nettie squeezed the small ball of leaves and rubbed them against each other. As she inhaled the tart smell, the nausea subsided.

Nibi gave her a hand up. "Stay focused on the work. It will help."

Nettie and Win crisscrossed the buck's legs and tied them to the hickory pole they'd brought. Hoisting it to their shoulders, they hiked down the mountain, the buck swaying in tandem with their steps.

"He's heavy. Nibi, how do you get them down the mountain when you're by yourself?"

"I make a litter of evergreen branches and drag them. The foliage protects the fur and is smooth enough to slide. If an animal is too heavy to drag, I dress it out where it falls, take the meat home, then come back for the rest."

Reaching the barn, Nettie and Win eased the pole down, then dropped into the grass.

"Up, girls. We're just getting started."

Nettie started to moan but stopped. Nibi did this kind of work day in and day out and never complained.

Hanging the buck's hind legs from a tree limb, Nibi explained how to skin the hide off the muscles in one piece. "Split the skin on the legs and peel upward. Then split the belly and peel toward the back. Finish by peeling it all toward the neck."

Nettie concentrated on keeping a tight grip on the slimy pelt, ignoring the nauseating smell and the sucking sound as the hide separated from the burgundy flesh.

Nibi handed Win and Nettie pieces of flint with sharp edges. "Take the hide to the barn and scrape the lining with these until it's smooth. Work from the edges in. Go slow. A damaged pelt serves no one."

Nettie and Win pulled open the double doors of the old barn and latched them to the outside wall. When their eyes adjusted to the dim light, they brushed dirt, feathers, and mouse fur off the old farm table. Nibi stood in the doorway, watching as they stretched the pelt across the table and began scraping off the filmy membrane.

When they'd finished, Nibi inspected the hide, running her hands over every inch.

"Smooth. No nicks or cuts. Good. I'll make you two some moccasins after it's tanned. There's a bag of curing salt by the door. Rub it into the pelt."

Nettie picked up a handful of the coarse grains. "Should we use gloves?"

"No. The salt will toughen your hands."

"Why do we need tough hands?"

"For the work yet to come."

When salt covered the hide, Nettie and Win pumped water over their red and stinging fingers.

"Come on, girls. We need to start the deboning. Trim off the fat and put it in this bucket. The oil will soothe your hands. Tomorrow, I'll mix it with lavender and make you some soap."

Nibi pulled a washtub close to the skinned deer. "Once the fat is off, cut the meat in long strips. Start with the legs, move to the back and neck, then finish with the ribs. Be careful not to cut the tendons. We want them long."

Nettie forced the image of the beautiful buck to the back of her mind and focused on moving the knife through the thick meat. Her queasiness didn't leave, but it didn't worsen. Halfway through, her knife found the bullet that had killed him. She cleaned it and stuck it in her pocket.

"When you're finished, take the venison to the barn and rub it with salt, like you did the hide. Then hang it in the cellar."

By the time they had carved and salted the last bit of usable meat, Nettie's fingers were raw, but there wasn't a drop of blood. Carrying the tub to Nibi's root cellar, she and Win eased down the steps into pitch blackness and set the tub on the dirt floor. Nettie rubbed her arms against the cold as Win ran her hands along the wall to find the hook holding the kerosene lamp. The scratch of a match and flare of the wick against filmy glass threw shadowy light around the earthen room. Shelves holding colorful canning jars lined the walls; partially filled baskets of roots, dried corn, berries, and nuts filled the center.

"Her supplies look a little low," Nettie said.

"When her garden comes in, this room will be stuffed."

Turning toward the shelf behind her, Nettie jumped backward as slanted red eyes met her gaze.

"Damnation!"

It took a moment for her to realize the satanic eyes were attached to a big white snake coiled in a large canning jar.

"I've never seen a snake with red eyes."

Win moved the lamp closer. "It's an albino."

"Wouldn't Nibi cut the head off and skin it before she canned it?"

"If she were planning to eat it, she would. She must have another reason for keeping it."

Nettie shivered and stepped back. Win raised the lamp toward the ceiling, where dozens of antler hooks hung empty. Suspended at the far end were a couple of large slabs of meat. "Looks like a turkey and what's left of her last deer."

Standing on crates, Nettie and Win hung the salted venison, then carried the tub up the steps. Nibi came around the corner as they lowered the cellar door.

"What's with the evil-eyed albino down there?" Nettie asked.

"It died shedding its skin."

"Why keep it?"

"As a reminder."

"Of what?"

"That you can't always tell good from bad by the outside."

Nettie rushed down the steps to answer the doorbell before her father but ended up two steps behind him. Still dressed in his state police uniform, he opened the door. Following her breakup with Andy, Nettie's father had become increasingly interested in meeting the new boys in her life.

Ethan's and Cal's eyes widened as they traveled from her father's face to his badge, then to his gun holster, and back. Their expressions confirmed they'd received her father's unspoken message.

Stepping up, Nettie quickly introduced Ethan and Cal. They'd come to pick her up for the weekly neighborhood softball game she and Win had invited them to.

Ethan took a deep breath and held out his hand. "Nice to meet you, sir." Cal followed suit.

Her father nodded as he shook their hands. "Boys."

Ethan pointed to the shiny, decked-out police cruiser sitting in the driveway. "Sir, is that the new Plymouth Fury?"

"Yes, it is."

"It's a sharp-looking car. I like the rounded fenders better than the angled ones in the older models."

"Me too." Her father relaxed a little. "Your dad used to drive an old Fury."

"You know our father?" Cal asked.

"We used to pal around together in high school. I haven't seen him since he moved out West."

The easy-going conversation took Nettie by surprise, but she interrupted it before the divorce could come up. "Dad, we need to get going. We've got to pick Win up and get to the softball game."

"You all have a good time."

"Thanks. We're going to the Courthouse Café afterward for dinner."

"Boys, give my best to your father."

"Yes, sir, we will." Ethan looked back at the door as they went down the sidewalk. "That got my attention."

"Don't worry—he likes you."

"How do you know?"

"Because he told us to have a good time. If he didn't like you, he would have told me not to be late."

"What? You two have a secret code?"

"Not really. It's just what he does."

"What happens if he changes his mind?"

"You don't want to know."

Ethan stopped walking.

"I'm kidding. He's a nice guy."

"I still wouldn't want to mess with him," Cal added.

Nettie chuckled. "Wise move."

Ethan cocked his head at Nettie. "Does he like Andy?"

"A lot."

Win hurried down her porch steps as Nettie and the others crossed the yard. "Come on. We're going to be late."

Scottie Wilson's house was one of the nicest in town, complete with tall white columns and a front yard big enough to hold a softball diamond, a reasonable-size outfield, and a couple of team benches. Thanks to the generosity of Scottie's parents, the neighborhood youth had been allowed to play in the yard long enough for the base paths to become permanent and to help their socially awkward son develop into a decent catcher.

Heads snapped as Nettie and the others entered the yard, everyone sizing up Ethan and Cal. Nettie quickly searched the crowd, Andy wasn't there, again. He hadn't been to a game since they'd split up. She couldn't decide whether she was glad or not. "Hey, everyone. This is Ethan and Cal. They're visiting Mrs. Smith for the summer." Nettie introduced the players using first names and positions.

As the team welcomed the newcomers, Scottie slid close to Nettie. "Good to see you've moved on. I ran into Anne Johnson yesterday. Seems Andy's moved on too—or so she says. Looks like he'd rather spend time with her than play ball."

Scottie's mean-spirited baiting hurt, but Nettie refused to give him the satisfaction of knowing. "That's too bad. He's a much better coach than you are."

Scottie smirked and turned to Ethan and Cal. "You two have decent throwing arms?"

Both nodded.

"Good. We're short outfielders. Ethan, you take right field. Cal, you go to the center. The rest of you, take your positions."

Nettie put on her glove and jogged to second base while Win positioned herself at shortstop.

The first batter had just stepped to the plate when Andy's car pulled up. Grabbing his glove from the backseat, he trotted toward his customary right-field position but stopped short. Everyone froze as his gaze went back and forth between Ethan and Nettie.

Scottie lifted his catcher's mask. "Hey, Andy, take the bench. We'll rotate you in."

After a long look at Nettie, Andy waved off Scottie and walked back to his car. Nettie took a step to go after him, but the memory of Anne snuggling his arm in the hardware store's parking lot stopped her.

Scottie grinned and lowered his mask. "Play ball."

By the fourth inning, Nettie had missed three pop-ups and let several grounders get by her, and now her team was down two runs. Scottie's repeated calls for her to get her head in the game didn't help. He finally benched her, despite not having a replacement. He waved in Win and the first baseman, but it didn't help—they still lost. Scottie threw his mask in the dirt and stomped over to Nettie. "Next time, don't come if you're not going to play."

Win started to back him up, but Nettie stopped her. "He has a right to be mad. I cost us the game. Let's go."

Ethan didn't speak until they were almost downtown. "Thanks for inviting Cal and me to play."

"You're welcome. Come again next week. Maybe I'll play better."

"Andy's a good-looking fellow."

"Ethan, please."

"But I bet my throwing arm is better than his."

Nettie came to a halt. "Will you stop?"

Ethan grinned from ear to ear and raised his hands. "Easy. I'm just trying to get you to laugh."

She gave him a weak smile as he grabbed her hand. "C'mon. I'll race you to the traffic light."

Nettie felt better by the time they reached the Courthouse Café. Selecting a shaded, outdoor table, they placed an order for Cokes, burgers, and fries. People were bustling around the square, doing last-minute shopping before the stores closed. Across the way, Pic hurried from the direction of the train station, a rectangular piece of paper in his hand. Nettie waved.

"Hey, girls."

"Hey, Pic." Nettie introduced Ethan and Cal.

"Nice to meet you boys."

"Want to join us for a burger?" Nettie asked.

"Thanks, but I need to get to the bank before it closes." He waved the piece of paper. "Today's payday." Pic scurried toward the bank with his bindle tight under his arm.

"He seems like a nice fellow," Ethan said.

Nettie watched as Pic held the door of the bank open for other last-minute customers. "They don't come any better."

"How'd you all get to know him?"

"He's just always been around. I think we met him at church."

"Do you know how he lost his hand?"

"An accident of some kind when he was young."

Nettie and Win took turns sharing some of Pic's hobo stories.

"Why did he end up staying here?" Cal asked.

Nettie looked at Win with a blank expression. "I don't remember him ever saying."

"I can't imagine he earns much," Ethan said. "Where does he live?"

"He has a room at the train station," Win said, "and he helps out at the church and other places around town when he's not working."

Nettie couldn't think of any place where Pic wasn't welcome. "The whole town is his home." She'd seen Pic rummage through boxes of clothes and shoes in the church's thrift room and knew he often bought two-day-old bread at the bakery for pennies. He had been on the periphery of Nettie's life for as long as she could remember. She knew he'd grown up in South Carolina, but for the first time she realized how little else she knew about his past. More important, she didn't remember ever having asked him about it.

Nettie rolled one of the buck's tendons between her fingers, before handing it to Nibi. Separating the long, gray-white strings from the buck's joints and leg muscles had been painstakingly tedious.

"They're so small."

"Don't be fooled by their size," Nibi said. "One is strong enough to lift you off the ground. They're made of thin, tough fibers called sinew." She took a flat rock and pounded the tendon until it separated into frayed-looking fibers that pulled apart like licorice. Peeling several, Nibi soaked them in a bucket of water, then twisted them together in a rhythmic, back-and-forth locking pattern to form a single, braid-like string. She handed it to Nettie. "Try to pull it apart."

Nettie wrapped the string around her hands and pulled hard. It didn't break. She handed one end to Win while she held on to the other. They pulled at the string until it hurt their hands.

"It didn't even start to break."

"That's the strength you want. You can also make the string longer by weaving in more fibers as you twist." Nibi's expert fingers seamlessly wove a piece of sinew to twice its length. "Now you two try."

It took the rest of the day for Nettie and Win to master the peel, soak, twist, and weave pattern and make enough string for their webs. When they finished, their fingers were red and full of tiny, bloodless cuts.

"We're nowhere near done with the dreamcatchers, and our hands are already as rough as corncobs," Nettie lamented.

Win handed her an almost empty jar of salve. "Split the last of it with me. It will keep the blisters away."

Nibi came out the door with a pitcher of raspberry tea and a plate of molasses cookies.

Sitting on the top step, Nettie sipped her tea. "When do we start weaving the webs?"

"The sinew needs to cure first, which gives you and Win time to go get your amethysts."

"Do we have to use amethysts?"

"Yes. It is believed to be a dream stone."

"A what?"

Nibi turned to Win. "Would you like to explain?"

Win nodded. "Throughout history, purple has been considered the color of royalty, and amethyst the most noble of all stones. Together they symbolize the power to separate good thoughts from bad, good dreams from bad."

"That's correct. Amethysts have been used as spider mothers for centuries."

"Spider what?"

"Spider mothers. According to legend, spider mothers protect and guide the young."

The thought of a protector seemed comforting, even if it was nothing more than a stone. So far, she and Win had been able to do everything Nibi had asked of them, but Nettie couldn't shake the feeling that the real tests were yet to come. "So, there's an amethyst mine up here somewhere?"

"Yes. It's hidden on Spy Rock."

"How'd you find it?"

"I didn't. Monacan elders have known about it for centuries."

"Since I'm not Monacan, can I know where it is?"

"Yes. I trust you to protect what you know. Spy Rock is a full day's hike from here, so you two will have to camp overnight."

Nettie glanced at Win. They'd camped many times, but not in an unfamiliar area that far away.

Win nodded. "We can't go this weekend because it's May Day, but we can go next week."

"I'll start gathering the camping gear when I get home," Nettie offered.

"No, don't bring any gear. You'll take food and what you need to mine the stones. Nature will provide the rest."

Chapter 6

Nettie and Win hurried across the lush campus of Sweet Briar College, passing oversize brick buildings, arched colonnades, sculpted lawns, and boxwood gardens. The grounds of the all-girls school teemed with hundreds of people setting up for Amherst County's annual May Day celebration. The afternoon festivities would begin with the announcement of the May Day king and queen, selected from Amherst County High School's upcoming senior class; the May Day planning committee kept the names secret until the coronation.

May Day also included a community-wide picnic, booths full of treats and games, a maypole, a medieval jousting tournament, and a concert in the dell. A dance in the pavilion followed at sunset.

For senior girls interested in attending Sweet Briar after graduation, May Day included a formal luncheon hosted by the college's president. In addition to their academic abilities, attendees would be evaluated on appearance, social etiquette, and ability to converse.

Ringing the doorbell of the president's mansion, Nettie tugged at the stiff lace scratching her neck and wrists. For luck, her mother had insisted she wear the same dressy dress her sister, Sam, had worn to the luncheon last year, despite its being a size too small. Sam had been accepted at the prestigious college and would start classes in the fall. "Hell's fire! Who'd wear this stuff on purpose? It itches worse than chiggers."

Win tried to flatten the fabric ballooning from the empire waist of her dress. "At least you have curves. I look like Humpty Dumpty."

"I know Amherst County girls can attend Sweet Briar for free, but if it means doing this more than once, I'm not sure I want to. I don't even know if I want to go to college."

"Which I'm sure is driving your parents nuts."

"You better believe it. Momma threatened to ground me forever if I screw up this luncheon. I'm still on thin ice with her because of the Pastor Williams thing."

An unsmiling, pasty woman in a black uniform with a starched white apron and cap ushered Nettie and Win across a two-story foyer and into a grand dining hall. A large crystal chandelier hung over the center of an elegant dining table that ran the length of the room. Long mirrors lining the walls traded miniature rainbows with hundreds of prisms on the chandelier.

Two dozen girls were already seated as Nettie and Win slid into the last two empty chairs near the head of the table. Each place setting included crystal goblets of different sizes and numerous pieces of shiny silverware surrounding a blue-trimmed, white china plate. Matching blue linen napkins, each folded in the shape of a peacock, rested in the middle. Dozens of Waterford rose bowls coursed down the middle of the table, each filled with miniature pink roses in full bloom. Underneath everything sat a brilliant white tablecloth with a long, silky fringe.

"Great," Nettie mumbled. "We have to sit next to the president."

"That's what we get for being late."

Nettie carefully rubbed the swirly curls her momma had bobby-pinned on top of her head; her scalp still smarted from the accidental jabs. "Momma made me read Emily Post last night. That lady tells you how to do everything: dress, walk, sit, eat, when to talk, when not to. She even tells you what to say."

Anne Johnson sat across from Nettie. Her long fingernails were painted pink to match her tailored dress. A pink bow accented her elegant updo.

"Nice to see you dressed up, Nettie. Who did your hair? Your little brother?"

"Nice to see you polished your red horns and pointed tail for the occasion, Anne. It's a shame you still smell like sulfur."

Anne's eyes narrowed. "You know, I really enjoy working with Andy. We're together all the time now and have such interesting conversations. Just last week, he said he appreciates a girl who pays attention to her appearance."

"Why, you hateful—"

Nettie cut short her retort as a dozen servers dressed in black and white entered the room, led by a tall man wearing a tuxedo and a white bow tie.

Nettie glared at Anne and whispered to Win, "As soon as this is over, I have to find Andy."

"Did he call back last night?"

"No. I called twice. His dad said he wasn't expected until late. I hope we can find him before the Wicked Witch of the West over there gets her claws into him any deeper. He usually helps with the jousting tournament. Let's head over there as soon as we get out of here."

The white–bow tie man clapped twice, sending most of the other black-and-whites snapping to attention along the back wall. Two servers at the far end of the room opened double doors and escorted the president in.

Nettie couldn't help but stare.

Dressed from chin to shin in form-fitting, cream-colored lace dotted with hundreds of tiny pearls and matching high heels, the woman walked gracefully to the head of the table, not one blond hair out of place in her tight French twist. Waiting until the white–bow tie man adjusted her chair, she sat as straight as she walked.

Nettie leaned forward and pulled her shoulders back.

With two fingers, the president raised a glass bell the size of an egg and tinkled it twice to garner the attention of those at the table. She needn't have bothered. No one had spoken or taken their eyes off her since she had entered the room.

"Good morning, ladies. I am Dr. Mariah Woods, president of Sweet Briar College. On behalf of the board of trustees and the faculty, I'd like to welcome you to our annual luncheon. As you may know, the founders of Sweet Briar were committed to educating the young women of Amherst County. To that end, our charter states that any young woman from here who meets the admission criteria may attend this college for free. Today's luncheon is the first step in the admission process and provides us with an opportunity to get to know one another. After lunch, faculty members will be available to tell you more about what it means to be part of the Sweet Briar community."

The white–bow tie man scanned the room to see if the servers were ready, then nodded to the president.

"Ladies, please bow your heads."

As soon as President Woods uttered, "Amen," the white–bow tie man unfolded her napkin and placed it on her lap, signaling a wave of black-and-whites to do the same for the rest of the table. A second wave swooped in to deliver small plates containing a few pieces of lettuce and a paper-thin slice of tomato.

That's it? Nettie placed a hand on her growling stomach. She hadn't eaten anything since the night before.

Win fingered the multiple forks next to her plate and whispered. "Which one do I use?"

"Emily Post said to start at the outside and work your way in. And don't start eating until the host does."

President Woods slipped a small fork under a piece of lettuce the size of a quarter. Placing the hint of green between barely opened lips, she set the fork on the edge of her plate and placed both hands in her lap while she chewed.

Nettie took a bite, laid down her fork, and tried to chew as daintily as the president. She had just enough time for two more tiny bites before a gloved hand whisked away her plate and replaced it with a small bowl of lemon-colored ice.

The president addressed the quizzical looks around the table. "The sorbet is to freshen your palates before the next course."

Wishing for a bowl of oatmeal, Nettie nibbled on a thin, rolled-up pancake the president referred to as a crêpe; a couple of warm, almost raw green beans that she described as al dente; a dab of sweet potatoes she didn't have another name for; and a rainbow of unsatisfying ice.

Win leaned toward Nettie. "I'm eating but starving."

Gloved hands set plates with ham and bite-size pieces of pine-apple in front of them.

"Finally," Win whispered.

When everyone had been served, Win speared a corner of the ham and started cutting. "This stuff is tough as leather," she whispered. Struggling to get the knife through the meat, she gave it one last, big push. The knife's blade hit the plate's juicy surface, tilted, and slid, lifting the slice of ham into the air and spinning it toward President Woods. It landed with a splat in the middle of her plate, sending juice and bits of pineapple across the front of her elegant dress.

Win gasped and turned deadly white.

Eyes wide, Nettie silently screamed, *Oh, sh—*.

As if in slow motion, the stunned president dabbed pineapple juice from her face, looked down at her spotted dress, then laid her napkin on the table. "Would you ladies excuse me, please?"

Rising, President Woods walked toward the door, not realizing the fringe of the tablecloth had captured some of the pearls on her dress. The cloth, along with everything on it, slid with her. Vases tumbled, crystal crashed, china shattered, and silverware clanked as it hit shiny hardwood. Pulled off balance, the president slipped in her high heels and landed on the floor with an unceremonious plop. Girls scrambled to escape the chaotic table as some of the black-and-whites rushed to save plates and glasses while others scurried to assist the president.

Win and Nettie jumped up to help but were waved away.

Smirking, Anne Johnson stopped in front of Nettie as she and the other attendees were leaving the dining room. "Tweedledee and Tweedledum strike again."

"Take a break, Beelzebub. Being so hateful must be exhausting." Nettie ignored the middle finger pointed in her direction.

As the rest of the black-and-whites picked up remnants of the luncheon, the white–bow tie man escorted Win to President Woods's office. Nettie followed, despite his insistence that she not. Sitting primly in the waiting area, she refused to meet his eyes. Summoned back to the noisy dining room by a timid underling, he instructed Nettie to stay put and left.

The sliding doors to the president's office were ajar enough for Nettie to peek inside. President Woods sat ramrod straight at a long executive desk. Win stood in front of her, the hem of her balloon dress quivering.

"Young lady, not only did you disrupt a respected tradition, you also ruined hundreds of dollars' worth of china, crystal, and linen, not to mention my dress. What do you have to say for yourself?"

"I'm sorry, ma'am."

"As you should be."

"It was an accident."

"I'm sure it was. But you are still responsible."

"Yes, ma'am. I am responsible for the flying ham."

"And the rest."

"No, ma'am. It seems to me your dress and the tablecloth did the rest."

"Are you saying the damage is my fault?"

Win went silent as her balloon dress stopped quivering and started swaying.

Nettie took a deep breath and slipped through the door to stand next to her friend. "No, ma'am. She's just telling the truth as she saw it. She's as honest as the day is long."

The incensed president started to speak but paused to study Nettie. "Do you normally involve yourself in other people's business, young lady?"

"No, ma'am."

"I see. Then I assume you two are friends?"

"Yes, ma'am, since we could walk."

President Woods leaned back in the chair, her shoulders relaxing, face softening. She looked back and forth between Nettie and Win. "Telling truth to power is not easy. It takes confidence and courage. As does standing up for a friend." President Woods rose and walked to the front of the desk. "While I would have preferred to discover these admirable personality traits another way, I'm impressed. You two may be exactly what Sweet Briar is looking for."

Slipping through the back door of the boathouse, Nettie and Win changed into the shorts and shirts they'd stashed earlier. Hanging their dresses on oar hooks to keep them wrinkle-free for the dance, they pulled the bobby pins out of their hair and traded their shiny patent leather shoes for flip-flops.

Hurrying past the booths and gaming areas, they headed to the far end of the quad, where jousting riders were mounting their steeds. The first rider galloped by on a tall gray Appaloosa. The power of the horse shook the ground, while its gracefulness allowed the rider to stand steady in the stirrups. Toes straight, knees tight, the rider leveled his lance and raced to the far end of the course, where he speared the middle of an inch-wide ring dangling from a pole. The crowd cheered as horse and rider cantered back.

Win shook her head. "I don't know how they do that. Those lances are really heavy."

"When there's a lot at stake, you'd be surprised at what you can do. First place gets five hundred dollars." Nettie scanned the crowd. "I don't see Andy anywhere. C'mon. Maybe he's already at the pavilion. They should be crowning the king and queen anytime now."

Winding through throngs of people and up the steps, Nettie and Win arrived as trumpeters in feudal costumes played the royal fanfare. Jostling to see, Nettie froze. Coming to a standstill under a canopy of pink and green streamers, Andy and Anne Johnson awaited their coronation.

Nettie stared at Anne while Anne stared at Andy, her hand wrapped around his finely suited arm, again. Andy met Nettie's gaze just as Win pulled her backward through the crowd.

Sunset pushed the leafy shadow of the chestnut tree up the copper roof of Sweet Briar's long stable. Mesmerized by the glow, Nettie had lingered in the tree's shade most of the afternoon, numb. Music floating up from the concert in the dell forced her back to the here and now. "I can't believe I lost Andy to that snob."

Win lay in the grass nearby, an arm over her eyes, almost asleep. "Don't jump to conclusions."

"Are you kidding? You saw them."

"I saw what you saw: two people being named king and queen. Nothing more. Nothing less."

"Dammit, Win. Andy and Anne aren't just any two people."

Win pushed up onto her elbows. "Look, I think you have this all wrong. Most people our age don't have a clue about what love is, including me. But something tells me Andy does. He made up his mind about you a long time ago, and I don't think Anne or anyone else is going to change that, despite what we saw at the hardware store and the pavilion."

"He sure has a funny way of showing it. No wonder Anne smirked at me all during that stupid luncheon."

"I still say don't jump to conclusions. Besides, maybe you need to figure out what you're more upset about, the possibility of losing Andy, or of losing him to Anne."

"What do you mean?"

"You know what I mean, and, to be fair to Andy, you need to figure it out sooner, rather than later."

"Leave it to you to make my head hurt even more."

"You want to go home?"

"No. Let's go to the boathouse and change for the dance. I may have been dumped, but I don't have to act like it."

Lights strung around the pavilion twinkled as Nettie and Win came up the steps. Folks milled around, talking, sipping punch, and waiting for the dancing to start.

Nettie forced smiles and feigned indifference as friends sent *I'm sorry* looks and uncomfortable little waves. "This was a mistake." She turned for the exit.

Win grabbed her arm. "Oh, no, you don't. You had the strength to get here; now find the courage to stay. And, for gosh sakes, don't give Anne Johnson the satisfaction of seeing you cry. Time to choose happy."

"Now's a hell of a time to bring that up." Choosing to be happy when you didn't have a reason to be was something Nettie had learned the previous summer, during her family's vacation in the Alabama Wiregrass. Mitchell, the young man who'd changed her life, had been a great teacher.

"It fits," Win said.

Nettie spotted Ethan coming up the steps and relaxed a little. His handsomeness struck her now as much as it had the day they'd met. Now that they'd arrived at a hands-off understanding, they enjoyed spending time together.

"Hey, Nettie. You look great."

"You look pretty good yourself."

He took off his jacket and loosened his tie. "Gram's idea. Would you like some punch?"

"I'd love some."

Ethan headed across the dance floor to the punch bowl; admiring looks from around the room followed in his wake.

Trumpeters announcing the arrival of the king and queen pushed the crowd into a semicircle. Nettie's chest tightened as Andy and Anne led folks onto the dance floor. Swaying stiffly, Andy searched the crowd while Anne tried to follow his gaze.

Ethan reappeared with a cup of foamy green punch, which Nettie downed in two swallows. She wiped the stickiness from her lips just as Andy spotted her.

She might not have a date, but he didn't need to know. Nettie grabbed Ethan's hand. "C'mon. Let's dance." Nettie and Andy watched each other over Ethan's shoulder until other dancers got in the way.

A midnight stroll around Sweet Briar Lake marked the end of May Day for most. Nettie took Ethan's arm as they led Win and Cal along the shoreline. "Keep your eyes peeled for Daisy."

"Who?" Ethan asked.

"Daisy. Sweet Briar's ghost."

"You're kidding."

"Not at all. They say she's the daughter of the original landowner. She died young but apparently decided to stick around and play tricks on folks."

"Like what?"

"Locking unlockable doors, slamming windows, turning lights on and off, spinning chandeliers, and stirring up the horses. Supposedly, she even lets them out of the barn occasionally." Nettie paused to look behind them. "Some folks say they've seen a wispy white figure floating along this path, carrying a torch. If anyone gets close, she disappears."

"Have you ever seen her?" Ethan asked.

"I think so. A few years back, the night of May Day, I heard laughing and saw a little girl in a white dress come out of the woods. She picked up one of the ribbons on the maypole, wrapped it around and around the pole, then disappeared into the trees."

"Did anyone else see her?"

"Win saw the ribbon moving."

"Were you scared?"

Nettie shook her head. "Not really. She's not scary; she just wants to play. I doubt she'll show tonight. Too many people around."

"I hope she does. I've never seen a ghost, much less a happy one." Ethan stopped to throw a rock into the moonlit lake. He teetered on the soft, uneven bank.

Nettie grabbed his arm. "No swimming at night."

"That was close. Thanks."

Win cleared her throat. "We have company."

Strolling toward them were the king and queen. Anne stuck to Andy like a tick. The path wasn't wide enough for the four of them to pass, but no one moved. Face to face, Andy and Ethan stared at each other as Nettie and Anne traded glares.

"Enough." Pulling Cal behind her, Win pushed through Ethan and Nettie, then wedged her way between Anne and Andy, pushing them off the path.

Anne spun around, hands on her hips. "Just who do you think you are?" As she stepped toward Win, her foot slid sideways in the muck. Struggling to keep her balance, she slipped farther down the bank. Nettie and Andy made a grab for her as she tumbled backward, but missed. Anne's shriek became garbled as she hit the brackish water. The commotion sent lightning bugs and other marsh dwellers scattering among the cattails.

Anne spat and sputtered as Ethan and Andy fished her out of the water. She shook free and made a beeline for Win as soon as her feet hit solid ground. "How dare you push me?"

"I didn't."

"You most certainly did."

"Look, I'm sorry you fell in, but I didn't push you."

"You're lying."

Nettie moved next to Win. "She didn't push you, Anne. I saw the whole thing."

Anne's eyes sparked. "What makes you think I'd believe you? You're just protecting your friend. Your Indian friend."

Nettie charged at Anne, but Andy quickly stepped between them. He spun on Anne. His withering look spoke more loudly than words.

Anne backed up. "I'm sorry, Win. But I know someone pushed me. I felt it."

Nettie could barely control her anger. "Maybe it was Daisy. She doesn't like mean people either."

"Mean? Me? You're a fine one to talk."

Win took Nettie's arm. "Let's go."

Nettie refused to turn away. "Where are your manners now, Miss Perfect? Shouldn't you thank these guys for pulling your prissy butt out of the water?"

Anne's gaze moved from Andy to Ethan. "Thanks." Pulling her sloshy shoes from the muck, she headed down the path in a huff. When Andy didn't follow, she stopped. "Are you coming?"

Andy ignored her and turned to Ethan. "Thanks for the help. Sorry you had to get wet."

"No problem."

Andy looked at Nettie. "Just what were you going to do if I hadn't stopped you?"

"Put her butt right back in the water."

Chuckling, Andy ran to catch up with Anne. Putting his hands in his pockets, he ignored her attempt to take his arm. Glancing back at Nettie, he winked.

Win gave Nettie a hug. "Thank you."

"No thanks necessary. That girl is in desperate need of a baptism."

Ethan pointed to a faint light disappearing into the woods. "Maybe it's Daisy we should be thanking."

Chapter 7

Nettie pulled a can of cleaning powder and a sponge from under the sink in the church kitchen. The baptismal pool had to be sparkling before the eleven o'clock service; she had little time. Climbing down the narrow steps into the shoulder-high pool, she wet the marble, generously sprinkled cleaner on it, and started scrubbing. She had most of the marble greened up and gritty before she noticed the sign on the wall: Do Not Use Abrasive Cleaners. Mild Soap Only.

As she quickly rinsed the pool, Nettie's heart sank. Hundreds of tiny scratches crisscrossed the basin.

"That's just great."

Slipping and sliding, Nettie hurried back to the kitchen. She grabbed a jug of dish detergent, hoping it would wash away the grit and help minimize the scratches. Following the directions to use it sparingly, she poured the thick liquid on the sponge and rubbed it over the marble.

"Want some help?" Andy stood in the doorway.

Nettie's heart sprinted for a fleeting moment, then slowed at the memory of his playing king to Anne's queen. "No."

"Look, I'd like to explain."

"Explain what? It's all out there."

"No, it's not. You don't understand."

"Understand what? That you've ignored me since that night at River's Rest and that yesterday, in front of God and everybody, you officially dumped me for the most hateful girl in town?"

"No. Honey. It's not like that. Let me explain."

"Don't you dare call me honey, not now. Not after yesterday." Nettie started scrubbing again. "Just leave. I have to finish cleaning the pool so your new hypocrite girlfriend can get baptized, this time in clean water."

Andy's jaw tightened. "My *girlfriend*? What about you? What's with this new guy, Ethan? You sure connected with him fast, kissing him in the middle of the drugstore."

Nettie whirled around, struggling to keep her balance. "I didn't kiss him. He kissed—"

Pastor Williams stood grim-faced over Andy's shoulder.

"Nettie, is the baptismal pool ready to fill?"

"No, sir. Not yet."

"Then hurry it along, please. It takes twenty minutes."

"Yes, sir."

"Andy, you'd best leave so Nettie can finish up."

"Yes, sir."

As Pastor Williams left, Nettie quickly debated what to do. Did she really want to blow the chance to talk with Andy alone?

"Andy, wait. I—"

Anne came around the corner, dressed to the nines, her hair in a French braid, the one style that looked as good wet as it did dry. Giving Nettie a disgusted glance, she turned to Andy with a smile. "There you are. Grandfather wants to know if you'll sit with him."

Nettie squeezed the sponge until nothing dripped. "You'd better go, Andy. You don't want to keep your boss or his whiny granddaughter waiting." Nettie went back to scrubbing, pretending she could see.

"Have it your way." Ignoring Anne's grab for his hand, Andy left.

Red-faced, Anne kicked the jug of detergent into the sudsy pool, barely missing Nettie's foot. "Make sure you get everything nice and clean for us, Nettie. You're good at dirty work. Maybe you could make a career of it, since you're obviously not college material."

"Careful, Anne. Wicked witches melt in water."

"Loser."

The soapy sponge barely missed the back of Anne's head as she ran after Andy. Nettie stomped out of the pool, closed the drain, gave the water valve a hard twist, then made her way to the bathroom to change into her Sunday dress. Maybe the water would hide the damaged marble. Maybe it wouldn't. She didn't care.

Only adults sang in the choir during the GA baptismal service, so Nettie and Win sat with their parents in their usual right-center pew.

Win scanned the church. "Half the town is here."

"Figures."

Pangs of envy struck Nettie as the side door of the sanctuary opened and her fellow GAs filed in, wearing dazzling white dresses and kid gloves. Crossing to the center aisle, they turned and went up the steps to the altar, positioning themselves on the second tier of steps leading to the baptismal pool. In the middle of the front row, Anne struck a pose, smiling toward the back of the church. Nettie followed her stare straight to Andy. He met Nettie's gaze.

Pastor Williams stepped into the pulpit, nodded approvingly at the GAs, then turned to the congregation, welcoming saints, sinners, and seekers alike.

"As the New Testament tells us, on the seventh Sunday after Easter, Christians celebrate Pentecost, the moment when the Holy Spirit descended upon believers in the ancient world and marked the birth of the Church in exuberant fashion. This morning, we're privileged to offer a similar welcome to our Girls' Auxiliary class."

As Pastor Williams spoke, Nettie caught movement above the layers of white dresses. An avalanche of bubbles exploded over the edge of the baptismal pool and cascaded toward the unsuspecting GAs.

The congregation tittered and pointed.

Realizing she'd left the detergent in the pool and forgotten to turn off the water, Nettie bolted from the pew. By the time she passed the altar, the avalanche had formed a giant skirt around the disquieted GAs as it rolled toward the congregation.

As the girls scattered, Pastor Williams rushed into the bubbles, only to disappear beneath the suds with a splat and a long, low moan. Panicky GAs who failed to find secure footing took others down like dominos. Many of those who made it off the steps tripped over the invisible pastor. With each fall, shrill yells and shimmering bubbles shot up and out over the scrambling congregation.

Making her way through the white foam and around scurrying congregants, Nettie got to the hall, kicked off her shoes, and ran to the back entrance of the baptismal pool. Pushing the door open, she waded into hip-deep bubbles, stumbled over someone's legs, and landed on her hands and knees.

"Whoa." Andy's head and shoulders emerged from the suds. "I got it. Water's off."

Nettie sat back on her heels, not knowing whether to laugh or to cry at his bubble-covered face. She reached up to brush the white foam from his eyes but quickly dropped her hand as agitated voices came through the door.

Impatient to get the sanctuary back in order, Pastor Williams allowed Win, Ethan, and Cal to help Nettie clean up. The four worked for hours to corral the bubbles, but the harder they cleaned, the bigger the sudsy mounds grew.

Nettie plopped down on the squishy, carpeted steps, launching yet another white wave of bubbles. "There's so much of it. I wish we could just vacuum it up."

Ethan and the others joined her. "We can once it dries."

"Dries? That's a brilliant idea."

"What?"

"Drying it up. You all split up. We need to find every fan we can get our hands on, even if we have to bring them from home."

It took an hour for them to gather fans of all shapes and sizes. After they placed them strategically around the sanctuary, it took less than a minute to turn the chamber into a giant snow globe.

Pastor Williams and several congregation members stopped by to watch the show, including Mrs. Smith. "Pastor, I haven't laughed so hard in years. These bubbles are exactly what our stuffy old congregation needed."

Pastor Williams did not appear amused.

By afternoon, bubbles were dropping and popping every-where. When Nettie and the others returned the next morning, the suds had dried to a fine dust that could be vacuumed. By day's end, the clean and polished sanctuary sparkled more and smelled better than it had in decades.

Nettie peeked into the baptismal pool before she left. The scratches were still visible, but no one had mentioned them.

While some of the congregation appreciated Sudsy Sunday, Pastor Williams refused to see the humor. Using a cane, he limped into the follow-up meeting with Nettie.

"Pastor Williams, I'm really sorry you got hurt. I was upset and forgot to turn the water off."

"So I hear. However, I'm sure you understand there still have to be consequences."

"Yes, sir. I guess so. Is Anne Johnson going to be punished too?"

"Consequences are not always a punishment."

"Is Anne going to have consequences too?"

"She says she had nothing to do with putting the soap in the pool. In fact, she thought the incident was an intentional prank on your part."

"And you believed her? Sir?"

"She said you threw a wet sponge at her."

"I did, but only after she—"

"I understand that you and Anne are dealing with some kind of romantic conflict, which is unfortunate but not my concern. You were asked to clean the pool. Your inattention to this responsibility resulted in quite a mess. Someone could have been seriously hurt."

"Yes, sir."

"As we discussed at our last meeting, Pastor Danes has volunteered to work with you. He feels he can help you mature as a Christian and develop a better sense of social responsibility. I think it's time you two get started. You and I will meet again in August to see where things stand."

Nettie paced angrily in front of Win's front stoop. "If Pastor Williams is so concerned about social well-being, why the heck is he baptizing that hypocrite in the first place? She lied to him. Again. And he bought it hook, line, and sinker. Again."

"The man can only work with the words he's given."

"Then why can't he work with mine? He didn't even bother to ask me what happened. He just took Anne's word for it and assigned all the guilt to me. You'd think he'd be smart enough to know when he's being manipulated. If Momma wasn't so intent on me getting baptized, I'd walk away."

"No, you wouldn't."

"How do you know?"

"Because it's not in you to give up, especially on something as important as this. If obstacles get thrown in your way, you figure out a way around them, or over them, or through them. You always have."

"I bet John the Baptist didn't make Jesus attend a bunch of meetings before he dunked him in the Jordan. And if the New Testament is right, I'm damn sure—oops, sorry, I'm *sure*—Jesus wouldn't put me through what this old Bible-thumper is. Jesus keeps things simple." Nettie stopped pacing and stared at the night sky, trying to surrender the injustice. "It's so unfair."

"Yes, it is. Now, dust off your feet and move on."

Nettie shivered against an air conditioner running full blast and struggled to get comfortable in the straight-backed chair as she waited for Mr. Danes. His basement office looked bare in contrast with Pastor Williams's. Other than a picture of Adam and Eve under an apple tree and a bunch of water pipes, nothing decorated the walls. No books lined the shelves, nor were there any papers, notebooks, pens, or pencils on the desk. There wasn't even a Bible in sight. The Wednesday-night church ladies said Mr. Danes had graduated from the seminary in New Orleans, a city they likened to Sodom and Gomorrah.

Other than watching him preach every other Sunday for a few weeks, Nettie had been around Mr. Danes only one other time. After his first Wednesday-night church supper, he and Andy had compared their rebuilt car engines while Nettie waited in the shade next to the parking lot. Afterward, he came over to introduce himself, shaking her hand enthusiastically until she pulled it away. Up close, his blond crew cut, silver-gray eyes, and wide smile made him attractive, if not handsome. His warmth had been a nice contrast to Pastor Williams.

She jumped as the door closed behind her.

"Good evening, Nettie."

"Good evening, sir."

Dressed in khakis, a white button-down shirt, and penny loafers, Mr. Danes sat his church-supper Dixie cup on the desk, adjusted his chair, and leaned back. His chair didn't squeak like Pastor Williams's.

"It's good to see you again."

"You too, sir."

"I'm particularly glad to have a chance to work with you. Mrs. McDermott says you're a great student."

"I wish Pastor Williams thought so."

He nodded. "I understand you two have had some challenges."

"You could say that." Nettie didn't try to hide her annoyance.

"He thinks you need to be better prepared for baptism. What do you think?"

"I'm not crazy about having to do extra work, but I'm here."

"At least you're honest."

"That's what got me into this mess."

"No. I think lack of belief landed you here."

"I believe. At least, most of it. I just have questions that don't seem to fit with what I believe."

"Fair enough. Keeping the faith when you don't understand why is a good place for us to start."

"What do I have to do?"

Mr. Danes pulled a list of Bible verses and a composition book out of a desk drawer. "Each week, I'll give you specific readings to do. Afterward, write down any questions you have in this notebook, and we'll discuss them after the GA meetings on Wednesday nights. How does that sound?"

"Okay, I guess. How many weeks will it take?"

"That depends on you."

"Oh, that's right. I have to remember to give all the right answers, don't I?"

Mr. Danes laughed out loud. "Pastor Williams said you have difficulty holding your tongue."

"Holding it isn't the problem. Telling a lie with it is. Pastor Williams chose to believe the wrong person."

Mr. Danes's eyes widened.

"I'm sorry. I shouldn't have said that."

He sat up straight. "Don't apologize. You're spunky. I like that. But I think you're confusing the injustice of how you got here with the more important reason of why you're here."

"Injustice?" Nettie cocked her head. "Does that mean you believe me?"

He gave a quick nod. "Yes. I do. This whole situation started because you were honest about what you believed and what you didn't. That type of conviction about the truth doesn't usually come and go."

Nettie relaxed. Meeting with Mr. Danes might not be so bad after all. "I never thought about it as conviction. It's just wrong to lie."

Mr. Danes's penetrating gray eyes stayed on her for a long, uncomfortable moment. Emptying his cup, he stood and walked her to the door. "Yes, it is."

Nettie met Win on the church steps.

"How'd it go?"

"Not as badly as I thought it would. He's not as stuffy as Pastor Williams. He also thinks I'm telling the truth."

"Well, that's good."

"It is, but I still have to do the sessions to figure out the belief things. He wants to meet on Wednesday nights, when I'm already here for dinner and the GA meetings."

"That makes it easier, especially with all the other stuff we have going on."

"Like spending more time with Cal?"

The streetlight made Win's blush glow. "There's a dance Friday night in Oak's Landing. Want to go? Cal said Ethan would drive if we didn't want to take the train. His grandmother lets them use her everyday car."

"I guess."

"Don't sound so excited."

"Sorry. I like Ethan, but as a friend. I'd prefer to dance with Andy."

"That's not going to happen until the two of you stop being mule-headed."

"Has Cal kissed you yet?"

"No."

"Then let's go."

Nettie navigated while Ethan negotiated the road's steep inclines and switchbacks. As they crested the mountain at Walton's Pass, the sunlit valley lay before them like a colorful quilt. She had forgotten how different Oak's Landing looked from a car, as opposed to the train. Painted houses, trimmed lawns, flower beds, and tended vegetable gardens lined the road into town. Along tree-lined Main Street, shop owners rolled in awnings and swept sidewalks.

Ethan guided the big Chrysler into one of the angled parking spaces in front of Huffman's General Store. Jumping out, he came around to open the door for Nettie. "This place is something. It's like going back in time."

"Folks here like it that way," Win said, as she climbed out. "They even have a plaque in the park that says BLESSED BY GOD AND SHELTERED FROM THE REST OF THE WORLD. C'mon, Nettie and I will give you two the nickel tour."

Two by two, they made their way past the post office, the five-and-dime, Maggie's Diner, and the barbershop. Hundreds of locusts were in full vibrato as the four approached the foothill at the end of the street. Way up at the top sat the stone church Win's great-grandfather had built. Stopping at a large, flat boulder near the bottom of the steep drive, Win sprinkled small brown flakes across the top.

Cal rolled some between his fingers and sniffed. "Tobacco?"

Win nodded. "It's a Monacan tribute to my great-grandfather."

"What's a Monacan?"

"I am. Monacans are Native Americans who settled this part of Virginia centuries ago. My great-grandfather was a chief. He was also a Baptist minister. He preached from this stone every Sunday until he and the congregation had gathered enough river rock and raised enough money to build the church. He'd sit here in the evenings, smoke his pipe, and talk with whoever passed by. He baptized me here. My grandmother Nibi is his daughter. She lives in the mountains across the river."

"Will she be here tonight?"

"Probably. She enjoys the music."

Ethan's gaze tracked up the church's spire to the cross at the top. "It's tilted. What happened?"

"Good eye. Nibi said it tilted during a bad storm the day it was installed. Her father left it that way because he thought it spoke to the short distance between heaven and hell better than words could."

"I don't see anyone up there. Why are the doors and windows open?" Cal asked.

"They stay open most of the time. My great-grandfather wanted folks to come in to worship when they felt like it or find shelter when they needed it."

Darkness had settled in and the band had started playing as the four of them circled back to the park. Half a dozen children and a few couples made their way to the clearing in front of the gazebo to dance while Mrs. Loving set out treats on a gingham-covered table. "Nettie, Win, come taste these cookies. I have a new butter recipe."

Win introduced Ethan and Cal as they sampled the goodies. Spotting the Warren boys' bicycle nearby, Nettie slid her cookie back. On the next table sat two large punch bowls, one clear, the other red. The clear one had a dipper and cups set around it; the red one didn't. Mr. Meeks, the barber, stood behind the second bowl, a dipper and paper cups on a bench behind him.

Ethan nodded toward the red bowl. "Wonder how old you have to be to drink from that one."

"Old enough not to tell," Nettie said.

Win pointed to a cluster of rocking chairs near the gazebo. "Nibi's here." She led them over and introduced Ethan and Cal.

"Nice to meet you, ma'am," Ethan said, shaking her hand.

"Ma'am," Cal added.

"Nice to meet you boys. First time in Virginia?"

"No, ma'am, but it's been a while," Ethan replied.

"Do you like our valley?"

"Yes, ma'am. It's beautiful."

"You'll have to get Nettie and Win to bring you boys up to my home place sometime."

Cal nodded. "That would be great."

Nibi nudged Ethan's arm and nodded toward Nettie as another song started.

"Right. Nettie, would you like to dance?"

"Sure."

Ethan led her onto the dance floor, smoothly matching her step, then taking the lead.

"Where'd you learn to dance so well?" Nettie asked.

"Cotillion."

"My mother made me do cotillion too, but it didn't stick."

"My mother made Cal and me take it over and over again until it did. I finally learned how just so I didn't have to go anymore." As Ethan pulled her closer, a hand tapped his shoulder from below.

"May I cut in?" Wade Warren stood dressed in his Sunday best.

"Sure." Ethan winked at Nettie, then went to sit with Nibi.

Nettie studied Wade's scrubbed face. "Did you spike anything on Mrs. Loving's table tonight?"

"No. Honest. I didn't. I'm really sorry about doing it the first time."

"You already apologized, but I'll accept it again. How many others did you set on fire that morning?"

"Just you."

Standing a head taller than Wade, Nettie saw his cowlick shaking. "Do you know how to dance?"

"A little. I've been practicing. I figured you'd show up at one of the dances this summer." He timidly placed his left hand on Nettie's waist and took her left hand with his right. Shuffling out of step with the music, he repeatedly stepped on her toes. His faced turned beet red as he stumbled. "I'm really sorry."

"Don't be. If you take a wrong step, just start over. Go slow and take one step at a time. Like this: One, two, three. One, two, three. One, two, three."

When they were finally moving smoothly, Wade quit watching his feet.

"Did you ever apologize to Mrs. Loving?"

"Yes, but she still made us help clean the store. It was the only way she agreed not to tell Pop what we'd done."

"Good for her."

Wade nodded toward Ethan. "Is he your new boyfriend?"

"No. Why?"

His Adam's apple bobbed. "Because I want to be. My birthday is the fifteenth, so I'm almost old enough to have a girlfriend."

Nettie bit the smile from her lips. It took courage for Wade to put himself out there. "I'm a little old for you, don't you think?"

Wade's face drooped like wilted lettuce.

"I'll tell you what. If you feel the same way next year, call me, and we'll have lunch at Howell's in Amherst. Deal?"

Happy with better than nothing, Wade nodded as the music stopped. "Deal."

"Thanks for the dance." Nettie kissed him on the cheek, then rejoined the others.

Nibi winked. "Puppy love?"

"I guess. He's been following Win and me around for a while now."

"Poor thing. Young love can hurt."

Ethan whispered, "So can old love."

Nettie wasn't sure he knew he'd spoken out loud.

Nibi took Ethan's hand and pulled him to her, whispering in his ear.

He looked shaken as he stepped back. "Yes, ma'am. Thank you."

"You're welcome. Now, you two go dance and have a good time."

Ethan led Nettie onto the dance floor, slid his arm around her waist, and started swaying to the music, but he wasn't there.

Nettie turned his face to hers. "What's wrong? What did she say?"

"Nothing's wrong. She just surprised the hell out of me, that's all. She said my family was going to be okay and that Cal and I should be patient."

Nettie nodded, not surprised that Nibi had sensed his pain.

"Did you or Win tell her what was going on with my mom and dad?"

"I didn't. I don't think Win did either."

"Then that old woman's spooky."

"No. She's a shaman."

"A what?"

"A medicine woman. She's able to see things we can't and know things we don't."

Ethan looked back Nibi. "I hope she's right."

Nibi's gift to him had been exactly that: hope. Nettie didn't mention that Win had the same abilities. It wasn't her story to tell.

Joining Cal and Win at the unguarded red bowl, they quickly filled their cups, Mr. Meeks too busy dancing to notice or discreetly looking the other way. The four of them made their way through the crowd to the shadows along the river walk.

"I've never had moonshine before," Nettie said.

Ethan grinned. "Neither have I. But there's a first time for everything." He and Cal took their first sips. Cal started coughing, and Ethan's face contorted as if he'd sucked a lemon. "Oh, man."

Nettie sniffed her cup. It smelled tart and peachy. Taking a tentative sip, she puckered and swallowed hard. The slow burn went all the way to her belly.

Win gagged on her first sip, while Cal took another swig. "It tastes better the second time."

Ethan poured the rest of his liquor into Nettie's cup. "Grams will kill me if I wreck her car."

Cal lifted his cup. "All right, you all, time to chug. On the count of three. One, two, two and a half, three."

Nettie and Win joined him in downing the clear whiskey, making a sputtering chorus with the last drops.

Nettie shuddered. "I don't know why anyone would drink this stuff more than once."

Ethan tossed their cups in a trash can. "Just wait. You'll know why in a few minutes."

Win pointed up. "Look, there's a supermoon tonight."

"A what?" Cal asked.

"A supermoon. When a full moon occurs at the same time the earth and moon are at their closest point, it looks really big."

The oversize moon crested as they reached the river, its face reflected vividly in the unusually smooth, mirrorlike water.

"That's beautiful," Nettie said.

"When the water is calm enough that you can see two identical moons, it's called *manosa mani*, moon water," said a voice from the dark.

The four of them spun around. Nibi had come up behind them.

"It means the light and dark energies of the earth are in balance." Nibi stepped between them, staring at the moon in the water. "It doesn't happen very often."

"And if they're out of balance?" Nettie asked.

"Nature does what it has to do to restore it. The moon's face will become distorted or not visible at all."

Once again, Nettie heard something more in her words and voice.

"You all enjoy the night. I'm going to head up the mountain before it gets too late." Nibi pulled her shawl farther up her shoulders and winked. "Take it easy on the moonshine—it doesn't take much to do a lot." She disappeared down the river walk, humming along with the music coming from the gazebo.

"Busted," Ethan said, as they watched Nibi blend into the night.

"Don't worry," Win said. "She won't say anything more than she already has."

Cal took Win's hand and pulled her toward the gazebo. "Since all is right with the earth, let's dance."

Nettie wobbled as she turned to follow, the river walk wavy beneath her.

Ethan put his hand on her elbow. "You two go ahead. We'll be there in a bit." He guided Nettie to a park bench. "Have you ever had any kind of hard liquor before?"

"Are you kidding? My dad's a state trooper, remember? He'd kill me. I snuck some beer under the bleachers once, but it didn't cause anything like this."

"If the light-headedness doesn't pass, I'll run back and get you something to eat. That will help."

"I take it you've tried liquor before?"

"Put a bunch of high school boys together, and they'll find a way to drink."

"Do your parents know?"

"They do now. Mom had a fit when she found out. Dad was a little more understanding. He said drinking alcohol came with responsibilities he didn't think I was ready for and threatened to take away my driver's license if I did it again before I understood that."

"My mom says alcohol makes bad seem good and wrong seem right."

Ethan chuckled. "Now you know why people drink."

"I like the feeling, but the taste is awful."

"Here, have a Life Saver."

Nettie closed her eyes, enjoying the silky taste of butterscotch and the sensation of floating along with the river. As the last sliver of candy melted, she realized Ethan had her hand. His skin felt warm and tingly. His closeness stirred her; the moonlight accented the highlights in his hair and eyes. She touched his face and put her lips on his. He tasted peachy.

Ethan put his arms around her, deepening the kiss. Pulling her closer, his hand found bare skin at her waist.

Fighting wooziness, Nettie pulled away and straightened her blouse. "I shouldn't have done that."

"No worries. I figured it was the moonshine talking."

"Then why'd you kiss me back?"

Leaning forward, elbows on his knees, Ethan laughed. "You're kidding, right? You think I'd turn down a chance to get a kiss?"

"Okay. I started it. I'm sorry."

"I'm not. One of these days, you'll do it again, and you won't be thinking about anyone else when you do." Pulling Nettie to her feet, he put a steadying hand on her hip. "Let's go get some of Mrs. Loving's cookies and then dance our socks off."

Chapter 8

Win slipped Nibi's small hatchet through a loop on her waist-band. "I wish you were going with us."

Nibi continued to grind a handful of dried sage in her mortar. "Don't underestimate what you know. You two are smart. You're strong. You know how to hike. You know how to camp. And you know how to protect yourselves. Your parents and I wouldn't let you go if we didn't think you could do it."

Nettie slid the knife sheath onto her belt. "Making these dreamcatchers is a bigger project than I thought it would be."

Nibi stopped grinding. "It's not a project. It's a journey."

"Why a journey?"

"Because journeys force us to make choices that never leave our lives in the same place." Nibi added more sage to the mortar. Her pestle crushed the pungent leaves as rhythmically as a ticking clock.

Nettie wanted more—the real reason Nibi had started her and Win on the dreamcatcher journey. But she wasn't going to get it just because she wanted it. Nibi shared information in strategic layers.

When she had transformed the sage into a coarse powder, Nibi poured it into a small pouch. "The amethyst mine is special to our people. Burn this in the cave before you leave. It will give thanks for the stones and honor those who came before."

Ushering them to the back porch, Nibi unrolled a small leather map and laid it across an old drum table. "This is where we are, and over here is Spy Rock." She pointed to the real mountain in the distance. "That's it. If you don't dally, you can be there by suppertime." She marked another mountain on the map. "This is Devil's Peak. You have to cross it to get to Spy Rock. Be sure to watch the tree markings when you get to the top of this one. The Appalachian Trail goes to the left, but you want to take the unmarked trail on the right." Nibi moved her finger down the map. "It ends at a creek that sits at the base of Spy Rock. From this point, you'll see an outcropping of boulders about halfway up the face. The stones will look like a carved waterfall, tall and ridged."

Nettie searched the bottom of the map for a legend. "Was it? A waterfall?"

"Centuries ago. Its waters helped form the Tye River. Once you're inside the cave, you'll be able to hear the headwaters."

"I don't see a trail up," Win said.

Nibi shook her head. "There isn't one. You'll see why when you get there. The terrain is steep and rocky, so figure out your approach before you start up. At the base of the ridged boulders is a narrow ledge. Once you're on it, follow the wall into the deep shadows on the right. The wall looks like it ends, but it doesn't. Feel your way along the stone until it curves into the mountain. Just past the curve is a narrow crevasse. It's just big enough for you to slide through. The amethyst cave is on the other side."

"We don't have flashlights."

Nibi pulled a flint from her pocket and handed it to Win. "Do you remember how to make pine-knot torches?"

"Yes, ma'am."

"Good. You'll need several. You'll find plenty of pines along the tree line at the top of Spy Rock. Once you're in the cave, you'll see where others laid their fire. Use that site. It has the best draw for the smoke."

Nettie moved her foot out of the way as a spider darted across the porch toward a web full of egg sacs. "Anything live in this cave beside spider mothers?"

"Probably not, but be careful where you put your hands and feet anyway."

"Great."

Nibi handed Win a long shoulder sack. "There's a canteen and a hammer and chisel in here. Amethyst is hard, so be patient and chisel carefully." She handed a second sack to Nettie. "There's another canteen and enough pone and jerky in here to last two days. Your stones need to be about the size of your thumbnail. The darker, the better. Once they're mined, keep them in the sage pouch. You don't want to lose them on the way back."

Nettie and Win trekked to the top of Nibi's Mountain, stopping long enough to wave to her from Lookout Point, a stone extension of the mountain that provided an incredible view of the valley. Running the ridge, they turned north and descended into a gap leading to Devil's Peak.

Hours later, Nettie stopped to take a long drink from her canteen. "The mountain didn't look this steep on the map."

"It also didn't look this pretty or smell this good."

Something shimmered in the trees. Nettie moved closer. "Would you look at that." A giant spiderweb, sparkly with morning dew, ran from one tree to the next.

Win spread her arms to gauge its width. "That's some web."

The ordinary-looking spider that had created it sat in the middle, bundling an unfortunate bug. Dozens of other food sacks dotted the web.

"Wonder why she needs such a big web? And so much food?"

"Must be preparing for something."

"Just goes to show you what one spider can accomplish."

"We need to get moving. We not even halfway yet."

By midafternoon, they reached the unmarked trail. Two hours later, they made it to the creek at the base of Spy Rock. Nettie dropped her sack and stretched. "Water's running high."

"High enough that we're going to get more than our ankles wet."

"According to the map, the only footbridge is a mile downstream. We'd lose too much time getting there. We'll have to cross here."

Foraging two strong limbs to use as wading staves, Nettie and Win slid out of their jeans and socks and stuffed them in their sacks, then tied the sacks around their shoulders. Putting their shoes back on, they held hands and waded in.

"Damn! It's a lot colder than I thought it would be."

Their teeth chattered as the cold creek quickly went thigh high.

Moving across the current, they navigated around and over slippery rocks. Reaching the opposite bank, they rubbed their legs for warmth and refilled their canteens. Nettie started to pull her jeans from the bag, when Win stopped her, staring downstream. "Don't move."

"What is it?"

"A bear cub."

"I don't see it."

"It's coming."

Nettie scanned upstream. Nothing moved. Quiet surrounded them. Even the ever-present nosey squirrels went silent.

"Are you sure? I don't see a thing."

Forty yards away, leaves rustled and twigs snapped as a black bear cub burst playfully out of the bushes and scampered to the water's edge.

Win reached for the hatchet at her waist and whispered, "Momma's coming."

"Where?" Nettie eased her hand into the shoulder sack to get their food.

"She's following the cub."

Bigger brush surrendered noisily to the lumbering momma bear as she joined her baby. Straight up, she'd be six feet tall. The wind blew toward Nettie and Win, so she hadn't scented them, yet.

Win inched back toward Nettie; then, side by side, they moved farther away.

The momma bear caught their movement and pivoted with a guttural growl. Moving in front of her cub, she huffed and pawed the ground, shaking her big head.

Win yelled and waved as Nettie heaved their bag of food; its contents spilled around the bears' paws. Nettie and Win then dodged behind a long line of rocks and took off up the mountain, not stopping until they were high enough to see the bears still feeding at the water's edge.

Panting, Nettie sank to the ground, her sides cramping. "We were almost bear bait."

Win propped her hands on her knees, breathing deeply. She attempted a giggle. "Well, one of us would have been. I can outrun you."

"Jokes? Really? That bear was close enough that we could smell it, and you're cracking jokes?"

Win stood to check on the bears again. "Beats the alternative. Plus, I think we handled it pretty well."

"True. Unless you consider we have no food."

"We have plenty of food. We just weren't planning on eating nuts and berries for two days."

Nettie pulled on her jeans and socks. "I hope these blasted dreamcatchers are worth all this."

The ledge of the stone waterfall sat ninety feet above them; they had no way to reach it from below.

Win groaned. "We'll have to backtrack to where it's not so steep, hike up to the tree line, cross over the top, and come down from the other side before it gets dark."

"And we have to find pine knots for torches while we're up there, then get them, ourselves, and the bags down to that ledge without sliding all the way back down here."

"Right. Nothing to it."

Struggling to keep their footing, Nettie and Win backtracked to a lesser incline, then climbed parallel past the formation. Once they reached the tree line, the ground flattened. Gathering pine branches, they split the knots, then stuffed them with pine cones and twigs to make torches. Following the tree line, Nettie spotted a patch of blackberries. "Thank goodness. I'm starving."

After eating their fill, she and Win picked the remaining berries, wrapped them in large poplar leaves, and stored them in the sacks.

Moving to the edge of the stone face, Nettie kicked at the sandy gravel, sending a loud spray cascading down the slope beyond where she could see.

"We're going to have to sit to do this," Win said.

Nettie squatted to test one of several clumps of scrub brush growing amid the stones. It held when she tugged on it. "Dig your heels in and hold on to this stuff. It's not much, but it's all we've got."

Nettie sat, balanced the torch-filled sack on her back, and inched downward. Win followed close behind. Every movement caused currents of pebbles to flow ahead of them. As they neared the ledge, Win's brush broke loose, sending her sliding into Nettie.

"Dig in!" Nettie yelled, as she made a frantic grab for a cluster of craggy rocks near the ledge.

A cloud of dust and gravel swallowed them, but the craggy rocks held.

"Work your way over to the ledge, then help me over," Nettie said.

Win tossed her sack carefully onto the flat stone and inched her way across. Scrambling up, she got on her knees to give Nettie a hand.

Once on the ledge, Nettie peeked over the rim. "I don't want to think about how we're going to get down from here."

Win pointed to the corner of the formation. "There's the shadow Nibi told us about." She led the way into the darkness, feeling along the curved wall, searching for the crevasse that would lead them inside.

"Please don't let any snakes be in there," Nettie prayed.

"We've made so much noise getting here, any critters calling this place home are long gone."

"We hope."

Win stopped. "I think I found it. It's not very wide." She eased the sack off her shoulder and handed it to Nettie. "When I get to the other side, pass these to me; then you come."

"Be careful. You're brave to go first."

Nettie felt Win's smile more than she saw it. "I'm not the first." Win disappeared into the black wall.

Inching closer, Nettie waited, admiring Win's courage. The cool air coming through the crevasse felt damp and smelled like a litter box.

"Win? Are you all right?"

"Yeah. I think I'm in. I just can't see." Her words echoed. "It's pitch black in here. Hand me a sack."

Nettie inched into the crevasse, the sack in her outstretched hand. She felt Win take it.

"Hand me the other one."

Nettie inched back into the crevasse with the second sack. Handing it to Win, she continued to follow the curved stone. She could hear Win rummaging through their supplies.

"Found the flint."

Nettie stepped into open space as the torch flared and filled the cave with yellow light. Sudden, frenzied flapping over their heads made them duck.

"Gotta be bats," Win yelled.

"That explains the smell."

"Leave them alone, and maybe they'll leave us alone."

"Don't tell me—tell them."

When the bats had settled, Nettie stayed low to light a second torch. The boost of light increased the shadows dancing on the walls as the smoke surged up and out of the cave, through the top of the crevasse. The remaining haze made the cave's odor bearable. Lowering the torch, Nettie scanned the floor. It was covered in bat guano, but nothing wiggled. "So far, so good."

"Listen."

The soft roar of big water echoed from deep in the mountain. "That has to be the headwaters of the Tye."

Win moved the torch closer to the wall. Long, erratic dribbles of water mapped the stone. "Look." Symbols, names, and messages were scratched all over the cave. She pointed at a squiggly line. "This is the symbol for 'river.' The half circle with lines above it is a symbol for the moon. And the circle with horns covering it means 'strong medicine.' I'll bet some of these carvings are hundreds of years old."

They moved about the cave, reading the names and messages they could decipher. Most of the readable ones simply marked the writer's presence in the cave. Some spoke of love and longing, others spoke of fear, and still others spoke of those who had come before and their love of the earth.

"Oh my gosh." Win ran her fingers along some carved letters. "'Dell loves Nibi.'"

"Dell is your grandfather?"

Win nodded. "He must have been with Nibi when she mined the amethyst for her dreamcatcher."

"How'd he die?"

"An accident of some kind. Nibi doesn't talk about it."

"It had to be hard for her to raise your mother alone." Nettie did a double take at the next name. "Holy cow. Look at this. 'Piccolo loves . . .'"

"Pic? Who does he love?"

"I can't tell. There's a dark drip line staining the stone."

"Funny. I never imagined Pic loving someone."

"That I can imagine. What I don't understand is why he was here. Like me, he's not Monacan."

"Maybe when Nibi brought Dell here, Pic came too. After all, they're friends."

"Maybe."

Win studied the wall again. "Nibi knew we'd see this."

"What do we do now that we have?"

"We'll have to figure that out later. Right now, we have a job to do."

The far end of the cave narrowed to a tunnel with long, sparkling purple stripes. The veins of amethyst closest to the cave had been chipped smooth from the floor to well above their heads. Grabbing more torches, Nettie and Win made their way deeper into the tunnel in search of a vein with the desired color and enough roughness to anchor a chisel.

"I can't see the cave anymore or where the tunnel ends."

"Just remember the direction we came from," Win said.

Nettie broke off a piece of charred pine and drew an arrow on the wall, pointing to the cave.

Win sank to her knees. "I think this is a good vein."

The inch-wide stripe of black-purple anchored lines of fading violet.

"It's the right color. Go for it."

Win placed the chisel against one of the dark ridges and tapped gently with the hammer. Nothing happened. She tapped harder. The chisel still didn't mark the stone. She hit it again, harder. Still nothing. Sighing, she sat back on her heels. "It's going to be a long night."

"We're going to need more torches."

"I know. The smoke's not clearing out of the tunnel as well as it did in the cave. It's burning my eyes."

"We don't have a choice. We have to see what we're doing."

Cloudy moonlight cast eerie shadows across the face of the mountain as Nettie inched back toward the tree line.

Win steadied herself on the craggy rocks. "I'll catch the branches or you, whichever comes down the hill first."

"That's not funny."

"Yes, it is. But be careful anyway."

Reaching the top, Nettie scrambled to her feet. Searching for downed branches, she spotted something deeper in the woods.

"Win, what was the name of that plant that glows in the dark? The green one Nibi showed us growing on the Gospel Tree?" Her words flowed down the mountain in waves.

"Fairy fire," Win yelled.

"There's some up here. Maybe we can use it to light the tunnel." Nettie made her way through the woods toward the green glow. Breaking through the thick brush, she entered a village of trees and stumps covered with the effervescent moss. Magic.

"Sorry, fairies." She filled her sack with the glowing clumps, then pulled off her T-shirt, tied the bottom, and gathered more. Making her way back to the tree line, she carefully inched down to the ledge. Win's moonlit silhouette had one foot on the ledge and one on the craggy rocks, ready to give her a hand up.

"You're glowing."

"Let's hope this stuff works."

Inside the cave, Win got the canteen and dug more berries out of her bag while Nettie broke up one of the torches to keep the embers going. Once they'd eaten, they carried the sacks of fairy fire into the tunnel. Placing the glowing clumps in a semicircle around them provided enough light to see, but the low angle of the vein made chiseling difficult.

Struggling to get comfortable, Win stood and rubbed her knees. "This gritty floor is killing my knees and butt."

Nettie gathered their sacks, folded them in half, and handed them to Win. "Maybe these will help."

Taking turns, they chiseled into the night, stopping just long enough to change positions, stretch, or get a drink of water. To stay awake, they talked, covering everything and everyone they could think of. Then they sang. Song after song echoed through the tunnel in soft waves, accompanied by arrhythmic clicks. When they ran out of songs, Win hummed and chanted.

As the hours ticked by, Nettie lost count of the number of times they numbly switched places. When she slipped out of the cave for fresh air, the beauty of the full, creamy moon hovering over the sharp tips of the evergreens below took her breath away. The moon's face seemed close enough to touch.

In the wee hours of the morning, Win sprinkled the crushed sage on the low-burning fire; then Nettie slipped two dime-size chunks of amethyst into the pouch and tied it to her belt. Exhausted, they carved their names into the wall, along with the word "thanks," then lay on their sacks and slept.

At sunrise, seeing no sign of the momma bear and her cub at the creek, Nettie and Win took their jeans off and shook them. The somewhat-controlled slide from the cave had filled their pockets and fabric with dirt, gravel, and rips.

Stuffing her jeans and socks into her bag, Nettie groaned as she knelt along the creek to fill her canteen. She'd gotten stronger over the summer, but her muscles still complained about the long night's work, the hardness of the cave floor, and the lack of sleep. "I'm starving. We need to find something to eat before we start back."

Win scanned nearby trees and bushes. "There's some hazelnuts and wild asparagus across the creek."

Shaking her head in amazement at Win's knowledge of plants, Nettie fingered a nearby bush. "This smells like almonds. Can we eat it?"

"Only if you want to die. That's arsenic."

"Good to know." Nettie quickly rinsed her hands and sat on a downed tree to tie her shoes.

Finding the staves they'd used for balance during the first crossing, they waded into the creek.

Nettie shook all over. "If I wasn't awake before, I am now."

Climbing the bank, she and Win dressed, then gathered pea-size hazelnuts and stalks of wild asparagus for breakfast.

Nettie couldn't help but make a face at the bitterness of the green stalks. "This stuff's worse than broccoli. I'd rather have Momma's French toast and coffee with sweet cream."

"Me too. But, this will get us back to Nibi's with energy to spare. She'll be waiting for us with something good to eat."

Taking turns at the lead, Nettie and Win reached the top of Devil's Peak before noon. They stopped to rest and finish the last of the forest food in the shade of a large maple tree.

Nettie studied the mountainside as the maple dropped whirlybirds all around them. "It's too quiet. No birds. No chipmunks. No squirrels. Where is everything?"

"That's a good question, especially since we haven't seen the first eagle or owl all summer. Not even their nests. We need feathers, and soon."

Nibi refilled Win's bowl with venison stew and reached for Nettie's. "More?"

"Yes, ma'am. Please."

"Diverting the bear with your food was a smart thing to do."

Nettie cocked her head at Win. They'd decided there was nothing to be gained by telling Nibi or anyone else about the close encounter with the bears. They should have known she'd know.

"If I'd been really smart, I would have thrown half the food at them, instead of all of it. We had to eat nuts and berries for thirty hours," Nettie said.

"Don't forget the asparagus." Win made a face.

"I'm still trying to get the bitter taste out of my mouth."

Nibi put the Dutch oven back on the woodstove and stirred the remaining stew. "You got away. And, they didn't follow you, did they? There was danger, and your instincts kept you safe. Don't second-guess them now."

"We saw your name and Dell's in the cave," Win said.

Nibi eased into her chair. Picking up one of the amethysts,

she fingered the chiseled edges. "He was with me when I mined the spider mother for my web. We hadn't been married very long." Her face relaxed, as if flowing into a happy memory. "I loved him then as I do now."

Nettie couldn't help but be amazed. How'd she do it—hold on to that kind of love for a lifetime?

Nibi's deep wrinkles returned as she laid the stone on the table and rose to get more corn bread. "You two have done well."

After they'd eaten, Nibi handed Win and Nettie thin pieces of hard-drawn copper wire. She showed them how to spin-drill a small hole through the middle of their amethyst. "This will take time and patience. When the holes are all the way through, come back and we'll thread them into your webs."

Win nodded at Nettie's silent question. "Nibi, we also saw Pic's name in the cave."

"As I knew you would."

"Tell us about it?"

"Soon. You two should get going, or you'll miss the train home. I'm sure your parents will be glad to see you."

Nettie hid her disappointment. Whether she liked it or not, Nibi had the right to tell the story when and how she wanted.

Chapter 9

"Faith? Blind? Not hardly."

Mr. Danes leaned back, propped his loafers on the desk, and took a sip from his Dixie cup. Despite his cold, sparse office, Nettie had come to enjoy their Wednesday-night meetings. He had a commonsense way of explaining things.

"We get up every morning having faith in something: that the sun will rise and we'll be here to see it. That spring will come and those who love us will always love us."

"That makes sense."

"Just as faithful are our doubts, those moments when we question whether the sun really will come up. Will we be here to see it? Will winter ever end? Will those who love us always love us? Christians are no different. Even the most faithful have doubts."

"You?"

"All the time."

"About what?"

"Myself, mostly. Am I serving as I should? Am I doing all I can to avoid temptation?"

"Do you ever doubt God?"

"No, but I doubt my ability to understand him."

"Why?"

"Because I don't think human beings are capable of understanding the divine. Just as a child can't understand the mind of
Einstein, we cannot understand the mind of God. That doesn't mean
we can't know his love at some basic level. Even children know when
they're loved and when they're not."

"If he loves us, then why does he let bad things to happen to
good people?"

"You could just as easily ask why he lets good things happen to
bad people or why he lets good and bad things happen at all. We ask
those types of questions when we try to hold God accountable for
our definition of what is good and bad and right and wrong. It's like
me questioning Einstein's intelligence because I can't understand
his theories about how the universe works. Look at the story of Job.
His life was filled with love and joy; then fate delivered blow after
blow: loss, sickness, pain, ridicule. Job didn't understand why. In his
mind, he'd been forsaken. It took a while, but he came to realize that
his physical and mental well-being during his time on Earth were
not the same as his spiritual well-being for eternity. We can't force
all that is God into our small fishbowl of understanding."

"Why couldn't Pastor Williams have explained it that way? He
acted as if he didn't hear the question."

"Maybe he heard more than you think."

"What do you mean?"

"There's a difference between doubts that motivate us to search
for deepening belief and doubts that obstruct belief. Maybe Pastor
Williams heard more emphasis on the wrong kind of doubt."

"I think he was just being stubborn."

Mr. Danes laughed. "Well, that's always a possibility."

"Some of the GAs lied about believing, but he baptized them
anyway."

"That's none of your concern."

"What? Why?"

"If they lied, the issue is between them, Pastor Williams, and
God. You don't have a say in it."

"But it's not fair."

"It's not an issue of fairness. And there are no buts about it."

Nettie leaned back, exhaling like a pricked balloon.

"Don't misunderstand me. If those girls lied, I don't like it. But God loves them just as much as he loves you and me. Hopefully, at some point they will acknowledge what they did, and Pastor Williams can help them mend relationships, both spiritual and human. Until then, your job is simple: forgive it, forget it, and move on. Not only for their sake, but for yours."

"It's not that easy. What they did, what they continue to do, is wrong. They go around pretending to be something they're not."

Fire flickered in Mr. Danes's eyes; his tone hardened. "We're all tempted to be something we're not. We all lie. We all sin. And, more times than not, we choose to hide when accountability for those sins rolls around. It's what humans do. We're flawed. We make bad decisions when we let our lesser selves take the lead. Afterward, when the guilt hits, we try to hide from it and we can't. Good or bad, with choices come consequences." He drained his cup.

"Then how do we avoid being tempted in the first place?"

"You can't avoid it. Evil doesn't ask, it tells. And it remembers what works. The only thing you can do is hope you're strong enough to resist. And when you're not, don't run and hide. Evil seldom survives the light of day."

"I hadn't thought about it like that."

"Not many people do." Mr. Danes put his feet on the floor. "The thing is, even when you try to hide, someone's always watching." He propped his elbows on the desk and looked at Nettie as if he knew a secret. "Question is, what are you hiding?"

"Me?"

"I didn't stutter."

"I'm not hiding anything."

"Sure you are."

Nettie searched her memory but came up empty. "No, sir. I don't think so."

Mr. Danes moved to sit on the corner of his desk. Nettie slid back in her chair to keep their legs from touching.

"Think about it this week and see what you come up with. We're all tempted. We all succumb. And we all try to hide from it. But we can't. There are eyes everywhere, human and divine, watching."

Leaving the discomfort of Mr. Danes's office, Nettie ran into Pic as he shuffled from the dining room, his lone hand holding his bulging bindle tightly. Even when it wasn't stuffed with church supper leftovers, Pic never let that sack out of his sight. "It's the only pocket I have that doesn't have holes," he'd once explained.

"Hey, Pic."

"Hey, Nettie girl."

"What are you doing here so late?"

"Kitchen faucet's leaking again. I had to wait till the ladies finished cleaning up before I could get in there to fix it."

"That thing leaks a lot."

"It's just old, like me. A new washer, a little tightening here and there, and she works just fine, at least for a little while. What are *you* doing here so late?"

"Meeting with Mr. Danes."

"You've been doing that for a while now."

"Weeks."

"The baptism thing?"

Nettie nodded. "One of these days, I'll measure up."

Pic opened the door for Nettie, then locked it behind them.

"Mr. Danes is still in there."

"He has a key. Plus, he always goes out the back. Where's Win? Don't you two usually walk home together?"

"My meetings with Mr. Danes started running too long. It wasn't fair to ask her to wait."

"You shouldn't be walking by yourself this time of night."

"Streetlights are on. Besides, I've run up and down these side-walks all my life. They're safe."

"It's not the sidewalks I worry about. It's the strangers who walk them. Mind if I mosey with you?"

"I'd like that, but I don't want to make you late getting home."

"No worries. It's a nice night, my feet work good, and I don't have a family or television to hurry home to."

The town was silent as they crossed the intersection under the blinking red light.

"Pic, how long have you and Nibi been friends?"

"A long time. Why?"

"Just curious."

"Uh-uh. You saw my name in the amethyst cave, didn't you?"

"How'd you know?"

"Nibi told me she'd sent you and Win up there."

"So, you were in the cave?"

"I take it Nibi didn't tell you about it?"

"She said she would soon."

"Then it needs to be her soon, not mine."

"C'mon, Pic."

"Nibi knows what she's doing. Far be it from me to second-guess her."

Turning onto the Upper Road, they passed Allen's Hill, the mansion dark and quiet, as usual.

"Pic, have you ever met the lady who lives up there? I mean, before she disappeared into that house?"

Clouds moved across the moon, deepening the shadows surrounding the mansion.

"A dark beauty, that one. She was out of my league." Piccolo kept walking.

A Cracker Jack box with skinny arms and legs danced across the drive-in movie screen as Ethan guided the Chrysler down the crunchy gravel of the terraced slopes and into an open parking spot.

Nettie rolled down the passenger window to turn on the speaker. "It's crowded tonight."

Win leaned over the seat. "What do you expect? It's John Wayne and Glen Campbell."

"Don't forget Kim Darby," Cal added.

Glen Campbell's winsome voice floated into the car as a ring of stars framed the blue mountaintop on the screen.

"I love this song," Nettie said, singing along.

"I know. You've played the record a hundred times," Win lamented.

"I don't think I have it."

"What? The record?"

"No. Grit."

Win laughed. "I don't know about that. You're pretty fearless, except when it comes to snakes."

"Very funny."

Ethan interrupted. "You realize the song is about finding a man with grit, not having it, right?"

"Can you find it if you don't have it?" Nettie asked.

"Quiet, you all. I want to hear what they're saying." Win settled in the middle of the backseat, close to Cal. Nettie and Ethan stayed on their respective sides.

An hour into the movie, Nettie caught movement in the back-seat. Win and Cal were enjoying a leisurely kiss.

"You two coming up for air anytime soon? You're missing a great movie."

Win giggled. "Eyes on the screen, please."

Ethan squeezed Nettie's hand. "Want to give it a try?"

"Eyes on the screen, please." Most of the couples in the surrounding cars were not watching the movie. If she had been here with Andy, they wouldn't have been either.

The dancing Cracker Jack box reappeared to announce intermission. Cal and Win slid out of the backseat. "Let's go to the snack bar."

Ethan opened Nettie's door and pointed to the swings and picnic tables at the bottom of the hill. "I'll get some popcorn and cokes, then meet you down there."

"Great. I'll grab a couple of swings."

Weaving between cars, Nettie zigzagged down the remaining terraces. The dormant movie screen cast a silvery glow across the small park. Surrounded by sweet-smelling shrubs, cricket calls, and lightning bugs, she wiggled into one of the swings. Pushing to her tiptoes, she pulled back on the chains, then let go, kicking her legs to go higher and faster. Closing her eyes, she enjoyed the thrill and the breeze.

"Hi."

The swing jerked in half circles until Nettie could get both feet on the ground.

Andy stood close enough for her to smell his aftershave.

"Hi."

"I saw you come down here. I wanted to see how you're doing."

"I'm okay. You?"

"Okay."

"You here with Anne?"

Andy nodded. "You here with what's-his-name?"

"Ethan. His name is Ethan."

"I know. Sorry."

"No, you're not. What's-her-name know you're down here with me?"

"No. She went to the bathroom. Where's what's-his-name?"

"Getting popcorn."

Andy took a step toward her, placing his hand over hers on the chain.

"Nettie, I—"

Ethan cleared his throat as he cruised through the grass toward them.

Andy steadied her while she jumped from the swing. He seemed taller, broader.

A talking hot dog burst onto the screen above them, reminding viewers that the snack bar had their favorite treats.

"Ethan, this is Andy. Andy, this is Ethan."

Andy nodded once. "We met at the lake."

"That same girl is up at the concession stand, looking for you."

Chapter 10

Nettie and Win sipped steaming black coffee as Nibi explained how to bow-knot the sinew string to the red willow, coil-wrap the overlapping ends of the wood, then loop the string along the inside edge of the ring.

"Use the first row to anchor the next by interlacing each loop. Pull the sinew taut until each opening is diamond shaped."

After a couple of awkward starts, the precise but tedious work of weaving the webs was under way. Nibi moved back and forth between Nettie and Win, observing and guiding but not doing.

By noon, with half a dozen rows completed, Nettie noticed her diamonds beginning to lose their firmness. Holding the sinew so tight had irritated the calluses she'd developed while spin-drilling the hole in her amethyst.

Nibi handed her a wide-mouthed jar of fresh-smelling salve. "Rub this into your fingers, then redo that last row. Your web is only as strong as the weakest loop."

"But—"

"No buts. Tight weave, strong web."

Nettie knew better than to push. She stood and stretched, then dipped her hands in the jar. The cool, tingly balm gave her instant relief as she massaged it in.

"This stuff's great. What is it?"

"Ask Win. She made it." Nibi couldn't keep the pride out of her voice.

Nettie turned to Win. "You made this?"

"I did. It's a mixture of cayenne pepper, turmeric, and aloe."

"Isn't that the stuff Wade and Skip put on the rock candy?"

"And the same stuff Mr. Carter used in the swish-and-swallow to get rid of the burning in your mouth. Remember? One form causes pain, while another cures it. My formula helps the pain, softens the skin, and smells good in the process."

"Why didn't you tell me you were working on this?"

"I wanted Nibi to test it first. Last thing I needed to do was set you on fire again."

Nettie hugged her. "It's wonderful."

Shooing them back to work on their webs, Nibi continued the lesson. "The rows and loops get progressively smaller toward the center, so position your spider mother where she can spin easily. Once she's in place, keep weaving until there's a three-inch portal in the middle. Then tie off the sinew with a bow knot."

When they'd finished their webs, Nibi checked them again. "Perfect. Any tighter, and the ring would bend."

Nettie scooped more of the healing salve from the jar on the windowsill. Nearby, the feathers in Nibi's dreamcatcher shivered in a barely there breeze. "Nibi, we may have to wait until the leaves are off the trees in the fall to find nests with the feathers we need."

"You can find them now if you look in the right places."

"We've been all over these mountains and haven't seen an eagle of any kind, much less a golden one."

Win leaned against the porch railing. "We haven't seen any owls either, for that matter, much less a white one."

"You're looking but not seeing."

"What are we missing?" Win asked. "We've searched everywhere they'd feed. They're not here. In fact, we're not seeing much wildlife of any kind. Not even their scat."

"What does that tell you?"

"Something scared them off?"

Nettie remembered Nibi's comment the day they had visited the Gospel Oak. "Does this have anything to do with the mountains being restless?"

"Most likely."

"Do you know what they're restless about?"

"Not yet," Nibi answered. "But birds are the first to leave when there's a threat and the first to come back when it's over."

"I wish Nature would give us a hint about where they went." Frustration gave Nettie's voice an edge.

"Really," Win added. "What happens if we don't find them?"

Nibi stood, her mouth set in a straight line. "You two come with me." Going into the kitchen, she motioned for Nettie and Win to sit at the kitchen table while she strained a cup of dandelion tea. Cradling the cup as if warming her hands, she eased into her chair. "You'll not find what you're looking for by whining. The birds you're searching for are ancient, and they're smart. What makes you think they'd make it easy for you? You're going to struggle, as you should, but be smart about it."

"What are we missing?" Win asked.

"My father used to say, 'Experience builds the most reliable map.' You learn by doing. What works. What doesn't. Where to go. Where not to go. You've got to start over. So be it. At least now you know where not to go and what not to do." Nibi blew across her cup and took a sip. "The Blue Ridge Mountains form a tunnel for the northern winds, so the birds are here. Up to now, you've hoped they'd just fly by or that you'd get lucky and spot their nests. That rarely happens—a fact I'm sure you knew but chose to ignore. It's time to think beyond the obvious."

Nettie rubbed the calluses on her hands. "We're running out of summer."

"Time is the price, and time is the payoff. Your dreamcatchers need to be finished before the waxing moon of August becomes a supermoon."

"We've had supermoons before. Why is this one any different?"

Nibi took her cup to the window and stared into the mountains. "Because it will also be a blood moon."

Nettie cocked her head. "I thought those only occurred with eclipses."

"It's rare, but they can also occur when a supermoon rises at the same time the sun sets. This causes a powerful red aura to veil the moon."

"Why is that bad?"

"Because it precedes a darkness."

"What kind of darkness?"

"It hasn't revealed itself to me yet. There are many possibilities, human and in Nature."

"Will we know what it is before it happens?"

Returning to the table, Nibi put a mint leaf in her tea and stirred, the spoon not touching the sides of the cup. "I don't know, which is why I've not said much until now. Darkness thrives on deception. It will bait and mislead until it is primed and ready to do its worst. I sense ominous power in this darkness."

Win leaned in. "So, what do we do?"

"Exactly what we've been doing: ready ourselves."

Nettie exhaled, not realizing she'd been holding her breath. "This is getting scary."

Nibi pushed a stray lock of hair behind Nettie's ear. "Worry seldom accomplishes what being prepared does. Now, see if you two can figure out where to find those feathers." She went outside, letting the screen door slam.

Win followed Nibi to the door and watched as she walked up to the garden. "She's telling us not to worry, but she is."

Nettie rubbed her temples, trying to focus. "Okay. Whatever it means, one thing is clear: We need to finish these damn dreamcatchers. Let's concentrate on that. Nibi said to think beyond the obvious. What do we know and not know about eagles?"

Win turned and leaned against the door jamb. "They're loners. Except they mate for life."

"They're strong, high fliers."

"They build nests in the tall peaks where it's safe. Rocky peaks."

"Not the rocky peaks around here. We've looked."

"Wait a minute." Win perked up. "The highest peaks in this mountain range are north of here. If the eagles aren't here, maybe they moved up there."

"What would make them move?"

"Predators?"

"Like what?"

"Bigfoot."

"Very funny."

"We've had cougars around here before. They chased everything out. But we haven't heard anything about farmers losing stock, and we haven't seen any carcasses."

"Hunters."

"It's illegal to kill eagles. Plus, we haven't heard any shots."

"Weather."

Win shrugged. "It's been rainy, but Nibi said eagles like to fly in storms."

"Fire."

"No big fires around here that I know of."

Nettie slumped. "Then we're back to food. Eagles eat small animals. Mice. Squirrels. Chipmunks. Rabbits."

"We haven't seen many of those all summer. Not even around water."

"Water? If land animals aren't available, won't eagles eat fish?"

Win jumped up. "That's it! Find higher peaks, find water. Find water, find fish. Find fish, find eagles. Crab Tree Falls is north of here, and it's on one of the highest peaks in the Blue Ridge. Guess what's near there? A fish hatchery."

"Isn't Crabtree Falls way up near Montebello? That's a two-day hike."

"Maybe Ethan and Cal will drive us up there."

Nettie and Win sailed out the back door, across the yard, to the garden.

Nibi nodded as they explained their plan. "Crab Tree Falls has five drops spread over two miles. Getting to the base isn't hard. Getting to the top is. The trail is steep, rocky, and wet. Plan carefully."

"Is it cheating if we get a ride to Montebello?"

"No more than riding the *Weak and Weary* up here. The challenge isn't getting to Montebello; it's getting to the top of the falls. You need to do that under your own power. And you'll need to get the feathers yourself."

Nettie dropped cross-legged in the shade. "Why couldn't we have thought about this weeks ago?"

Nibi tossed her a ripe tomato. "Some of the most important journeys start in the wrong direction."

Hurrying back across the Route 56 bridge, Nettie and Win headed for the train station. They paused next to the rumbling engine to toss a fresh bag of remedies to Mr. Roberts, then dodged crates and workers to make their way to the caboose.

Pic sat up and felt for his bindle, then rubbed his beard as they came inside. "Hey, girlies."

"Sorry to wake you, Pic."

"Wasn't napping, just checking my eyelids for leaks. You two have a good visit with Nibi?"

Win handed him a package. "Yes, sir. She sent you some blackberry jerky."

Pic pulled a piece of the dark, dry meat out of the wrapping. Taking a bite, he closed his eyes, savoring the taste. "I'd never had blackberry jerky till I came here. Nibi made me some that first summer and has every summer since."

Nettie winked at Win. Pic told them the same thing every time he got a new batch. She grabbed the back of the bench in front of her as the train lurched. "How long have you been here, Pic?"

"Where? The train?"

"No. Amherst. Oak's Landing."

"Since the Great Depression."

Win propped her feet on the bench in front of her. "I never understood why it was called the Great Depression. Seems like it was anything but great."

"You're right. It was awful. It cost my family a lot."

Nettie caught a change in Pic's voice. "You grew up in South Carolina, didn't you?"

"I did. Pa used to call it the better Carolina to tease Ma. She was from North Carolina."

"How'd you find your way up here?"

"My brother and me got turned out."

"Turned out?"

"Pa lost his job. The bank took our house. He and Ma couldn't afford to feed us, so they turned us out."

"How old were you?"

"Old enough to understand. Nobody was hiring for farm work. Pa said we'd have a better chance of finding a job in a city. We started riding the rails around the South, looking for work and food. Those were some mighty hungry days. If it weren't for orchards, soup kitchens, and hobo camps, we would've starved to death."

The *Weak and Weary* shuddered as it started the long climb into the mountains. Nettie lowered another window to recapture the breeze.

"Were you able to find work?"

"Odd jobs here and there. When we made it to the Richmond railyard, one of the old-timers said the pulp mill in Oak's Landing had put out a call for log loaders, so we hopped a train up here. The mill's foreman needed young men with strong backs and hired us on the spot. Job didn't pay much, but he fed us good. He also let us sleep in his barn as long as we helped him with farm chores."

"Who was the foreman?"

"Nibi's father."

Win's eyes widened. "I never knew that."

"Wasn't no secret. He preached good on Sunday and worked at the mill the rest of the week. We helped him with the stonework on his church. When it was done, he'd leave the door open in case any of the workers needed a place to sleep."

The train crested the mountain, picked up speed, and rode the backside of the swell toward the valley, turning the breeze into a loud, pine-scented wind.

"Where's your brother now?"

"He died a long time ago." Pic rubbed his stump. "'Bout the same time I lost my hand."

A pang of guilt gnawed at Nettie. She'd never bothered to ask Pic about his family. "I'm sorry."

"It was a long time ago. Don't pay to dwell on it."

"Did you ever go back? To see your parents, I mean?"

"I went back after my brother died, but my parents were gone. Neighbors said they left town soon after we did. No one knew where they went."

"Is that why you came back here?"

Pic nodded. "I liked this place. Folks treated me nice. After I lost my hand, I couldn't load logs anymore, so Nibi's father helped me get a job cleaning the train stations. The yardmaster in Amherst set up a little apartment for me in the stone storage building behind the station as part of my pay. It keeps me warm in the winter and cool in the summer. It's dry. I have a bed to call my own, food every day, and a reason to get up every morning. It felt like home. Still does."

"What was your brother's name?"

Pic didn't answer. He'd turned toward the window, lost in memories.

Nettie's stomach flip-flopped as she stood at the base of Crab Tree Falls. The noise of the pounding water had started as a smooth hum at the trailhead below. Now, it roared like a locomotive at full throttle.

"That's some mean-looking water," Win said. "Must be all the rain we've had."

An agitated mist floated above them, before settling in the surrounding woods like remnants of a storm. Higher up, hidden among the dense blue-green dips and swells, were four more falls and the large creek that connected them. In the peaks, splashes of gray pinpointed where the mountain's forested coat had surrendered to millennia of wind and rain.

Cal leaned over the railing to look up. "Grams said these falls have the steepest drop of any waterfall east of the Mississippi."

Nettie pulled him back. "She's right. And climbing up is more than a walk in the park."

Ethan stood at the base of the rugged vertical trail paralleling the falls. "You've got to be kidding. We're hiking two miles up this?"

"All the twists and turns make it more like three, but who's counting?"

"This isn't a trail; it's an obstacle course."

"All the more reason to get started." Nettie climbed the stair-like ledge of the first boulder and shuddered as a slithering, pointed tail disappeared over the back edge. "Dammit, Win. I wish you'd get back to seeing those things before I do."

"I'm trying. Cal, you and Ethan watch where you put your hands and feet."

Thirty minutes later, they stood beside the second fall that formed a massive figure eight. At the top, spread-out water cascaded down a stone staircase like a white lace veil following a royal bride. In the middle, the fall narrowed, overlapping the lace to race through a crown of shimmering quartz, only to explode into another lacy veil below.

Cal whistled. "It looks like that math thing we studied in Calculus."

Ethan punched his arm. "It's an infinity symbol, bozo."

"Same difference. It's math."

"It also symbolizes power," Win added. "A balance between forces, such as male and female, light and dark."

Cal turned and headed up the trail. "That's easier to understand than the math. I almost flunked Calculus."

By midmorning, Nettie had a new appreciation for her increased strength. She and Win outclimbed Ethan and Cal, who seemed to stay with them by sheer determination. She slowed the pace as the trail dropped through a dense, tree-covered hollow filled with thick variations of green on green and sounds that seemed of another world.

Ethan did a slow turn. "This is incredible."

Nettie had spent so much time in the woods of late, it took a minute for her to appreciate the moment. "It is."

As they climbed out of the hollow, Ethan ran into Nettie's backpack when she stopped short.

"A little warning would be nice."

"Hear it? We must be getting close to the third fall. It sounds different than the first two."

Rounding the next bend, Ethan pointed. "That's why."

Unlike the mirror cascade of the second fall, the third one dove through a long, deep crevice bordered by thick trees and rocks covered with shiny algae.

Cal whistled. "It took some powerful water to carve that out."

"Keep moving, y'all." Win cracked an invisible whip. "We have a long way to go."

Falling in behind Win and Cal, Ethan slowed the pace. "So, when do I get to see this dreamcatcher we're risking life and limb to help you make?"

"I'll give you wet and muddy, but life and limb?"

"The day's young."

"Maybe you two can go with us to Nibi's next time and watch."

"Watch?"

"Nibi says we have to make them ourselves. But I'll take you out to dinner as a thank-you for getting us here. Fair?"

"Fair."

As they caught up with Win and Cal, the trail turned into a steep, distorted tree-roots staircase that had them all breathing hard by the time they reached the top. The four of them stopped in their tracks as a powerful echo circled them.

Nettie's skin tingled at the view. An enormous, shallow cavern had been scooped out of the mountainside, its richly colored, concave wall a chronology of time. In front of the cavern flowed the fourth waterfall. A long, vertical island of boulders filled with craggy crevices housing trees and walking ferns split the fall into two distinct sides. Whitewater churned angrily down the steeper grade on the right, while on the left, calm water flowed into a lagoon fronting the cavern's rocky, narrow beach.

Ethan threw a pebble into the lagoon, adding another layer of ripples. "What a great place to swim. Wish we could get over there."

"Even if we could cross those rocks, it's too dangerous."

Win inched sideways down the bank to check out a small, high-water pool. "There are minnows and small fish in here."

Nettie gave her a hand up and scanned the empty treetops. "Hopefully, we'll find big fish and eagles higher up."

Cal headed toward an off-trail tree with root knees big enough to sit on. "C'mon, let's take a lunch break. My legs feel like Jell-O."

Nettie and Ethan settled on one side of the tree while Win and Cal rested on the other. After eating their sandwiches, Ethan dug two apples out of his pack. He handed one to Nettie.

"So, have you and Andy made up?"

Nettie chewed slowly, then swallowed hard. "Let's not talk about that. Okay?"

"I realize your relationship is none of my business, but seeing him at the movies the other night made me realize he still cares. You two should talk."

"Look, it's nice of you to—"

"I'm not being nice. As long as Andy's in the picture, I haven't got a snowball's chance in hell. Talking with him will do one of two things, either get you two back together or end it, which at least gives me a shot."

Nettie looked away.

"I'm not kidding. If I have a shot, I'll stay with Grams and go to school here in the fall."

"Ethan, you're a nice guy, whether you want to admit it or not. And don't think I haven't given the possibility of us some thought. I have. I like you. A lot. But Andy's part of me. I miss him. I didn't realize how much until he wasn't around anymore."

"So, you *are* in love with him."

"I am. At least, as much as anyone my age can tell. I just don't know if it will last. With graduation and college coming up, who knows what will happen?"

"Don't be silly. Nobody knows if love's going to last. You can promise it will, you can even plan for it, but you never know for sure. Look at my parents. Don't base your future on what-ifs. Talk with Andy."

"I've tried. Anne's in the way every time."

"That says more about her than it does about him."

"It takes two to tango."

"No. In this case, it's taking three. Talk with him."

Nettie didn't answer.

"Regardless of what happens, this summer had disaster written all over it until you rang my grandmother's doorbell. You've made it bearable. I want you to know that."

"Just bearable? Gee, thanks."

"I'm serious."

"I'm kidding. I feel the same way."

Win came around the tree. "Y'all ready to get going?"

Ethan gave Nettie a hand up and winked. "Just know that if it doesn't work out, I'm going to be knocking on your door."

The trail leading back to the water twisted through a roofless tunnel of boulders that ended at a bend in the rambling creek. Nettie barely noticed the beautiful upstream view as they continued to climb; Ethan's words kept fighting for her attention.

The fifth and final fall, the most beautiful and most dangerous, loomed ahead. A continuous wall of smooth water plunged off a wide, straight-edged cliff to thrash in a rocky pool a hundred feet below. Karst walls with moss-covered ledges towered on both sides. Little caves pocked the upper walls, some tall, some wide, some deep, but all accessible only to those with wings.

"Win, if we don't find golden eagles here, we're not going to find them anywhere."

"If they're living up in those walls, we're still out of luck."

The trail paralleling the cliff elevated so sharply that the trunks of some trees appeared to grow out of the canopies of others. Nettie used whatever she could find to hold on to as the gravel and mud trail rolled beneath her feet. When she finally pulled herself to the top, the vastness of the plunging valley stole her breath. Swells of vivid patchwork colors rolled toward the horizon, ultimately fading into a blue ridge.

"This view is worth the climb, even if we don't find the feathers."

Win huffed and puffed as she and the others pulled themselves over the edge. "Bite your tongue. We are going to find those damn feathers."

Near the edge of the trail, Nettie stopped in front of a National Forest Service sign warning climbers to stay out of the water and off the algae-covered rocks. To Date, Sixteen People Have Been Killed Going Over These Falls.

Cal groaned. "Now they tell us."

Farther up, the headwaters split around another island, longer and wider than the first one they'd seen.

"Oh my gosh. Win, look!"

In the middle of the island rose a tall hickory tree with a large, V-shaped nest centered at the top of its bare crown. In it flopped two eaglets, the white patches flashing under their wings confirming their youth.

"Hallelujah!"

Shrill birdcalls bounced off the canyon walls. Two large eagles with variegated brown-black feathers and gold necks paced the lip of a big cave, their wings poised in an alarmed arch. "There's Mom and Dad. Mom's the big one."

Ethan shielded his eyes to study the nervous birds. "They obviously don't want company. Question is, what are they going to do about it?"

Win's gaze bounced between the parents and the nest. "I don't think it's us they're worried about. They're watching something on the island."

"Whatever it is, we still have to get over there." Nettie moved along the bank until she paralleled the narrowest point to the island. One slip, and she'd be the next Forest Service statistic. A thin strip of stone barely breached the surface of the water. "Hey, look at this. It goes all the way over." Nettie eased down the bank to get a better look at the land bridge. "We can cross here."

Ethan put up his hand. "Whoa. You saw the sign. That stone is slippery as ice."

"Not if you go across on your butt."

Nettie and Win dropped their backpacks and double-tied their shoelaces. "If this bridge isn't solid all the way down and there's a current underneath, we don't want to lose a shoe or get pulled off."

Ethan and Cal followed suit.

Nettie shook her head. "Uh-uh. You and Cal stay here."

"Like hell. We've come this far. We're going."

Nettie pulled a plastic bag from her backpack and stuffed it in her pocket. "Win and I have to do this. You don't."

"Nettie's right. You two should wait here."

"Either Cal and I go with you or we'll follow you. Your call."

Nettie and Win looked at each other, raised eyebrows, then nodded.

"All right. But we go first, and we have to get the feathers," Nettie said. "You two hang back until we see what the eagles are going to do. Deal?"

"Deal."

The twenty-foot span of narrow stone had rounded edges and a slick algae-green sheen. Silhouettes of dozens of fish flashed below the surface on the upstream side. "Look at all the food. No wonder the eagles are up here."

"I wonder if the same theory will help us find a white owl."

"One bird at a time, please."

Nettie shivered as she eased into the water, straddling the bridge. "It's cold, but I'm not feeling a bottom current." The algae made gripping the stone difficult, but it also helped her slide forward.

Win followed a few feet back.

They'd almost made it across when Ethan called and pointed up. The eaglets' parents were soaring around the top of the hickory. Their closeness and formidable wingspan sent a clear message.

Nettie picked up the pace. Once she and Win reached the island, they could hide among the trees and boulders, if necessary. When they got to the cay, she scampered to the top, then gave Win a hand up.

"Let's hope they molted close to the ground," Win said. "I really don't want to climb that tree."

"Me either, but we've climbed them before."

Nettie and Win kept an eye on the eagles as Ethan and Cal crossed the bridge.

Once ashore, Ethan picked at strings of green algae stuck to his pants. "This stuff doesn't want to come off."

"Can't waste time on it now."

Win put her finger to her lips. "Careful—we don't know if anything else calls this place home." Using her quiet walk, she led them farther into the island, skirting rocks, brush, and evergreens. Just ahead stood the hickory, fronted by a clearing containing a small pool and rimmed on the far side by an asymmetrical rock wall.

At the edge of the pool, two young bobcats lapped water and playfully pawed each other. Nearby, under a scrubby bush, lay their mother, thirty pounds of taut muscles covered with sleek black, white, and brown fur. Her tufted ears were relaxed, slanted eyes closed. Not far from where she slept were the bloody remnants of tiny bones and feathers.

"Uh-oh." Win pointed up as the mother eagle folded her wings and plunged with blurring speed toward the unsuspecting kittens. With a loud, sudden *whoosh*, she banked sharply, arching her wings to come in talons first. As she grabbed the neck of one of the kittens, the momma bobcat let out an earsplitting yowl and lunged, clamping her sharp teeth into the eagle's chest right below the throat.

"Oh, jeez!" Jumping back, Nettie and the others ducked behind some nearby brush.

Dirt and feathers flew as the eagle bludgeoned the bobcat with her powerful wings and stabbed at its face with her sharp beak. Screeches and howls roared out of the growing dust cloud. The big cat clung to the eagle's neck, clawing frantically. The brutal clash loosened the cat's hold, and the moment she relaxed her jaws to get a better bite, the eagle flared its wings and lifted off. The kitten, dangling from its sharp talons, let out a frightened cry as it disappeared into the face of the cliff. The bloody, limping bobcat grabbed the scruff of her remaining kitten and disappeared into a shadowy tunnel in the rock wall.

Ethan jumped out from behind the brush. "That was incredible! I can't believe we were lucky enough to see it."

Nettie shook. "Lucky?" Her voice barely rose above a whisper.

"Eagles don't feed on dead prey. They'll eat that kitten while it's alive," Win explained.

"That's cruel."

"To us. Nature doesn't have the luxury of caring." She grabbed Nettie's arm. "C'mon, we have work to do."

Scattered around the pool were tufts of bloody fur and feathers. Nettie picked through them to find gold ones. Rinsing the blood off in the spring, she and Win counted them into the plastic bag. "Thirty-four. Eight more than we need. Let's take them all; the extras may come in handy."

The hike down Crab Tree Falls took almost as long as the hike up. Everything ached by the time Nettie and the others collapsed at the base of the first fall.

Ethan roused himself enough to search his pockets for car keys. "I wish I knew what time it is. I don't want to drive that hairpin road out of here in the dark."

Win leveled the side of her hand at the bottom of the sun, then folded one finger at a time until the last one met the edge of the horizon. "We have about forty-five minutes until sunset."

Ethan raised his hand and did the same. "I get it. Each finger is fifteen minutes?"

"Just about."

"It's going to take us that long to get out of here." He pulled Nettie up and waved Win and Cal toward the path to the parking lot. "Up, you two. Let's go."

Nettie fell in step beside Win, their hair damp and matted, clothes muddy, skin scraped and scratched yet again. "We're a mess."

"Yes, but we're a mess with feathers."

"We're one big step closer to finishing."

"Enjoy tonight, because tomorrow we need to figure out what white owls like to eat."

Chapter 11

Mr. Danes slid behind Nettie's chair to close his office door as voices filled the hallway. She took a deep breath as he passed but didn't smell the usual hint of alcohol. It hadn't taken long to figure out that his ever-present Dixie cup held something stronger than sweet tea, but she'd stayed quiet about it. He never seemed affected. Plus, she didn't want to do anything that might extend the number of sessions she had to have.

Nettie turned her focus back to the conversation. "That's it? Choices and consequences? That's all free will is about?"

Mr. Danes sat on the folding chair next to Nettie and crossed his legs. "It's a little more complicated than that, but choices and their consequences are a good place to start. Think about it like this: If we make the choice to believe, the expectation is that we will also make the choice to turn away from earthly desires and live the life Christ wants us to live."

"By earthly desires, you mean sin."

"Yes. Sins of the mind. Pride, greed, envy. Sins of the mouth. Lying, hypocrisy, slander. Sins of the flesh. Lust and adultery. Believers are tempted by these as much as nonbelievers. And it's easy to give in, since human beings are sinful by nature. However, the consequence is separation from God, which no believer wants. The good news is that forgiveness is ours for the asking."

"John 3:16."

"Exactly."

"Sometimes it's hard to know what's sin and what's not."

"I think we know. At least most of the time, deep down. We just choose to ignore the possibility until it's convenient, which is usually after we've done what we were tempted to do."

"So, how do we stop ignoring it?"

Mr. Danes threw his head back and laughed, too loudly. "The simple answer is to obey God. The more realistic answer is to strive to obey and know we'll fail sometimes." Something flickered in his eyes as he fingered the raised rim of his desk. "Romans 7:19: 'For I do not do the good I want, but the evil I do not want is what I keep on doing.'"

"I guess it's a good thing we don't have a limit on the number of times we can be forgiven."

"It's a very good thing." Mr. Danes put both feet on the floor and leaned forward. "Now, are you ready to talk about your sins?"

"My what?"

"You heard me." Mr. Danes opened his hands the way Jesus did in pictures. "Baptism marks the beginning of a new life, which means you have to let go of your old one. Confessing is a part of letting go."

"Here? Now?"

"Sure. Why not?"

"Because."

"Because why?"

"Because I don't want to."

"We seldom want to do what we need to do."

"I may need to, but I'm not going to."

"What could you have done that's so bad? Sins of the mind? You don't seem greedy or prideful. Envious, maybe?"

Nettie shook her head as she thought about Anne Johnson being with Andy.

"You've already told me you're truthful, so sins of the mouth are unlikely. That leaves sins of the flesh." Mr. Danes leaned closer. "Are you having sex?"

Nettie blushed at the memory of Andy's hands on her at River's Rest. "Look, I know you mean well, but I'm not comfortable with this." She wasn't sure if the almost dances she'd had with Andy constituted a sin or not, but she wasn't about to figure it out with Mr. Danes.

"Confession is an essential step for forgiveness. To be meaningful, it has to be specific. We need to examine our sin and how it influences our lives. It helps to talk it out with someone."

"I get that. And I will." Nettie stood, positioning the chair between her and Mr. Danes. "But not here and not now."

He stood and put his hands in his pockets. "Confession is hard but needed."

Nettie put her hand on the doorknob. "Then I'll talk with God."

"Why just God?"

"Because Martin Luther, John Calvin, and Mrs. Mac said I could." The door banged the chair as she left.

"Nettie, wait."

She kept walking.

Moving through the ebb and flow of her streetlight shadow, Nettie stopped at a hedge of honeysuckle and buried her face in a cluster of blossoms. Unlike Nibi's Angel Water, the sweet aroma did little to clear her concern about the possible consequences of mouthing off to Mr. Danes. She didn't care what he said; she wasn't going to talk with him about River's Rest. Those moments belonged to her and Andy. And God.

Mrs. Smith's Chrysler pulled up to the sidewalk. Ethan leaned over and rolled down the passenger window. "Hey, cutie. Want a ride?"

"Perfect timing." Nettie climbed in, grateful for the diversion. "What are you doing out and about?"

"Going to the Tastee Freez. Want to come?"

"It's a little late for ice cream, isn't it?"

"It's never too late for ice cream. Besides, Grams and Cal are on the phone with my father. I didn't want to hear the arguing all over again."

"Situation isn't any better?"

"Judging by the number of phone calls and the amount of yelling, no."

"I'm sorry."

Ethan's hand dropped from the wheel. "You know what I don't understand? My father says he loves my mother, that the affair didn't mean anything—it was just sex. My mother says she loves him but the sex means everything. She can't forgive him."

"How about you?"

"How about me what?"

"Do you love him?"

"Of course I love him—he's my father. But right now I don't like him very much."

"Do you forgive him?"

"Sometimes I think I can. Then I hear my mother crying and I get angry at him all over again."

"How did you all find out about your father's affair?"

"He told my mother; then he told Cal and me."

"He confessed?"

Ethan nodded. "He said he loved us and had made a terrible mistake. He apologized and wanted to start fresh, but that doesn't seem to matter. My mother keeps saying that if he really loved us, he would never have cheated."

"Earthly desires."

"What?"

"Just something Mr. Danes said tonight."

"Grams told Dad it wasn't as much about sex and love as it was about trust and betrayal. The greater the trust, the worse the damage, even in the betrayer."

"Love turned inside out."

"Exactly."

"Think your mom will ever forgive him?"

Ethan shrugged. "I don't know. Grams says she needs to wait to make a decision, to let the storm wear itself out."

"Sounds like she knows what she's talking about."

"I hope so. Right now, she's the only thing holding my family together."

Ethan's pain tugged at Nettie's heart, but his confusion about love, sex, and betrayal just added to her already fuzzy thoughts. She needed to think about something else for a while.

"You're right. It's never too late for ice cream. Let's go."

As they turned into the parking lot of the Tastee Freez, Nettie spotted a familiar car. "Andy's here."

"Want to leave?" Ethan gave her a way out, but his voice dared her not to take it.

"No."

He glided the Chrysler into the space next to Andy's. Smoothing her hair, Nettie watched Andy watch her get out of the car. Two half-empty ice cream cups sat on his dash. Anne leaned against the passenger door, a napkin scrunched in her hand. She turned away, trying to hide red-rimmed eyes that glowed in the fluorescent light.

Ordering chocolate-and-vanilla swirls, Nettie and Ethan sat at a picnic table facing the parking lot.

Nettie glanced at Andy's car between licks. "Anne doesn't look happy."

"Doesn't take a mind reader to know what's going on."

"They're arguing."

"More like they're breaking up."

"How can they be breaking up? They weren't going steady."

"You know what I mean."

"How can you tell?"

"I thought girls were supposed to be intuitive about these things."

"Get serious."

"You're such a spoil sport."

"Ethan, please."

"Oh, all right. Andy's the only one talking. If they were fighting, the conversation would be going back and forth."

Nettie quit trying to be discreet. Ethan had nailed it. Anne stared ahead while Andy talked calmly, his brow slightly furrowed, his lips unsmiling. Nettie pretended to work on her drippy ice cream cone as Andy got out of the car to throw away the trash. His eyes didn't leave Nettie until he started the car.

For a fleeting moment, Nettie felt sorry for Anne, but that quickly changed as she met the girl's dagger-throwing eyes. "I think you're right."

"What are you going to do?"

"I don't know."

"Seriously?"

"Seriously. What do I say? 'Hey, Andy, I'm glad you broke up with Anne. I want to be in your life, but I'm not sure we'll be together a year from now'? That would go over well."

"You're making this a lot harder than it needs to be."

"Oh, really? How?"

"We've been over this. If you love the guy, tell him. Let the future take care of itself."

The lights of the Tastee Freez flickered off as they opened the doors of the Chrysler.

Maybe Ethan had a point. "Why does love have to be all or nothing?"

"Because we need to be able to count on it."

Nettie waved goodbye as Ethan pulled out of her driveway. The stars were vivid against the black-velvet sky, but their sparkle did little to clear her thinking. As she locked the front door, her father called out from the family room. "You're a little late tonight."

"Yes, sir. The meeting with Mr. Danes went a longer than usual; then Ethan and I went for ice cream."

"What did you all talk about in your session this time?" her mom asked.

"Sin, consequences, and confession." Nettie crossed her fingers, hoping her mother wouldn't press for details.

"That sounds pretty intense."

Nettie just nodded.

"Did Mr. Danes say how much longer you'd have to meet with him?" her dad asked.

"No, sir. But it shouldn't be much longer. Pastor Williams said we'd talk again in August." Nettie kissed them both. "Good night."

"Sleep tight."

Upstairs, her little brother's room was dark, but light still shone under Sam's door. Over the years, her sister's practical advice had helped Nettie make some tough decisions; maybe it would again. She raised her hand to knock, then lowered it. Deep down, she knew who she needed to talk with.

A wispy breeze filled Nettie's room with the calming smell of lilac. She pulled baby-doll pajamas over her head and turned out the light. Kneeling on throw pillows covering the window seat, she closed her eyes. Jumbled thoughts about Andy, Anne, Ethan, Mr. Danes, love, sex, betrayal, and confession vied for attention as she talked with God. She had no answers by the time she uttered "amen," but at least some of the questions had begun to take form, and she knew what she needed to do. She would call Andy in the morning.

Nettie opened her eyes to the warmth of a neighborhood bathed in moon milk. Across the street, in the shadow of a large maple tree, sat Andy's car. Sliding into her robe and slippers, she tiptoed down the stairs. Quietly unlocking the door, she eased outside just as the taillights disappeared toward Main Street.

Allen's Hill shimmered with thousands of yellow, blue, and violet wildflowers. Mixed with grass turning to hay, they provided a perfect ocean for the scattered islands of emerald trees and squatty bushes. In the distance, the farmer who bush-hogged the hill for winter cattle feed checked his blades. By evening, the flowers and grass would have to start all over.

Nettie and Win sat in the shade of their favorite tree, picnicking on cheese straws and Fanta. At the top of the hill, the housekeeper carried grocery bags into Alise Allen's side door.

Win snapped her fingers. "Will you stop staring at the house?"

Leafy limbs shadowed the mansion's Palladian window, making it impossible to see if anyone happened to be looking back. "You know she's watching us. One of these days, she just might wave or even stroll down here to say hi."

"Dreamer."

"We haven't seen the nighttime visitor in a while."

"That's no surprise. When was the last time we were on the hill at night? It's been a busy summer."

"True. I hope he or she is still coming. I imagine that big old house can get really lonely. Maybe we can start watching the path again when I finish with Mr. Danes."

"How'd the session go last night?"

Nettie twirled a dandelion between her fingers. "Weird. He wanted me to talk about my sins of the flesh."

"Your what?"

"Sex. He wanted to know if I was having sex."

"You're kidding."

"I wish I were."

"Was he asking about you and Andy or you and Ethan?"

"Me and Ethan? Are you nuts? Nothing's going on between us. And nothing happened with Andy."

"Mr. Danes doesn't know that. Maybe Pastor Williams told him you and Andy were having trouble. He might be trying to figure out if you're seeing someone else."

"That doesn't mean I'm having sex. Besides, what does it matter? He wasn't asking who; he was asking if."

"It seems logical that if he'd ask about one, he'd ask about the other. Just be prepared in case he does."

"It's none of his business if or who."

"Why was he asking about it in the first place?"

"He said to be baptized, I need to confess my sins."

"What did you tell him?"

"That I'd work it out with God."

"Good answer. Was he drinking?"

"I couldn't smell anything."

"I know you don't want to say anything, but Pastor Williams needs to know what he's doing."

"I can't. Not yet. Pastor Williams already thinks I'm the spawn of Satan. Plus, he hasn't believed me all summer—what makes you think he'll believe me now? He'll probably just use it as an excuse not to baptize me. Besides, I can't prove anything."

"What are you going to do?"

"Figure out how to get Mr. Danes to talk about something other than sex. Lord knows I have a pile of other sins he can choose from. If I can just hang in there a little while longer, maybe I can get these meetings over with."

"I'll wait and walk home with you next Wednesday. That way, if Mr. Danes gets weird again, you won't be by yourself."

"Ethan and I went to the Tastee Freez last night. Andy and Anne were there. She didn't look happy."

"Does she ever?"

"Good point. Ethan said they looked like they were breaking up."

"How can they break up? They weren't going steady. Were they?"

"How would I know? But Andy's car was sitting outside my house a little while later. He left before I could get out the door."

"At least he came. That's a good sign."

"That's what I thought until I called him this morning. His dad said he was going to be out of town for a while."

"Where'd he go?"

"I don't know."

"Did you ask?"

"No."

"Why?"

"It didn't feel right. It's not any of my business. I left a message asking him to call me when he gets home."

"Do you know what you're going to say when he does?"

"No. Let's talk about something else, please."

"Okay. I think I know where we might find owl feathers."

Nettie groaned and fell back, sending a flurry of bugs into the air. "Let me guess. The feathers are at the top of Mount Whatever, and it's a three-day hike straight up."

Win giggled and kicked her foot. "No, silly. Remember the fire on Afton Mountain a couple of years ago? My dad remembered firefighters talking about seeing a white owl when they were building a break line near the top. The fire never made it that far, so maybe the owl stayed. They're supposed to be territorial birds. Cal said he and Ethan would drive us up there."

Nettie pushed up on her elbows. "I assume we're looking for a deserted nest with feathers?"

"Unless by some miracle one decided to spend the summer down here."

"Now who's dreaming? We'll need to stop by Nibi's on the way. Ethan wants to see the dreamcatchers."

Chapter 12

Half a mile past the Route 56 bridge, Ethan turned the Chrysler onto an old logging road with deep ruts that rocked the car like a slow-moving boat. Nettie put her hand out the window to skim leaves still damp with morning dew. The last time she'd come to Nibi's the back way, Andy had been driving. "It gets a little rougher at the top."

"Rougher? You're kidding. How often do you all come this way?"

"Not often. If it's just us, we take the train and walk up from the river. It's steeper but a lot shorter."

Thirty minutes later, Ethan stopped the car when the rear bumper scraped dirt at the turnoff to Nibi's. "I'm afraid we're going to lose Gram's muffler if we drive much farther. Can we walk the rest of the way?"

"Sure. It's not far."

Ethan pulled to the side of the road and parked under low-hanging limbs and vines. The four of them climbed out the driver's side and headed down the long dirt driveway.

As they rounded the first turn, the forested slope opened onto a rocky overlook, the gift of a long-ago mudslide. Rockfish Valley lay before them in all its summer glory.

"Welcome to Lookout Point." Win pointed to two specks

halfway down the mountain. "There's Nibi's house and barn, and across the river is Oak's Landing."

Ethan whistled. "That's some view. No wonder your grand-mother likes living up here."

"You should see it when the colors change."

Strolling back into the shaded part of the lane, Nettie and Ethan took the lead, chatting for a while, then letting the peace and quiet of the forest surround them. Halfway down, Ethan stopped. "I need to make a pit stop. Wait for me." Leaving the road, he pushed through heavy, tangled brush and disappeared behind a large hackberry tree.

He'd been gone several minutes, when the low-lying brush around the tree began to rustle.

"Ethan, watch your step," Win said calmly.

Nettie squatted to see if she could get a better look under the brush. "Can't see anything, but the noise is too soft to be a bear."

Cal scanned the woods. "Deer, maybe?"

"Smaller," Win said.

"Small is good. Can't be too serious if it's small, right? C'mon, Ethan, what's taking so long?"

With his back and hands tight against the trunk, Ethan slowly circled to the front of the tree, face ashen, eyes wide. Rustling brush surrounded him.

"What is it?" Nettie whispered, as she and the others backed up.

Ethan gave a nervous shake of his head. Time went into slow motion as he eased through the brush and onto the road, sur-rounded by a large family of skunks.

Nettie and Win froze, but Cal's screechy "Oh, shit!" and sudden turn interrupted the peaceful migration of the black-and-white family. The startled mother hissed, stamped her paw, and raised her tail in a stiff salute. She and her half dozen offspring filled the air with a repeating chorus of *psssssst*s, accurately sending an oily green cloud of noxious fumes over everyone.

Partially blinded by burning, weepy eyes, and hampered by gagging and coughing, Nettie yelled, "Run!" Then she and Win took off before the furry family could douse them again. They hadn't gone far when Cal stopped, retched, and dropped to his knees, vomiting. Ethan tried to help him up but struggled to find good air. He pulled his saturated shirt over his nose, then quickly pulled it back down. His eyes pleaded for help.

Doubling back, Nettie and Win turned their shirts around and pulled their collars over their noses. The lack of a direct hit lessened the smell just enough that they could breathe.

Ethan fought to turn his shirt as Nettie gave him a push down the road. "Keep going." She and Win got Cal to his feet, half-dragging him down the road and around the bend.

When they were away from everything but their own stench, Nettie and Win sat Cal down.

"Ethan, you stay with Cal," Win said. "Nettie and I'll be right back."

Splitting up, they dove into the woods. From experience, they knew which plants would cut the smell.

"Win, here's some wisteria."

They each stripped a vine, crushed some of the leaves, and rubbed the sticky liquid under and in their noses. Taking the rest of the leaves, they hurried back and did the same for Ethan and Cal.

Once Win painted Cal's upper lip and nose, he lay down in the road, pale but breathing. "Thank God for whatever that stuff is. I thought I was going to die."

"Why'd you run like that?" Win snapped. "Don't you know you're supposed to freeze?"

"How would I know that? I live in a city, remember?" Sitting up, he stared at his brother. "Besides, Ethan's the one who led them straight to us."

"I'm sorry. They came up from behind and surrounded me. They were digging holes all around the tree, eating some kind of fat white worm. They didn't seem to mind me being there, so I figured I could ease my way out, but they followed me. I hoped they'd just keep going."

"Well, they didn't, did they?" Cal snapped.

"Shut up. They might have if you hadn't turned sissy and started screaming."

"If I could see, I'd throttle you."

"My eyes are stinging too."

Win pinched the back of Cal's arm, hard.

He jerked away. "What the hell? What did you do that for?"

"You need to cry. Bite your tongue. Hard."

"What? Are you nuts?"

"No, silly. Tears will rinse the skunk oil out of your eyes."

Cal shook his head. "I don't believe this. We're in the twilight zone."

Ethan smirked at his brother. "You're the one who said smaller was better."

"Smart-ass."

Ethan turned to Win. "What do we do now? We can't get in Gram's car like this. We'd never get the smell out."

"Nibi will help us."

"Great. We get to visit your grandmother smelling like three-day-old roadkill seasoned with sulfur and garlic."

Nettie laughed. "You're going to do more than visit her."

"What do you mean?"

"You'll see."

Nibi stepped from her back porch and waved as the four rounded the corner of the barn. She laughed and shooed them back as soon as she got a whiff. "I thought I taught you two how to avoid skunks."

"Sorry. They surprised us."

Cal gave Win a grateful smile for not throwing him and Ethan under the bus.

"Go stand by the garden," Nibi called. "It's going to take a few minutes to get things ready." Chuckling, she headed for the barn.

"What does she mean 'get things ready'?" Cal asked.

Win giggled. "Just wait."

Nibi dragged three washtubs from the barn, placing them in a row next to the clothesline.

Eyes wide, Ethan looked from the tubs to Nettie and back. "What's she doing?"

"Getting our baths ready."

"Baths? Outside? In front of everyone? You have to be kidding."

"Nope."

Nibi made several trips to the cellar, bringing back baskets of jars filled with tomato juice and jugs of cider vinegar. She poured the tomato juice into one tub and vinegar into the other two. She went inside the house and came back with scrub brushes, towels, a bowl of white cream, and bars of homemade soap. She set some near the water pump and others near the washtubs. Last, she clipped an old, holey barn blanket on the clothesline in front of the tubs. Pinching a eucalyptus leaf, she rubbed the juice under her nose. "Okay, boys, you first."

Nettie nudged Ethan forward. "Go on. She doesn't bite."

Ethan and Cal walked down the hill as if going to the gallows.

"Go behind the blanket and strip down."

"Everything?"

"Everything. Put your clothes, tennis shoes, and socks in the first tub of vinegar. Make sure everything is covered. Then get into the tub of tomato juice, one at a time. Help each other wash. Don't miss an inch, and don't forget your hair. When you finish, get into the tub of vinegar and do the same, then wrap yourself in a towel, wring out your clothes, and go to the well pump. Put some baking soda paste from the big bowl on the scrub brush and wash yourselves and your clothes again. When that's done, rinse off, then wash with the bar soap. The last rinse should take out any remaining smell. If it doesn't, then you get to do it all over again. I'll warn you, well water is cold."

Once the boys were behind the blanket, Nibi built a fire in the pit at the far end of the clothesline.

"Boys, when your clothes are scent free, hang them here to dry."

Nettie's eyes stung from the skunk oil, but she could still see Ethan's and Cal's bare feet moving behind the blanket.

Finally, wrapped in towels and looking embarrassed, Ethan and Cal emerged, their hair sticking up at odd angles and their exposed skin bright pink from scrubbing.

Nibi waved to Nettie and Win. "Come on, girls. Your turn."

Ethan winked at Nettie as she passed.

When the deskunking was complete and their clothes were on the line, Nibi pointed to Adirondack chairs made of tree branches sitting in the shade of her old oak. "You all bring those chairs over to the fire while I fix lunch."

Holding their towels in place, the four of them moved the chairs closer. Settling in, they forgot about their state of undress as Nibi served hazelnut-butter sandwiches, peaches, and cups of raspberry tea while sharing some of her dancing-with-skunks stories.

"Aren't you afraid living up here by yourself?" Ethan asked.

"Why would I be?"

"Animals, snakes, things like that."

"I've lived my life surrounded by things like that, by Nature. It's what I know. What I understand."

"Does anything frighten you?"

Nibi shook her head, but her eyes told a different story.

Once their clothes were dry and everyone dressed, Nettie and Win triple-washed the towels and hung them on the line while Ethan and Cal cleaned the jars and put them on the porch. Together they scrubbed and rinsed the tubs and carried them to the barn, hanging them on pegs along the back wall. As they were leaving, Nettie passed the old farm table where she and Win had scraped the deer hide. Mixed in with new dust and dirt were little bones and feathers, white ones.

"Win."

"What?"

Nettie pointed.

Win walked over to study the table. "Oh, my gosh."

They both scanned the rafters.

"I don't see anything," whispered Nettie.

"Me either."

Ethan followed their gaze. "What are you looking for?"

Nettie and Win raced to the wide, built-in ladder supporting the middle of the loft.

"You and Cal stay down here."

Side by side, Nettie and Win peeked over the top. Bales of hay blocked their view of the corner. Climbing the rest of the way up, they slowly circled the stacks.

Nettie stopped and pointed. "There."

Gold eyes glowed from the shadowy corner. A white owl.

"I'll be damned."

Nettie inched closer. The owl's head and eyes followed her. With a loud flutter, he took flight toward the rafters. "He's huge."

"Who cares how big he is? He has white feathers."

Keeping an eye on the owl, they eased over and cleared the nest of white feathers, stuffing them in their pockets. Moving slowly back to the edge of the loft, they climbed down.

Nibi leaned against the door jamb. "I was beginning to think you two never would figure this out. Thank goodness for those skunks."

Nettie pulled the feathers from her pocket and laid them on the farm table. "This is what you meant when you told us we were looking but not seeing, isn't it? The owl's been here the whole time."

"Sometimes what we're searching for is right in front of us and we're too distracted to see it."

Win turned to Nibi. "What is he doing here? White owls aren't supposed to be this far south this time of year."

"I found him in the woods last spring. He had a broken wing and was almost dead."

"How in the world did you set it?"

"The only way I could: I folded it like his good wing and wrapped it to his body. He was weak and dehydrated, so he didn't fight me. Early on, I wasn't sure he was going to make it. But once I started trapping field mice and chipmunks, he started eating and getting stronger. He let me take the wrap off a couple of weeks ago. Now that I know he can fly, it's time for him to go home."

The owl, feathers fluffed and bell shaped, sat in the rafters, watching them. His left wing dipped slightly lower than the right.

As Nettie moved closer to get a better look, his piercing eyes rotated to keep an eye on her. "I can't believe we were this lucky."

Win glanced at Nibi. "Maybe luck had some help."

"Come, girls. Ethan and Cal can watch while you add the white feathers to your dreamcatchers."

Chapter 13

Rain poured off the blunted awning of the old Monacan school-house, splatted loudly against the stone stoop, then rolled into the muddy water surging toward Indian Mission Road. Nettie pressed her heels and shoulders tighter against the rough, slatted door, enjoying the sound of the rain but not its feel. Darkening clouds and the deepening smell of ozone had motivated her and Win to make the long walk from Amherst to the Monacan settlement on Bear Mountain in record time.

Win held on to Nettie's arm to keep from falling out of the doorway. "At least we got here before it started."

"That doesn't mean we're not going to get soaked."

The log-cabin school sat on a small triangle of land between the road and Rolling Rock Creek. Across the way stood a one-room church, a small brick medical clinic, and a cluster of houses.

A shuffling vibration behind them preceded a metallic *thunk* that released the door's old lock. Nettie and Win tumbled backward into the strong, copper-colored arms of the Monacan chief.

"Sorry, girls. Hope I didn't scare you. I came in the back way."

Win hand-signaled greetings to the chief. "No, sir, we're good. Thank you for giving up your Saturday to help us."

"Any day on the mountain is a day well spent. Besides, I'd never turn down a special request from Nibi."

The vintage room smelled of forest, not the mustiness Nettie expected. Hewn-flat logs with small gaps in the chinking spoke to the building's age, while scattered pictures of school children, pow-wows and homecoming celebrations, and Indian artifacts displayed its character. A long table sitting in front of several rows of folding chairs indicated that the building still served as a meeting place for the tribe.

"Have a seat." Chief Brannon took off his rain-soaked cap and turned one of the chairs to face theirs.

Nettie had met the chief at several of the tribal gatherings Win and Nibi had taken her to over the years. Tall, broad-shouldered, and in full ceremonial dress, he'd been an impressive sight. Now, in jeans, a short-sleeved madras shirt, and a crew cut, he still had a powerful presence.

"So, Nibi sent you to see me?"

"Yes, sir."

"She is doing well?"

"Very well." Win handed him a small pouch containing freshly cured pipe tobacco. "She asked us to give you this."

The chief opened a corner and took a long whiff. "Ahh. Bear-berry." He slid the pouch into his shirt pocket and leaned forward. "Nibi said you two are making dreamcatchers and need some arrowheads."

Win nodded. "Yes, sir. She said Bear Mountain is full of them."

"That's correct. Our people have lived and hunted on this mountain for hundreds of years."

"Nibi said her mother and father were born here."

"Yes, as were their mothers and fathers. I've often wished Nibi would find her way back."

"She loves her mountain."

"Yes, she does."

"A blood moon is coming, sir. We need to finish our dream-catchers before it gets here, and we're running out of time."

The lines in the chief's face deepened. "So she said." He went to the window, hands deep in his pockets. The rain had slowed to a drizzle.

"The last blood moon Nibi warned me about was forty years ago. It signaled the start of an influenza pandemic. I'd just graduated from medical school and returned here to start the clinic. Thousands died across Virginia, but we were able to isolate the settlement in time and didn't lose anyone. I pay attention when Nibi speaks."

"Yes, sir. So do we."

The chief's comments made Nettie's stomach churn. Questions were piling up. What danger would the blood moon bring? Who would be in harm's way? When would it hit and how? No one had any answers, least of all her and Win.

The chief returned to his chair. "Nibi said your dreamcatchers were to be exactly like hers, so you'll need thirteen arrowheads, one for each phase of the moon."

"Thirteen apiece, sir." Win glanced at Nettie. "We know that's a lot."

"It is, but the mountain's covered with old hunting camps. If you know where and how to look, you'll find them."

"Wouldn't collectors have scavenged these places already?"

"They would have tried, and would still be trying today if they were allowed, and if they knew where to look. Bear Mountain is sacred among the Monacans." The chief addressed Nettie. "You're not Monacan, but I can count on one hand the number of times Nibi has ever asked me for anything, and she asked me to help you and Win. I trust you will keep our secrets."

"I promise, sir."

"One of the oldest and largest hunting camps is about halfway up the mountain. We'll start there. Did you bring tools?"

"Yes, sir," Win answered. "Hand spades and a small pickax. They're in a bag outside."

"And do you have an offering of thanks for the arrowheads you find?"

"Yes, sir. We brought more tobacco."

"Good. I'll get a shovel and filtering pans and meet you out back. You all don't mind getting wet?"

"No, sir," Nettie said. "A little rain doesn't hurt anything."

"That's right. In fact, rain is a blessing. It helps uncover what is hidden."

The big man moved stealthily and gracefully up Bear Mountain. Following barely visible game trails, he led them upward for two hours, before stopping and putting his finger to his lips. He pointed to a ponded area surrounding the mouth of a large tributary flowing into Rolling Rock Creek. Slowly circling the marshy edge, a large, jagged beaver dam came into view. Inching closer, the chief pointed to a window-like hole in the middle of the roughly stacked logs. Fast-moving water poured through it, forming a small fall that churned white all the way to the creek.

"That hole is there by design," he whispered. "They build it that way to help keep the logs from being washed away during high water." He froze as two small beavers made their way across the top of the dam. "Watch."

Reaching the bridge over the opening, the first beaver slipped into the backwater. Seconds later, he surged out of the window on his back and tail first, riding the whitewater all the way to the creek. The second beaver followed; then both climbed back up the dam.

"They're playing?" whispered Nettie.

The chief nodded.

Again, the beavers slid all the way to the creek, then flipped onto their bellies and dog-paddled back to the dam.

"Why do they go down on their backs and legs first?" Nettie asked.

"Because it's safer. Their legs protect the rest of the body."

The chief led them farther up the mountain to where two branches of Rolling Rock Creek noisily remerged after splitting near the headwaters at the top. "Some of the largest hunting camps were located along splits like this."

Nettie and Win followed as he traced the rocky, Y-shaped shoreline, pointing out the best places to search for arrowheads.

"Watch for turbulent water and dark sediment lines, especially where the current hits angles along the banks. Rocks and debris in these areas trap the arrowheads. Once the creek bottom smooths out, they're harder to find."

Nettie put her hand in the clear water, running her fingers along the first layer of rocks.

"It's rare that you'll find arrowheads exposed and lying flat. Most of the time they're buried, which is good because it protects their shape. Watch for sharp points embedded among larger stones, and dig them out."

The chief climbed the bank and looked up and down the creek. "You'll find them faster if you split up. Nettie, you search here. I'll take Win up the north split."

Win grabbed a sifting pan and shovel and followed the chief, while Nettie took the pickax and hand spade to the south side of the merge point. Making her way along the edge, half in and half out of the water, she concentrated on looking for points, instead of stones, in the wavy glare. Spotting one, she pulled away the surrounding rocks and dug with her fingers. A perfectly shaped, brown-and-white arrowhead popped out of the hard sand. The three points and serrated edges were symmetrical and sharp. Two matching notches had been carved into the sides of its base. Nettie silently thanked the Indian who'd carved the stone as she turned and held it high to show Win and the chief. They were sitting on the bank, deep in conversation. She slid the arrowhead into the leather drawstring bag tied to her cutoffs.

By midday, Nettie's tennis shoes were no longer white, and her fingers were full of cuts and scratches. She'd found half a dozen intact arrowheads and lost count of the partials she'd thrown back.

Making her way to the bank, she took off her shoes, rinsed

out the sand, and stuck her feet in the water. The current flowing between her toes felt cooler than the ripples licking her ankles. Nettie studied her collection of arrowheads, a colorful mix of variegated quartz, jasper, and chert. Setting them in a shallow between her feet, she scraped off the embedded dirt with her fingernails. She didn't hear the chief coming but wasn't startled when he knelt beside her and studied her arrowheads.

"These are a good length and have deep notches, which will help them stay tied to the ring." He picked up one of the arrowheads. "See how its maker smoothed the curve of each notch? That prevents the stone from cutting through the sinew."

Nettie ran her thumb over the flat surface of the stone. "Chief, are you worried about this blood-moon thing?"

"Are you?"

"Yes, sir. I don't know if we can finish the dreamcatchers in time. And if we do, I don't know why it's so important. Something big is coming, and nobody can tell us what."

With a flick of his wrist, the chief skipped a stone downstream. "Are you worried or afraid?"

"What's the difference?"

"Worry is a choice. Fear can be a gift."

"What?"

"Worry is choosing to be stuck on what-ifs—what might happen, instead of what *is* happening. It's a choice you don't have to make." The chief skipped another stone, this time to the other side.

"No disrespect, sir, but you looked worried when you were talking about the blood moon back at the schoolhouse."

"That wasn't worry you saw. It was fear."

"I don't understand."

"I'm not worried about a blood moon. I'm afraid of what it's signaling. Fear is real, and it's focused."

"How's that a gift?"

"Unlike worry, fear has a cause we can usually identify and do something about."

"Like isolating the settlement when influenza hit?" Nettie asked.

"That's right."

Nettie propped her arms on her knees to stare at the mesmerizing glitter of the water. Her whole summer had been wrapped in worry about things she'd been able to do little about. "We don't know what the blood moon is signaling, so how can we do anything about it?"

"Act on the information we do have. We know it's signaling something, which tells us to be alert and watchful. Not worried, watchful. Nibi has some insight into what it is, and she may know more the closer the blood moon gets. She's preparing you. Do what she tells you, and do it well. Then deal with the fear as it comes. You'll be amazed at what you can accomplish when you choose not to worry about being afraid." The chief skipped a third stone, this time upstream. "Choice can be a powerful ally when you realize you have it."

"Yes, sir."

He nudged Nettie and pointed to a sharp edge sticking out of the creek bottom near her foot. Pushing the dirt away, she pulled out a long gray arrowhead, perfectly shaped.

Win joined Nettie and the chief on the bank, the leather drawstring at her hip hanging heavy.

"You girls learn quickly. I'm going to head back. Take a lunch break, then work your way downstream. It will lead you back to the settlement. Meet me at the schoolhouse by dusk, and I'll give you a ride home. If you need more arrowheads, come back tomorrow after church. We'll go to the other side of the mountain. There was another large camp over there. Most of the bad storms come from that direction. You're likely to find more arrowheads than you need."

By midafternoon, Nettie and Win had worked their way downstream to a wide turn and a long stretch of rapids.

Nettie headed for a toppled tree. "C'mon, let's take a break."

Win joined her on the wobbly trunk and started counting arrowheads. "I have seven. You have eight. Eleven more to go. That's a hell of a sight better than I thought we'd do."

"We'd still be looking for the first one if Chief Brannon hadn't helped us."

Win put the arrowheads back in the pouches. "You two talked for a long time."

"I asked him about the blood moon."

"And?"

"He said worrying about it was a waste of time."

Win nodded. "He told me the same thing. Nibi must have said something."

"His way is worth a try. Lord knows worrying hasn't helped anything."

Win hesitated. "The chief said something else."

"What?"

"He asked me to consider working at his clinic after school. He wants me to teach him things Nibi taught me. In return, he'll teach me about modern medicine. He thinks we can blend the two."

"That's so cool. Do you want to do it?"

"I think so. It feels right."

"Wonder what Nibi will say."

"The chief said she suggested it."

"Strange she didn't say something to you first. Are you going to talk with her about it?"

"I'm not sure. You know Nibi. There's a reason for what she does and what she doesn't do."

"What about college?"

"I don't know. Maybe I can do both. There's a lot to think about."

Nettie's heart dropped at the thought of going to college without Win. Ready or not, like it or not, they were heading for big changes.

"Uh-oh," Win said.

"What?"

"Lift your feet. High."

"Why?"

"Just do it."

Nettie's sneakers came off the ground at the same time a baby water snake slithered out of a knot hole in the tree trunk. It wiggled past Nettie's leg and down toward the grass as two more banded heads popped out of the hole.

"Damnation!" Nettie high-stepped away from the tree trunk. Win followed, albeit more slowly.

"Dammit, Win!"

"You knew when I knew. You also know better than to run."

"I could stay put for one, but three, maybe more? Not going to happen." She secured her bag of arrowheads to a belt loop and headed for the creek. "C'mon, let's get going."

"Nettie, wait."

"Now what?" As Nettie turned, the ground beneath her went spongy and quickly gave way, dropping her right foot and ankle into a hole. The stings started registering immediately. "Oh, crap." Her left foot sank into another part of the nest as she worked to get her right foot free. The harder she struggled, the deeper she sank.

Win headed for her at a dead run. "Grab my hands!"

With Win's help, Nettie scrambled out of the nest. They bolted for the creek, followed by a hard-charging swarm of yellow jackets. Diving in, they crawled to deep water, periodically coming up for air until the menacing insects retreated.

Nettie sat up and pushed strands of dripping hair out of her eyes. "You okay?"

Win rubbed the welts on her arm; a drowned yellow jacket clung to her tangled hair. "Yeah. That was frightening."

Nettie lifted her right foot out of the water, then her left. Both ankles were sprinkled with bites and already swelling. "Frightening and painful."

Win gasped and sat up straight. "I just realized something. My visions seem to come right before fear, danger. The bears, the snakes, the bees—visions came before all of them."

"Jeez, you're right."

"I can't believe I didn't make the connection before."

"I wonder what it means."

"I'm not sure, but just knowing there's a connection between the two should help."

"I hope so. Maybe you'll get a vision about the blood moon. It has fear written all over it."

Making sure the yellow jackets were nowhere in sight, Nettie and Win waded out of the creek. Win found some plantain leaves and made a poultice to ease the pain and swelling of the stings. Heading downstream, they walked along the water's edge and managed to find another intact arrowhead. They reached the schoolhouse as the chief pulled up in a navy-blue Wagoneer.

"Chief, do you have something we can sit on so we don't mess up your car?"

He opened the back door. His black bag and a stethoscope lay on the seat, along with a couple of little green towels and large bottle of Betadine. "Compared to the injured people and animals that are usually back there, a little water and sand won't hurt a thing."

Nettie scanned the faces of the congregation as she followed Win and the other altos into the choir loft. "Andy's not here," she whispered. "I wish I knew where he was."

"Anne's here. Right side, halfway back," Win whispered.

"I know. If looks could kill, I would've been pushing up daisies a long time ago."

"She might know where Andy is."

"Maybe, but I'm not going to ask her." Nettie abruptly stopped talking as Pastor Williams rose from his chair and glanced in her direction, before walking to the pulpit. She'd forgotten how close his chair sat to their side of the loft. She grimaced at Win. If the sessions with Mr. Danes were ever going to end, she couldn't risk antagonizing either of them more than she already had. She wrote a note to Win on the top of her church bulletin. "As soon as the service is over, we need to get out of here, fast."

Pastor Williams must have known the morning would be unusually hot and humid. The hymns he'd selected were only two or three stanzas, and he cut his sermon mercifully short. At the end of the benediction, Nettie and Win scampered down the loft stairs, hung up their robes, and were hurrying toward the exit when Pastor Williams stepped into the hall. "Nettie, a moment, please."

She skidded to a stop at the door. Damn. Turning around, she gave Win a look of surrender. "I'll be back in a minute."

Nothing had changed in Pastor Williams's office. Stacks of books and papers and a thick layer of dust still covered everything except the open, dog-eared Bible on his desk.

"I understand your study sessions with Mr. Danes have been going quite well."

"Yes, sir."

"Are you getting the understanding you were looking for?"

"I think so. At least, most of the time."

"You and Mr. Danes are, uh, getting along?"

Nettie's heart pounded. Pastor Williams hadn't asked about the sessions with Mr. Danes since they'd started. Why did he want to know now? Had he heard she'd walked out of the last session? Did he know why? She decided not to deal with the consequences of a wrong answer. "Yes, sir. We're getting along just fine. He's a good teacher. He explains things in a way I understand."

"You're sure."

"Yes, sir."

Pastor Williams seemed relieved. "I'm glad to hear that." He leaned back. "I'm hoping you'll be able to finish up soon and we can baptize you before school starts."

"Me too, sir."

"Let's talk again next week."

"Yes, sir."

Nettie almost skipped down the hall toward Win.

"What are you so happy about?"

"Let's get out of here first."

Scurrying down the church steps, they crossed to the shady side of the street and headed toward town, returning waves to passersby.

"Tell me. What did Pastor Williams want?"

"He wanted to know if I was getting my baptism questions answered."

"That's it?"

"And he wanted to know how Mr. Danes and I were getting along."

"Finally," Win said, coming to a dead stop. "Did you tell him? About the drinking and sex talk, I mean?"

"Are you nuts? I want these sessions to be over with, not have more added on."

"I can't believe you didn't tell him." Win seldom raised her voice.

"And I can't believe you don't understand why."

"Dammit, Nettie, this has gone on long enough. Pastor Williams needs to know."

"What makes you think he'd believe me? He hasn't taken my side on anything all summer. Besides, I may have only one more session to get through."

"For a smart girl, that's a dumb move."

Nettie shook her head. "Not dumb, desperate. I want it over with, and the quickest way for that to happen is to not make waves."

"I hope you know what you're doing."

"Me, too."

As they rounded the corner to Main Street, Anne Johnson rose from a bench in front of the bank.

Nettie turned away, pulling Win with her.

"Nettie, wait. Please. Can we talk?"

"I don't have time."

"It won't take but a minute."

Win nudged Nettie toward the bench. "Go on. I'll wait for you at the corner."

Nettie crossed her arms but didn't move any closer to Anne. "What do you want?"

"Would you like to sit?" The mean part of Anne didn't seem so mean at the moment.

Nettie shook her head. "What do you want?"

"Do you love Andy?"

Nettie froze for a split second. "What business is that of yours?"

"He quit dating me because of you."

"Andy would never say that."

"But it's true."

The sandy grit on the sidewalk crunched as Nettie spun to leave.

"If you don't want him, tell him."

Nettie stopped short. Ethan had said the same thing. She turned to face Anne. "Why? So he'll come running back to you?"

"At least I'd have a chance."

Years of dislike for Anne melted into pity. "No. I don't think you would."

"Why not?"

"Because you're mean, just because you can be. Andy doesn't have a mean bone in his body."

Anne slumped onto the bench. "You're the one being mean. You always have been."

"Me? Mean? There's a difference between being mean and being honest."

"You could help me."

"Andy's a big boy. He makes his own decisions."

"So, you *do* love him."

"As I said, that is none of your business."

Anne's face turned dark. "I should have known you'd be a bitch about this."

"That's your job description, not mine."

"I'm not giving up."

"Suit yourself."

"You don't know where he is now, do you?" Anne flounced her skirt and turned away. "I do."

Nettie bit her tongue and ran to catch up with Win. "Did you hear that?"

"Most of it."

"She's such a snake. I wish she'd just go away."

"That won't happen. Enemies are harder to lose than friends."

Nettie shaded her eyes against the midday sun. She stood with Win and Chief Brannon at the mouth of a long, ugly washout that snaked down the back of Bear Mountain into Tyree's Creek. "Would you look at that?"

The chief picked up a clod of dirt. Still damp from last night's downpour, it broke into smaller clumps. "We've gotten so much rain this summer, I'm surprised we haven't had more slides. This one is recent. It wasn't here last week." He walked to the edge of the creek and pointed to where a peninsula of mud and rock from the slide lay just below the surface of the water. "Big slides can dam up the creek bed and redirect the current. See how the creek has bulged out on the other side?"

Nettie and Win nodded.

"It can be a real problem if the creek dams up completely or if the redirected current alters the downstream path significantly. Folks live down there."

"Do you want us to warn them?"

"Thanks, but that's not necessary, at least not yet. Right now, I'm going to get you two started; then I'm going to hike up to the headwaters and make sure there are no more slides coming into the creek." Squatting, the chief pointed to the jagged sides of the washout. Layered in colors, a wide ribbon of dark sediment sat closer to the surface than what they'd seen the day before. "Slides unearth lower layers of soil and redistribute them along the top. You won't have any trouble finding arrowheads here."

Nettie and Win nodded. "We've been pretty lucky already."

The chief winked and headed upstream. "You can never have too much luck."

Nettie and Win climbed halfway up the washout and began searching their way down, Nettie on one side and Win on the other. By midafternoon, they'd found six more arrowheads and hadn't yet reached the mouth of the washout.

"Four more to go." Spotting a point, Nettie tried to pull it out of the dirt, but the mud held fast. She pushed the tip of the spade under the point and worked the soil until a long arrowhead popped out, along with a big clump of mud that stayed stuck to the bottom of the spade. She found a tuft of grass and cleaned the worst of the dirt off the stone, then used her cutoffs to finish the job. "Hey, Win, look at this one. It's solid white."

"Looks like milky quartz. It's beautiful."

Nettie checked the points and the smoothness of the notches, then put the arrowhead in her pocket. Scraping the mud off the spade and back into the hole, she balked and stumbled backward, landing on her bottom. "Damnation!"

Win hurried over to help her up. "What is it?"

Nettie pointed at the hole with a trembling finger. "I'm not sure, but I think it's a face."

"A what?"

"You heard me. A face."

They approached the muddy hole timidly and peeked inside. Staring back were two empty eye sockets and a deep nose cavity sunk in a dirty, moon-colored skull.

Nettie sank to her knees. "That's no animal skull." She slowly reached into the hole to dab the loose dirt away from the lower half of the face.

Win poked her shoulder. "Boo!"

Nettie jerked back. "Dammit, Win! That's not funny."

"It's not going to bite you."

"Then you pull it out of there, smart-ass."

"Maybe we should leave it."

"It's too late for that." The chief came up behind them. Kneeling, he cleaned out the area around the large skull and lifted it from the hole. Turning it one way, then the other, he gently probed the wide-set eye sockets, broad nose opening, and movable jaws, which held a few remaining teeth. He carried the skull to the water's edge, let the current wash away layers of dirt, and examined it again. "The skull is intact. Based on its size, it was most likely a male. We have to rebury him."

"Where?" Nettie asked.

The chief studied the trail of the long washout again. "There are burial mounds all over the mountain; one of the largest is near the top of this ridge. The washout must have breached it. Summer rain brought him to us. Now we must take him back to his place, his time."

"May I go with you? I mean, I know Win can go, but may I?"

"Of course. You found him. You should be the one to take him home." The chief walked to the wood line. "Win, there's some sweetgrass growing over there. Break some stalks to take with us. Be careful not to pull the roots. Nettie, just behind the tree line is a downed cedar. Pick up some of the broken branches. We'll need it for kindling."

Nettie raised her eyebrows at Win, who shrugged and whispered, "Guess we'll know soon enough."

As she approached the top of the washout, Nettie spotted what was left of the burial mound. The tree- and brush-covered bump on the mountain stood ten feet tall and would have been forty feet across if the washout hadn't taken off one end. At first glance, the gaping wound revealed a maze of roots and rocks. When she stepped closer, she saw layers of bones of different sizes and shapes.

Most of the higher ones were whole, while the lower ones were little more than shards or long lines of fine powder.

The chief laid the skull on a nest of pine needles and walked the circumference of the burial mound, surveying the damage. "I need to get the elders up here. We need to search for more displaced remains, restore the mound, and figure out a way to divert the wash-out before it rains again."

The enormity of the job left Nettie speechless. Covering and reseeding the mound and diverting the wide rain channel would have to be done by hand, given the steepness of the slope, and tons of soil and rock would need to be moved and shaped. "May we help?"

"It's kind of you to offer, but you two have dreamcatchers to finish. Once I can get in touch with the elders, they'll notify the tribe. We'll have a meeting tonight at the schoolhouse to figure out our approach and will be back up here early tomorrow morning with specialized work teams. We'll have this taken care of pretty quickly."

Nettie and Win followed the chief to the south side of the burial mound. Dropping to his knees, he dug a hole as deep as his arm would go, sifting the dirt for bones as he went. He retrieved the skull and lowered it into the fresh burrow. "Nettie, bring me the cedar."

He scraped a second, shallower hole, added dried leaves, and covered them with a small tower of cedar kindling. Pulling a lighter from his pocket, he lit the tinder. It didn't take long for the fire to flare, then reduce itself to glowing embers.

"Now, the sweetgrass. Win, tear the stalks into small pieces and sprinkle them over the ashes."

Vanilla-scented smoke flowed up and over the mound as the chief began a low-pitched chant. The richness of his voice and the haunting, hymnlike cadence made Nettie shiver. With the last notes, the chief began refilling the hole, tamping each layer until it was firm.

Nettie recalled her last conversation with Mr. Danes. "Chief, was that a prayer?"

"Yes. For the ascension of his soul to the Great Spirit."

"Sir, you're a Christian, right?"

The chief stripped leaves from a bush, then used them to clean his hands and arms. "I am."

She nodded toward the smoldering fire bowl and burial mound. "How does Jesus fit into all of this?"

The chief settled against a tree and motioned for Nettie and Win to join him. "They fit together naturally. Monacans are deeply spiritual people, as are most Native Americans. In fact, we believed in Jesus before we knew his name."

"How do you mean?"

"The presence of the Great Spirit lived among us long before we ever heard the name God. And we believed in an eternal spiritual journey, life after death, before the New Testament put resurrection into words. To us, smudging with cedar smoke and sweetgrass is a ceremonial prayer. The cedar represents immortality. The sweetgrass is an offering of gratitude. Together, their smoke drives away dark spirits, honors those who have died, and shows them the path to follow into the next life. Christianity gave this path a name: Jesus."

Nettie kicked at pebbles. "So, did your ancestors understand sin?"

"They understood the battle between good and evil, as did yours. Just as there is no light without darkness, no life without death, there is no good without evil. The universe exists as opposites. Good and evil occupy different sides of the same face—our face."

"We can't escape it?"

"No. But we do have a choice about which one we feed."

Nettie repeated his words from the day before. "Choice is a powerful thing when you realize you have it."

"Indeed." The chief stood and brushed himself off. "I'm going to head back and get in touch with the elders. You two find the rest of your arrowheads, then work your way back to the creek. Follow it down the mountain until you come to an old logging road. Turn left, and it will bring you back to the settlement. If you find any more bones, put them near the smudging bowl and I'll rebury them when I get back."

The *Weak and Weary*'s whistle sounded in the distance as Nettie and Win turned onto the Upper Road and headed for Allen's Hill. Tall, gold-tinted grass once again covered the rolling knoll, harboring a myriad of summer bugs that scurried ahead of them like panicked escorts. Passing tufts of goldenrod, Nettie smelled licorice, a sure sign that summer would soon come to an end. As they moved into the shade of their favorite tree, the sweet smell of wisteria replaced the licorice. The lush green vines draping the limbs were heavy with seedpods that would bloom the following spring.

Nettie pulled off her tennis shoes and rubbed her sore feet against the soft undergrass while Win poured the arrowheads out of their pouches and counted them, twice. "We're missing one. I thought you had thirteen."

"I do."

"No. You have twelve."

"Wait a minute." Nettie stretched out so she could dig into the pocket of her cutoffs. Pulling out the white arrowhead, she handed it to Win. "I forgot I stuck this one in my pocket."

Win fingered the quartz, still sparkly in the low light. "This is the prettiest one."

"I found it near the skull."

Win's head snapped up. "Was it buried with it?"

"I don't think so. Why?"

"Because of what the chief said about the sanctity of burial. If it was buried with the dead, it should stay with the dead."

Taking the arrowhead, Nettie rubbed her thumb over it. "It's not likely they'd both get washed down to the exact same spot even if they were buried together, is it?"

"You're right."

"What happens if I'm wrong? Bad luck? Should we take it back?"

"We can check with Nibi or with the chief the next time we see him. I really don't want to hike to the top of Bear Mountain again for a while if we can help it."

"Me either. Why don't we take a break and go to the lake tomorrow? Nibi's not expecting us back until the day after tomorrow."

"A little rest would do us both good."

"Want to invite Ethan and Cal?"

Nettie hesitated. After their conversation at the Tastee Freez, Ethan would want to know if she'd been able to talk with Andy, and she hadn't. She had finally talked with his mother, who said Andy would be home soon. She'd seemed genuinely happy to see Nettie, but made a point of not saying where Andy was. She promised to have him call.

Win cocked her head and waited for an answer.

"I guess so."

"You guess?"

"Andy's supposed to be back in town soon."

"Okay?"

"Maybe he'll call."

"Or maybe you can see him at church on Sunday. Let's go swimming tomorrow. The break will do us good. Plus, Ethan and Cal are fun to be around. We need to laugh for a while."

"You don't think I'm being unfair to Ethan?"

"Not at all. You've been straight with him all summer. You're friends."

"Okay. You're right. It'll be fun."

They got up and were gathering their things when Win suddenly stopped. "Oh my gosh! Look at the house."

The angle of the disappearing sun cast a soft glow on the Palladian window, where two silhouettes stood shoulder to shoulder.

"Who's that with Alise Allen?"

"Maybe the housekeeper?"

"Too big."

"I didn't see the gardener's car in the driveway. Did you?"

"Nope."

"Then he, or she, got by us."

"The shadow dweller?"

"Who else?"

"I wonder if they realize we can see them?"

The silhouettes quickly backed into the shadows of the room.

"They do now."

Chapter 14

The sunny beach at Sweet Briar Lake bustled as Ethan backed the car into a shady spot and opened the trunk to get the picnic basket. Nettie and Win grabbed towels while Cal got the blanket and Frisbee. Finding an open space in the sand, they spread out the blanket, dumped their stuff, and headed for the water.

Nettie dove in and glided down through the cool, silky darkness, then, with mermaid kicks, turned upward toward the wavy light. She needed to do this more often.

She popped to the surface near Ethan. "Boo."

"Race you to the floating dock."

Taking off, Nettie made it a race but lost.

Pulling themselves up onto the bouncy wooden platform, they dangled their feet over the side.

"You surprised me," Ethan said. "I'm pretty fast, but you almost caught me."

Nettie pulled her hair back. "And would have if my arms were a little longer."

"Seriously, you're pretty strong."

"If you'd been climbing around the mountains as much as Win and I have this summer, you'd understand why."

"Did you talk with Andy yet?"

"He hasn't been home."

Ethan studied the water. "So, you still haven't figured things out."

"No."

He bumped her shoulder playfully. "Maybe no news is good news for me."

Win and Cal climbed out of the water before Nettie could respond.

Stretching out on her stomach, Win shaded her eyes and nudged Nettie. "Did you see who's on the beach?"

"You mean Anne and her posse? Can't miss them."

"She's had eagle eyes on you since we got here."

"Ignore her."

"That's hard to do with that hot-pink bikini she's got on."

Ethan leaned over. "Did you say 'hot-pink bikini'?"

Nettie pointed to the cluster of girls on the beach.

"They're here for show." He pulled Nettie up and over to the far side of the dock. "Is that a boathouse over there?"

"It is."

"Race you."

He hit the water before Nettie, but they were almost head to head by the time they reached the entrance. Their wake rocked a dozen rowboats tied to cleats inside. Making their way along the wall into the dank darkness, they climbed the ladder on the inside dock. Oars, life jackets, fishing poles, and other various sundries hung on the walls. Along the back were built-in bench chests, ropes, bumpers, and buoys.

"Are we allowed to use these boats?"

"Not really. They belong to the college."

"Will they stop us if we do?"

"There aren't any lifeguards or monitors."

Ethan put two oars in the first boat.

"Maybe we shouldn't."

"Chicken?" He stepped into the boat and held out his hand.

Nettie stepped in off-center, causing the dinghy to rock. Ethan put his arm around her waist for balance, then pulled her closer.

"My, my. When the boyfriend's away, the country bumpkin will play."

Nettie pushed away from Ethan and spun, almost dumping them both in the water. Anne stood in the doorway, her hot-pink bikini effervescing in the dim light.

"Turned to spying now, Anne?"

"You're such a hypocrite, keeping Andy dangling while you play touchy-feely with your summer boy."

"Look, Barbie, I don't know what you think you saw, but Nettie wasn't doing anything wrong."

"My name's not Barbie."

"Tacky, blond, and plastic—if the shoe fits."

Anne gave Ethan the finger and slammed the door so hard, it banged twice.

"Nettie, I'm sorry."

"Don't worry about it." She grabbed an oar. "Come on. Row. I'm not giving her the satisfaction of messing up a nice day."

Ethan maneuvered out of the boathouse and angled over to the floating dock to pick up Win and Cal; then the four of them set out to row the perimeter of the lake. On the beach, Anne and her posse were in a tight huddle.

It was lunchtime by the time they rowed back into the boathouse.

"Uh-oh," Nettie whispered. One of Sweet Briar's elderly security guards sat on the bench chest, relaxing and smoking a pipe.

As the four of then climbed out of the boat and up the ladder, he pointed to a sign on the wall that said the boats were private property. "You folks read?"

"Yes, sir."

Ethan stepped forward. "Sir, it was my idea, my fault."

The old guard chuckled. "I used to do the same thing in my younger days. The way I figure it, if they really didn't want folks using 'em, they'd lock 'em down." He stood up and stretched. "But I gotta do my job. Consider yourself warned."

"You mean we're not in trouble?" Ethan asked.

"Not this time," he said with a wink.

"Sir, did someone turn us in?" Nettie asked.

He nodded. "Girl out there on the beach. The one in the 'look at me' pink bathing suit. Seemed pretty arrogant about someone using a boat she didn't own." He walked them outside and, in front of everyone on the beach, shook their hands. "You all have a blessed day."

"Thank you, sir. You too."

Tipping his hat, he climbed into his golf cart and buzzed off.

Ethan looked over at Anne and her posse. "What a lowlife."

"C'mon," Win said. "Shake it off. Let's eat."

When they reached the blanket, their picnic basket, towels, and Frisbee had disappeared. Neighboring sunbathers pointed to Anne and her posse.

"Dammit." Ethan took off with Nettie close behind. He kicked sand onto Anne's blanket as he came to a stop. "What did you do with our stuff?"

"I don't know what you're talking about."

"Like hell you don't."

"Nettie, call off your dog."

Nettie crossed her arms. "What's wrong, Anne? Start something you're not up to finishing?"

"Bug off. And take California Boy with you." Anne's posse tittered.

Ethan stepped on the blanket, leaning close enough to Anne that she pulled back. "It must be miserable being you."

Anne turned blotchy red as she hissed and stuttered.

Win called from their blanket. Picnic basket in hand, she pointed to the neighboring sunbathers. They'd revealed the posse's hiding place.

Ethan took Nettie's arm. "Come on." Back on their blanket, he fumed as he ate. "I can't believe the nerve of that girl."

"You don't know the half of it."

"She wasn't born that way. What turned her mean?"

Nettie hesitated. "I don't know. In fact, I never thought about it that way."

"Are her parents mean?"

"Prissy, maybe, but not mean. At least, not that I know of."

"Brothers and sisters mean?"

"She's an only child."

"That may be part of the problem. Spoiled brat."

"Her friends sure don't bring out her good side, if there is one."

"Okay," Win said, "let's change the subject. The day's too pretty to get stuck in the muck."

When they finished eating, Nettie packed up the leftovers. "I'm going to give the rest of these cookies to the folks who helped us, then put the picnic basket in the car. I'll be right back."

She also wanted a minute to collect her thoughts. Anne would find a way to tell Andy what had happened and twist the truth about Ethan into something ugly, and there wasn't anything Nettie could do to stop it. Walking slowly across the parking lot, she put the basket in the trunk and headed back to the beach.

"Nettie, wait up." Andy came trotting across the gravel, his handsome face beaming. Tanned and fit, the muscles of his bare shoulders were more defined than she remembered. "Hey."

"Hey, stranger." Nettie's heart pounded.

"I was hoping to find you. Your dad said you and Win had come here for the day."

"It's really good to see you."

"You too. How've you been?"

"Okay. You?"

"Okay." My mom said you called and came by the house while I was gone."

"I did. You've been gone a long time. Where'd you go?"

Andy stepped closer. "It's a surprise. Can we—"

Anne's barbed voice rang out again. "Oh, so now you're making nice with Andy while just a little while ago, you were in the boathouse, playing handsy with your blanket buddy, Ethan."

"You don't know what you're talking about."

"I most certainly do. I saw you. In fact, I've seen you two doing a lot more than that."

"That's a lie, and you know it."

Following Anne off the beach, Win stepped beside Nettie. Ethan and Cal stopped a few feet back.

Andy turned to Anne, his anger obvious but controlled. "We've had this conversation. Nettie is free to see who she wants and do as she pleases. She's not accountable to me. And she's certainly not accountable to you. Leave her alone." He glanced at Ethan. "Leave them both alone." Andy headed for his car.

Nettie stepped so close to Anne, she could smell the baby oil. "You're a malicious liar."

Anne snickered. "I told you I wasn't giving up."

Nettie took off across the parking lot. "Andy, please wait."

He opened his car door but didn't get in.

"What she said, it's not true."

"I figured as much. I don't think she knows what the truth is anymore."

"Ethan and I are friends. That's all."

"Like I said, you don't owe me an explanation. I gave up that right."

"But I want you to know. It's important. I'd like to talk."

"Me too. But this isn't the time or the place." He glanced over her shoulder at Ethan. "You have folks waiting."

Nettie's heart sank as Andy's car disappeared around the turn.

Win put her arm around Nettie's waist. "Anne's doing what Anne does: making trouble just because she can."

"At least he's home."

As they left the parking lot, Ethan dropped in step beside Nettie. "Want me to talk with him? Guy to guy?"

"And tell him what? That you tried to make another pass at me?"

"Good point."

"I appreciate the offer, but Andy and I are the ones who need to talk."

Back at the beach, Anne stood on her blanket, arms crossed, staring at Nettie.

Nettie's eyes narrowed, anger building. "I'm sick and tired of this."

Win grabbed her arm. "What are you going to do?"

"Stay here." Nettie marched across the sand.

Anne turned back and forth to keep from being face-to-face with her, but it didn't work. "Will you stop? People are staring."

"What do you care? You're the one that turned this day into a three-ring-circus."

"What do you want?"

"I want to know why you are so blasted hateful."

Anne pushed past her. "Get real."

Nettie caught her arm. "Either tell me or I'm coming to your house and asking again, in front of your parents. I'll bet they'd be surprised to learn how their precious little girl behaves when they're not looking."

"You wouldn't dare."

"Watch me."

"You're a fool, Nettie."

"You and I both know Andy's only part of the reason you're so hateful to me."

Anne hissed through gritted teeth, "It *is* Andy. You don't want him, but you won't get out of the way so someone else has a chance."

"I'm not standing in his way. I couldn't if I wanted to. If you really knew Andy, you'd know that."

"You *are* standing in his way—you just don't know it."

"Walking away from you was his call, not mine."

"That's a lie." Anne's voice lowered to a whisper, as if she didn't believe her own words.

"It's not a lie. Straighten your halo, Anne. Maybe then you'll be able to recognize the truth when you hear it."

"You are so hateful."

"Me?"

"Yes, you. You always have been. Ever since we were kids, you've been just as hateful to me as you could be."

"That's not true."

"It is."

"Look, I know we've never gotten along, but—"

"Never gotten along? Are you kidding?" For an instant, Anne's eyes looked more sad than angry. "You never gave us a chance to be friends. Not once. Even when we were little. You laughed at everything about me, just because I didn't dress and act like a tomboy. On top of that, you get the one guy I want and dangle him on an invisible leash just so I can't have him. If anyone needs to straighten their halo, it's you." Anne stormed off toward the parking lot.

Nettie wobbled as Win hurried up. "Are you all right? What was that about?"

Nettie didn't answer, her thoughts reeling. Had she really been the spark that had ignited all that hate?

Win took Nettie's elbow, guiding her toward the path circling the lake. Ethan tugged Cal back to the blanket. "Give them a few minutes."

Away from the crowd, Win pressed. "What in the world did she say to you?"

Nettie shivered, despite the late-day heat, as she relayed the conversation.

"Don't do this," Win warned. "You are not responsible for that girl's meanness."

"I know, but she's right about one thing: I don't think I ever gave her a chance."

"Did she ever give you one?"

"I don't remember ever wanting her to."

Nettie and Win held tight to their pouches of arrowheads as they jumped from the caboose. Scurrying along the shaded river walk toward Oak's Landing, they stopped by Huffman's to get a Coke before heading to Nibi's to finish their dreamcatchers. Hearing lively bluegrass music coming from the park, they joined the crowd gathered on blankets, benches, and lawn chairs in front of the gazebo. The mayor sat on the steps, puffing into a jug, keeping time with his foot, while Dexter Carter plucked a banjo, Alma Carter strummed a guitar, and Sheriff Tanner played a red-tinged fiddle tucked under his chin. Behind all of them stood Mr. Huffman, plucking an upright bass.

Mr. Meeks stood guard over the red punch bowl, while at the next table Mrs. Loving advertised chocolate fudge, lemon drops, and an assortment of taffy.

A familiar bicycle stood propped against one of the old oaks. Wade and Skip sat on a low branch, hidden partially by leaves. Seeing Nettie, Wade did a backward flip off the limb, sticking the landing for a split second before falling on his butt. He jumped up and hurried over, not bothering to brush himself off. "Hi, Nettie. I didn't hear the *Weak and Weary*'s extra whistle. Must have been the music."

Nettie smiled at his assumption that she had expected him to meet her.

"Did you come for the concert?"

"No. Did you hurt yourself getting out of that tree?"

Wade blushed. "Uh-uh. Are you going to Miz Nibi's?"

"In a few minutes. Just thought we'd enjoy some music before we head up."

"Is it okay if I walk up with you?"

Before Nettie could say no, Wade's father called to him and Skip. "Hamburgers are done. Time to eat."

"Figures." Wade looked disappointed. "Maybe I'll see you on the way back?"

"Maybe."

Win grinned at Nettie as the boys ran to join their parents. "I must say, he's persistent. Are you sure you don't like younger guys?" she teased.

"Good grief."

Pushing uphill past brush, trees, and boulders, Nettie and Win came to an abrupt stop at the bottom of Nibi's clearing. The running cedar had become so thick, they had to take big hopscotch steps to avoid trampling it.

"Isn't this stuff off the endangered-plant list yet?"

"Not that I know of."

Clanging and banging echoed from the back of the house as their knocks on the screen door went unanswered. When they entered, the doors to the kitchen cabinets were wide open and the counters covered with clutter. Nibi's head and shoulders were buried in the bottom of her Hoosier cabinet.

Win knocked on the wall. "Hi, Nibi. Isn't it a little late for spring cleaning?"

"Hey, girls." Nibi inched out of the cabinet. "Found it." She sat on her heels, holding a carved wooden pipe, the bowl black and worn. "It was my father's." Nibi climbed to her feet, using the chair for support. "You girls have your arrowheads?"

"Yes, ma'am. Thanks to Chief Brannon."

"He's a good man. I want to give him this pipe as a gift for helping you."

"Want us to take it to him?"

"Thanks, but no. I'll see him soon. Get those two balls of sinew and the scissors off the table and come with me."

Nibi had hung the dreamcatchers on the same low limb as the buck. "Both of you cut thirteen pieces of string. The longest should be about eighteen inches; the next two should be sixteen inches, the next two fourteen inches, and so on. Keep going until you have two six-inch ones. Tie the longest string at the very bottom of the ring, then come out two inches on either side and tie the next longest strings. Keep going until the six-inch strings are on the ends. Tie them with bow knots—they don't let go."

While Nettie and Win tapered the strings, Nibi laid their eagle feathers out in rows by size. "When you're finished, tie the biggest feather in the middle of the longest string and work your way out, adding the next two biggest feathers to the next two longest strings. Save the extras."

Next, Nibi organized the arrowheads into two rows. Pulling the solid white one out of the bag, she studied it from both sides. "Nettie, did you find this one?"

"Yes, ma'am. I found it near the Indian brave's skull."

"Near what?"

Nettie and Win explained what had happened on Bear Mountain.

"Should I not use it?" Nettie asked. "Should I take it back?"

Nibi shook her head. "White arrowheads, quartz ones in particular, are symbols of great strength. But what's most important is that it was delivered to you."

"Pardon?"

"You heard me."

"You think this arrowhead was meant for me? That I was supposed to find it?"

"Not only was it meant for you, I think you met the brave who made it and delivered it."

"But why me?"

"We don't always know why things happen, good or bad. But for this to come to you at this moment in time is no accident."

Nettie fingered the arrowhead as Nibi moved on, demonstrating how to use bow knots to tie the arrowheads onto the ends of the sinew. When they were finished, she examined each stone to make sure the fibers rested in the smooth curve at the base and that each knot was tight, especially the white quartz.

When she had examined and approved the last details of the dreamcatchers, Nibi touched both spider mothers, closed her eyes, and chanted a beautiful melody using words Nettie didn't understand. Then she stepped back. "Well done, girls."

Win took Nettie's hand. "I can't believe we're actually finished. Thank you, Nibi."

"It is I who should thank the both of you. The journey to complete these was difficult and dangerous, with much to learn along the way. You did it, and you did it well. For that I am grateful."

"Is that what the chant was about?" Nettie asked.

"It was a prayer for continued wisdom and strength for both of you."

A rustling in the barn caught their attention.

"Is the white owl still here?" Win asked.

"No. We must have another visitor." Moving quietly to the barn door, Nibi led the way inside.

Nettie blinked as she waited for her vision to sharpen. "There." She pointed to the top of the ladder.

A black owl with piercing yellow eyes sat on the top rung. His jet-black feathers were tipped in white.

An ominous feeling wrapped Nettie like a blanket. "Nibi, I know you said Nature doesn't play either-or, but since the white owl has come and gone and the black one is here now, could that mean . . ."

"Don't say it," Win whispered.

Nibi stared at the black owl, then left the barn. Her hands were shaking when Nettie and Win caught up with her.

"You two go sit down. I'll be back in a minute."

Nettie grabbed Win's arm as Nibi disappeared inside. "Does this mean what I think it means?"

"Is it a bad omen? Yes."

"What kind of bad omen?"

"I have no idea."

Nibi returned shortly with three cups of blackberry tea. Composed, her hands steady, she settled into a chair, looking resolute. "The black owl warns that the darkness is approaching. Yet it remains veiled. For months, the mountains and wildlife have hinted that it bodes from Nature, but the exact form remains distorted, confusing. What I can see clearly is that it has an emerald aura, which makes no sense." Nibi leaned forward, cradling her cup. "In the spring, when the darkness first appeared, there was a spiderweb in front of it. The web was ringed with red willow and wrapped in grapevine. A real spider sat near the portal as a white owl and golden eagle came forward, offering gifts of their feathers. As they disappeared, the spirit of an Indian brave appeared and laid thirteen arrowheads at the foot of the web. The largest one was solid white."

Nettie shivered as she tried to process the connections. "The spider was building a dreamcatcher?"

Nibi took a deep breath. "No. You and Win were."

It took a moment for Nibi's words to sink in.

"In the vision, we were building it?" Win repeated.

"Yes. Piece by piece, the two of you put together the symbols of faith, wisdom, courage, hope, strength, and commitment and placed them in front of the coming darkness."

"But it had a white arrowhead. Does that mean my dream-catcher is supposed to stop it?" Nettie asked.

Nibi shook her head. "The only thing I know for sure is that the two of you have important roles to play."

The breeze flowing from the peaks made the suspended dreamcatchers dance, the spider mothers sparkling as they spun. Nibi watched them, deep in thought.

Win moved to sit at her feet. "You're afraid we may not have done enough, aren't you?"

"This darkness is deceptive. There is much I do not know."

"Is that why you had us make a second dreamcatcher?"

Nibi stroked Win's hair. "The time is coming when you will take my place among our people. Your dreamcatcher will serve you, as mine has served me. As for the darkness, we must continue to prepare as best we can and continue to remember the lessons we've learned. Hopefully, the darkness will reveal itself before the blood moon rises."

"Why before then?" Nettie asked.

"Because that's when Nature's energies are most out of balance and destructive. The full moon peaks midweek; the blood moon will follow."

"What do we do until then?" Win asked.

"Live your life. And do it unafraid. We will deal with what comes as it comes."

"When do you want us to come back?"

"When the darkness appears. You'll know."

Nettie and Win moved their dreamcatchers to the front porch and hung them next to Nibi's. With rings two feet wide, intricate webs, and shining spider mothers, they made an impressive combination.

"Would you like us to help you put the kitchen things away before we head home?" Win asked.

"Thanks, but I'm still going through them."

Nibi gave both of them a long hug.

"Nettie."

"Yes, ma'am."

"Are you finished with your Wednesday-night study sessions?"

"Almost. One more, I think."

"You have good instincts. Trust them."

"Yes, ma'am."

Nibi turned and went inside.

When they reached the bottom of the hill, Nettie stopped. "I didn't realize Nibi knew about the sessions with Mr. Danes. Did you tell her?"

"Not that I remember, but who knows? It's been a long summer."

Chapter 15

Nettie and Win dried the last of the plates and stacked the clean trays on the counter, completing their turn at church supper cleanup duty on the last possible day. Wednesday-night suppers were to be suspended until after school started.

Nettie peeked under the sink at Pic. "Were you able to fix the leak?"

"For a little while. Pipes are shot. Leak won't stop for good until they're replaced." Pic climbed out and wiped his hand on his pants. "Church's building committee moves slower than I do. I'll leave the bucket here, just in case. You two headed home?"

"Not yet. I have my session with Mr. Danes. How about you?"

"In a bit. I'll wait and walk you home. Exercise will do me good."

"That's nice of you, Pic. Ethan and Cal should be here in a few minutes. As soon as I'm done, the four of us are going out."

"Double date, huh? I remember those days. My brother and I used to double date."

Nettie baited him. "Anybody we know?"

Pic shook his head. "Too long ago."

Win nudged her. "You're going to be late for your session."

"Right. Gotta go. See you later, Pic." Gliding among the almost empty tables and chairs, she and Win stopped long enough to thank

Mrs. Mac for sponsoring the GA class again. She'd been teaching it for as long as Nettie could remember.

"You are most welcome. It's been a pleasure. See you again in mid-September." Before Nettie could turn away, Mrs. Mac touched her hand. "How's the baptism prep going?"

"Okay, I guess. It's almost over."

"Good. Don't second-guess yourself or your faith. Sometimes adults just get it wrong."

"I don't think Pastor Williams feels that way."

Mrs. Mac winked. "He's coming around, slowly but surely."

Nettie hugged her teacher's thin shoulders. "Thank you."

"You're welcome, dear. See you Sunday."

"Yes, ma'am."

Once they were in the hall, Nettie turned to Win. "I bet she's the reason Pastor Williams is ready to let me finish. I wonder if he's already talked with Mr. Danes. With luck, this really could be my last session."

"Let's hope. I'll wait for you on the front steps. Ethan and Cal are picking us up there. I think we're going to the Tastee Freez."

"Good. Maybe we'll have something to celebrate."

Nettie knocked on the partially open door and peeked in. "Mr. Danes?"

He wasn't at his desk. The air conditioner hummed at full blast in the window while the back door leading to the staff parking lot stood wide open. Stepping outside, Nettie started to sweat; the rising heat and humidity had become so oppressive that the swallows were flying low and the insects had disappeared. In the waning light, Mr. Danes fiddled with something under the hood of his car. Pulling the office door closed, she crossed the almost empty parking lot.

"Engine trouble?"

"It's been misfiring for a couple of days. I just changed the spark plugs. Let's see if that fixes it. Get in."

"What about our study session?"

"I'll drive, you talk. We'll kill two birds with one stone." Something strange flickered in his eyes, before he looked away.

Nettie didn't like the analogy. "I don't mind waiting until you get back."

"No need. Let's go." Mr. Danes slammed the hood and opened the door for her. A suitcase and other odds and ends lay on the backseat.

"I can come back tomorrow."

"Nope. This is it. Our last class." He opened her door. "Hop in."

Last class? Relief told Nettie to get in the car, while fear told her not to. She hesitated, then stepped in. Mr. Danes slid behind the wheel and started the engine, gunning it twice. Pulling out of the parking lot, he headed away from town.

"Engine sounds pretty good," Nettie said. "No misses."

"So far." Mr. Danes kept his attention on the narrow twists and turns in the country road. When they reached a straight stretch, he spoke. "So, this is it? You think you're ready to be baptized?"

"Yes, sir."

"Have you given any more thought to our discussion from the last session?"

"If you mean did I talk with God about my sins, yes, I have, several times."

Mr. Danes reached under the seat and pulled out a flask. Unscrewing the top, he took a long swig and rolled it around in his mouth, before swallowing. "Funny thing about sin. It never seems to let go of us."

"Shouldn't we head back to the church?"

"Not yet."

The sliver of sun over the mountains flashed metallic green and disappeared.

Mr. Danes turned the headlights on and took another swig, showing no signs of being ready to turn around.

"Really, sir, we should get back."

"There's no hurry."

Slowing, he turned onto a dirt lane lined on both sides by tall grass. Nettie knew the lane all too well.

"Mr. Danes, there aren't many places to turn around in here. This is the back way to the Piney River."

"That so?"

"Yes, sir."

"You like going to the river, don't you?"

"Yes, sir, but not at this time of night."

"Now, that's not exactly true, is it?"

The rough lane curved, paralleling the river. The usual comforting sounds of the lapping current were anything but. She knew where they were going.

"Like I said, you enjoy coming here in the dark, don't you?"

Nettie leaned away as Mr. Danes rubbed her arm with the back of his hand. "What do you mean?"

"You know exactly what I mean."

Mr. Danes pulled into a glade facing the river. The headlights cast a harsh glare on the mossy clearing she and Andy called their special place, River's Rest. He turned off the engine. Despite the sultry heat, Nettie shivered.

With a soft click, the headlights went out. Moonlight and shadows from the tangled canopy played against the shimmering black river.

Nettie eased her hand along the door, trying to find the handle. In the shadowy darkness, Mr. Danes took another gulp from the flask. She could see a smirk on his face.

"I know all about your sins of the flesh."

"Please take me home."

"You were right here. You and your boyfriend."

"I don't know what you're talking about."

"Oh, yes, you do. What's his name? Andy? You two used to have a good time down here."

His guttural laugh burned. Nettie whirled on him. "You were here? Watching us?"

Danes grabbed her wrist. "Every slow, sexy move."

"You sick bastard. Let go of me." She frantically grabbed for the door handle.

Danes slid his hand behind her and pushed the lock down, then wrapped his arm around her shoulders, pinning her arms. "Tsk-tsk. There goes your language again." He put his hand on her waist.

"What are you doing? Stop it!"

"You and I can have a good time too, Nettie. In fact, we can have an even better time, because I know how to finish what you started."

Nettie jerked her head away as Danes tried to kiss her; his day-old whiskers tore at her face. She struggled to push his arm away as he fumbled with the buttons on her blouse. "Stop it!"

He put his hand over her mouth as she tried to scream. "Shh. There's no one around to hear you." His hands found skin and pushed the cotton strap off her shoulder. "Just relax. You're going to enjoy this." He lowered his head.

Jerking one hand free, Nettie dug her fingernails into Danes's face, dragging them all the way to his neck.

Rearing back, he grabbed her hair. "You little tease. I saw you. You enjoyed being touched. Remember? You wanted more, but your boyfriend didn't want to deliver, did he?"

Nettie fought to push his hand away, but he held her tighter. Probing fingers slid under the band of her shorts.

Danes put his mouth to her ear. "Let me in, Nettie."

Nettie rammed Danes's nose twice with her forehead. Blood spurted through his fingers as he grabbed his face with both hands, freeing her arms. She landed a knuckled punch to his groin. He yowled and fell back against the steering wheel just as the driver's-side door flew open. Hands grabbed Danes by the neck and arm, dragging him from the car and slamming him to the ground.

"You son of a bitch!" Ethan shouted.

Someone pounded on the window by Nettie's head. Win tugged on the handle as she yelled, "Unlock the door!"

Nettie pulled the lock and scrambled out.

Win gave her a quick hug. "Thank God you're okay."

Leaning against the car, Nettie felt relief battling anger as she caught her breath. Sharp blows, dull thuds, moans, and scraping sounds came from the other side of the car. Pushing past Win, she dashed around. Ethan had Danes pulled up by the collar, primed to deliver another punch. Danes wasn't fighting back. Nearby, Cal knelt in the dirt, his hands bloody.

Nettie grabbed Ethan's arm. "Stop!" He tried to shake free, but she held tight. "Let him go. Please."

Ethan shoved Danes to the ground. "You sack of shit. She trusted you."

Pushing himself sluggishly up on one elbow, Danes wiped his bloody nose with the back of his hand. His wobbly gaze stopped on Nettie.

Ethan grabbed Nettie's arm. "Let's get out of here."

"Wait."

Nettie dropped to her knees beside Danes. Ethan, Cal, and Win stepped closer. "How long were you following Andy and me? Since you came here? Since the night we met in the parking lot? Back in the spring? You followed us that night, didn't you?"

"What does it matter?"

"It means you've been planning this all along."

Danes spat blood in the dirt. "What if I did?"

"That night when you said, 'The evil you don't want is the evil you keep doing'—you've done this before, haven't you?"

Danes turned away.

Nettie jerked his face back to hers. "Answer me."

He knocked away her hand. "You think you're any different? Any of you?" He turned back to Nettie. "You and your boyfriend were right here, doing the same thing."

"Not even close. I chose to be with Andy. I didn't choose any of this. You did." Nettie stood.

"What are you going to do?" Danes asked.

"Didn't you say with choice comes consequences? That it's not my job to play judge and jury? We leave that up to God, right?"

Danes nodded, hopeful.

"Well, in this case, it's God and the police."

Danes sat straighter, eyes narrowed. "You're not going to turn me in."

"I'm not?"

"No. You'd embarrass yourself, your family, and your church. Not to mention dear old Pastor Williams. You could forget about being baptized."

"That's the best you've got? Embarrassment's been my summer companion, and my family and church know it. Besides, I'm not embarrassed; I'm pissed off. I'd think after all these weeks you'd be able to tell the difference. I'm not worried about getting baptized either. Not anymore. Forgiveness is mine for the asking. It is for you too. You'll just be asking from a jail cell."

Ethan pulled Nettie back as Danes struggled to his knees. "What about your precious Andy? You want him to know you teased me like you teased him?"

"Andy knows that would never happen. Nothing you can do or say will ever change that."

Danes got to his feet, shoved Win out of the way, and ran for his car. Ethan and Cal started after him, but Nettie stopped them. "Let him go. He can't get far. The police can deal with him."

Danes gunned the engine and spun the tires, creating a rooster tail of dirt and leaves trailing the car's bobbing lights.

Ethan took Nettie's hand. "C'mon. We need to go to the police station before that sicko gets too far away."

Streaks of smoky moonlight broke through the trees as they hurried toward the main road and Ethan's car. As the four of them piled into the Chrysler, Nettie hugged herself for warmth. "How did you all know I was in trouble?"

Win grabbed a jacket off the floorboard and draped it around Nettie's shoulders. "Pic. He saw Danes drive off with you. He came running out the door to get help as Ethan and Cal pulled up. We took off to follow Danes while Pic headed to the police station. We almost didn't find you. If Cal hadn't seen Danes's taillights going toward the river, we would've driven right past."

As she got out of the car at the police station, Nettie wiped the sweat rolling off her forehead. The night had gone beyond oppressive. Pic hurried up the sidewalk to meet her.

"Nettie girl, I'm so glad you're okay. Nibi and I knew that man was up to no good."

Nettie gave Pic a grateful hug. "Thank you for watching out for me. Who knows what would have happened if you hadn't?"

Nettie looked around for Win, but she wasn't there. She'd stopped in the middle of the road, eyes locked on the western horizon, where a translucent red veil had begun to inch its way across the cream-colored supermoon. Below it churned the blackest storm clouds Nettie had ever seen, so black they looked green, layered in rolls like a hornet's nest and blowing in from the west. Nettie couldn't tell where the clouds ended and the mountains began.

Win broke from her trance. Her voice faltered as she said, "It's starting. Nibi needs us."

Nettie struggled to pull her eyes away from the blood moon. "We can catch the *Weak and Weary* to Oak's Landing if we hurry." She turned to Ethan and Cal. "We have to go. Please tell the police what happened."

Pic stepped up. "I already gave them a description of the car and his license plate."

"Good. Tell them I'll come back tomorrow to answer questions."

Ethan shook his head. "No. You stay and talk with the police. I'll go with Win."

Nettie cupped his face and kissed him. "Thank you. For everything. But Win and I have to do this."

Pic put his hand on Win's arm. "Is Nibi in danger? What's wrong?"

"The blood moon."

"What did you see?"

"Nibi was calling for me, but I couldn't see her."

Pic hurried toward the Upper Road, his bindle sack tight under his arm. "I have to tell Alise."

Nettie froze. Alise? Pic? Taking backward steps toward the train station, she struggled for a moment to put the two together, then took off running after Win. She couldn't think about them now. "Ethan, tell our parents we've gone to Nibi's. We'll spend the night there."

Chapter 16

The *Weak and Weary*'s last, short whistle of the day had sounded and the pulp mill's night-shift workers had already boarded as Nettie and Win scrambled up the steps of the caboose. Wisps of dark clouds raced across the red, distorted face of the moon. Heat lightning lit the sky as jagged bolts of purple and green flashed inside the hornet's nest and speared the ground.

"I've seen wicked lightning before, but nothing like this. We'll be lucky to get to Nibi's before this monster hits. We may get stuck at the train station."

"I've got to get to Nibi," Win said.

Nettie counted Mississippis each time thunder clapped. They were going to get wet. She squeezed Win's hand. "We'll get there." Turning to the window, Nettie felt her concern about the pending storm swirling along with other questions. Nibi. The darkness. Danes. Repulsed at the memory of his rough hands, she wished Andy were next to her. *Please, Lord, help me find my way back to him, keep Nibi safe, and help the police catch Danes.* Curiosity about Pic and Alise Allen did not warrant prayer, but she made up her mind to ask him about it when they got back to town.

The *Weak and Weary* complained as it climbed the mountain more quickly than usual, rocking precariously as it split the winds whipping around the peak. On the downslope into Rockfish Valley, the wind quickly changed to thick humidity that smelled of pending rain mixed with smoke. Moonshiners' fires glowed across the mountain, dulled by the damp air. Scattered porch lights offered fuzzy snapshots of families shelling peas, smoking pipes, and strumming banjos.

Win's brow furrowed as she watched passengers waiting on the platform mingling nervously, watching the approaching storm and the slowing train.

"These folks have been through bad storms before. Lots of them. So has Nibi. So have we," Nettie said.

"I don't think experience is going to matter this time. Remember what Nibi said? This blood moon brings the unknown."

As soon as the *Weak and Weary* stopped, Nettie and Win jumped from the caboose. Weaving through scurrying passengers and around workers rushing to unload and load freight, they came to an abrupt stop as a bicycle skidded in front of them. As usual, Skip sat perched on the back.

"Wade Warren, what are you two doing here? Can't you see a storm's coming?"

"We just delivered some supplies to the train for Pop."

"You two need to beat it home."

"Are you and Win going to wait it out at the station? We'll wait with you."

"No. We're going to Nibi's."

"You don't have time to get there."

Win kept moving. "Nettie, come on!"

"We will if we run. You two go home. Now!"

The night sky grew blacker the farther Nettie and Win got from the bright lights of the station. High over the mountains, a ragged, fiery ring burned through thickening clouds; sharp winds tossed treetops violently in one direction and then the other. Guided by shadows and memory, Nettie and Win ran toward the bridge.

Behind them, the hornet's nest filled the sky, banking so high they couldn't see the top. Multicolored lightning bolts, too numerous and fast to count, gave the black mass a variegated glow. Nettie couldn't stop staring. "I've never seen anything like that."

"I don't think anyone has. C'mon."

Whitewater slapped angrily against the bottom of the bridge as they ran across.

"It's not even raining yet, and the water's this high."

"Runoff's leading the storm. Hurry."

Their footsteps went silent as they stepped onto the soft dirt path to Nibi's, hurrying past familiar trees and boulders until the uphill turn forced them to slow down. The bumps, rocks, twists, and turns of this part of the path were rough enough when Nettie could see them. Now, they were almost impossible. She jumped as a bolt of lightning struck a tree near them. Thunder cracked, shaking everything around them; its cannonade pulsed across the valley.

"That hurt!" Nettie could smell wood burning.

As they reached the edge of the clearing, a flickering lantern outlined Nibi's silhouette on the porch.

Win grabbed Nettie's arm. "There she is."

Quickly navigating the parameter of the clearing, they avoided the prickly blackberry bushes but kept tripping on the long, low strands of running cedar. Picking herself up a second time, Nettie rubbed her scraped knees. "Damn this stuff!"

"We're almost out of it."

"Listen."

"What?"

"Where are the wind chimes? All this wind, and they're not making a sound."

"Nibi must have taken them down."

"Why would she do that?"

"I have no idea."

Reaching the porch, they went up the steps two at a time. In the low lantern light, Nibi appeared tired and worn. Swathed in a shawl, despite the heat, she held tight to her dreamcatcher. "I'm glad you're here," she said, her voice surprisingly calm.

Win hugged her. "What is the darkness? Lightning? Fire? Wind? Rain? All of it?"

"I still don't know what poses the danger. My portal has gone dark." She laid her dreamcatcher down and stepped toward Win, cupping her cheek. "But yours is awakening."

"What? What is it showing?"

"The visions, good or bad, are for your eyes, child, not mine."

Win stepped back. "But . . ."

Nibi took Win's hand and pulled her closer to the dream-catcher. "Some things have to end for others to begin. Time is precious. Tell me what you see."

Every part of Win shook. "Nibi, I can't."

"Yes, you can." Nibi put her arm around Win and pulled her close. "You're not alone. Generations are with you."

Nibi and Win locked eyes, then Win turned toward the portal. Her shivering slowed as she became engrossed in what only she could see. It stopped completely when she began to speak. "There are three rings circling a red moon. The first is tinted brown, the second green, the last blue."

Nibi's frown deepened. "The danger is water, drawn from the earth, sea, and sky."

Win continued as the vision unfolded. "The rain is thick, pounding. Landslides are everywhere; they're washing away the mountains. The river is so high." Win gasped and stepped back. "The cross. The tilted cross. It's barely above the water."

Nibi spun toward the valley. Freakishly colored lightning flared like fireworks from one end to the other, surreal in its close-ness to the ground. She grabbed the railing for support. "Many will not survive this night."

Nettie's chest tightened. "There has to be something we can do." She headed for the steps. "C'mon, Win. We can warn those in town to get to higher ground."

Nibi grabbed her arm in a viselike grip. "No, child. This darkness comes from all directions. Some will die because they stay; others will die because they leave."

"We have to do something!"

Nibi's gaze went down the hill. Two shadows, one large, one small, entered the lantern's field of light. "Now I understand," she whispered to the night. "We save those we were meant to save."

"What do you mean? Who were we meant to save?" Nettie asked.

"Say nothing more for now." Nibi called into the darkness, "Boys, come up here."

"Boys? What boys?"

Nibi turned to Nettie and Win. "They followed you, and because they did, they have a chance."

As Wade and Skip crossed the clearing, Nettie's thoughts spun between anger and relief. "Dammit, Wade. What are you two doing here?"

Wade shifted his feet uncomfortably. "I . . . we just wanted to make sure you and Win made it up here okay."

Walnut-size raindrops began falling. Slow enough to count, they hit the ground with audible splats.

"Get up here," Nibi said.

"Naw, we don't melt. We gotta get home. Pop doesn't like it when we're out too late."

Nibi motioned to the boys. "No. Come. Get out of the rain."

Reluctantly, they made their way up the steps, wiping fat drops from their faces, then drying their hands on their jeans. "Sorry, Miz Nibi. We didn't mean to cause you any trouble."

"You haven't."

The giant drops started falling faster and closer together. Nibi opened the screen door and ushered everyone inside. "Win, Nettie, bring your dreamcatchers."

Drumming on the tin roof marked the moment the thudding raindrops turned into a downpour.

Following Nibi through the house, Win and Nettie lagged

behind, shocked to see the familiar rooms standing empty. The kitchen shelves were bare, the counters clear, the table and chairs gone, the constant kettle of simmering nettle tea absent from the cold woodstove. Even the fireplace in the sitting room harbored no glowing embers; the slight scent of sage was the only remnant of the home they knew.

Win ran her hand along the counter. "Where is everything?"

"Where it needs to be."

"What do you mean?"

"I'll explain later."

The drumming on the roof grew louder.

Wade and Skip stood wide-eyed. "Miz Nibi, we've got to get home."

"Not now. This storm's too dangerous."

"But we've gotta warn Mom and Pop."

Nibi's voice softened. "Tell me what your parents would say if you asked them what you should do right now."

Wade's gaze went from Nibi to Skip to the floor. "They'd say for us to stay put and do what you tell us to do."

Nibi gently cupped each boy's cheek. "I've known your parents for a lifetime, and that is exactly what they would say. It's time for you both to be brave." She looked at Nettie and Win. "It's time for all of us to be brave."

Win crossed to the rain-blurred window. "Someone's coming."

As they clustered on the back porch, the already intense downpour worsened. Blurred car lights inched down a driveway of streaming mud. Passing the barn, the lights pulled close to the porch.

Nettie recognized the car and pushed past the others to the door. "It's Andy."

The car's interior light snapped on and off as Andy jumped out and ran for the porch. Soaked to the skin, he gathered Nettie in his arms.

Nibi's voice forced them apart. "Inside. Quickly."

Holding tight to Andy's hand, Nettie wanted answers. "What are you doing here?"

"Ethan. He came looking for me. Said you and Win were headed up here and might be in trouble. He told me what Danes tried to do to you at River's Rest. I'm so sorry I wasn't there, and beyond grateful that he was."

A monstrous crack of thunder shook the house.

"We must go" Nibi said. "It's not safe to stay here."

"Can't we drive out?" Nettie asked.

Andy shook his head. "I don't think so. My car slid most of the way down here. The logging road was already washing out in places, and the Tye was cresting the bridge as I crossed. Sheriff Tanner was putting road blocks up when I got there. He wasn't going to let me cross until I told him I was coming to get you all. He said to tell you to stay put, that he's already had reports of flooding in the mountains west of here."

Rolling thunder rocked the house again as rainwater began dripping from under the door of the woodstove and pouring out the sitting-room chimney, sending ashes and bits of wood flowing across the floor and into the kitchen.

Nibi herded them toward the kitchen door. "Win, Nettie, Andy, I need you to get the boys up to Lookout Point. The overhang is part of the mountain's granite face, so it will be stable. Underneath it is a shallow cave. You'll be safe and dry there."

The rain's roar surrounded them as Nibi opened the door. A wall of water obscured everything beyond the back porch. Lifting the lid of a storage barrel, Nibi pulled out strands of fairy fire wrapped in sinew netting; the green glow lit the porch. "Tie these over your shoulder," she shouted. "They'll help keep you from getting separated."

Andy looked skeptical. Nibi touched his face. "Trust me." Moving quickly to Win, she took off her ever-present moonstone cross and placed it around her granddaughter's neck. Kissing Win's cheek, Nibi held her close. "Do what you were born to do, daughter. And remember, you are not alone."

Nibi turned to Nettie next. Sliding the braided copper bracelet off her arm, she placed the malleable metal around Nettie's wrist and squeezed it tight. Cupping Nettie's face in both hands, she kissed her forehead. "You're braver and stronger than you realize. Just as Win is not alone, neither are you."

Win's voice trembled as she fingered the moonstones. "Nibi, what are you doing?"

Nibi didn't answer but turned to talk with everyone. "Wet skin is slippery, so don't hold hands. Hold on to each other's belts or clothing. Win, you go first. Skip, you hold tight to her. Wade, you hold on to your brother. Then Nettie. Then Andy. Keep going right until you're past the barn; then turn uphill. Stay in the clearing, and keep going straight up. Lookout Point is just before you reach the ridge. The entrance to the cave is just below the overhang. Wait there until the rain stops, then make your way across the top of the mountain and down to Route 56."

Nibi moved to open the screen door, but Win stopped her. "What about you?"

"I'm going to town to help who I can."

"Let me go with you."

Nibi took Win's hand and kissed it. "Fate has other plans for you, daughter. You and Nettie hold tight to your dreamcatchers. Remember the lessons you've learned, and when this is all over, go to the church. Now hurry." Nibi opened the screen door and pushed Win forward, motioning for the rest to follow.

Win stepped into the torrent, followed by Skip, then Wade. Nibi hand-signaled "Godspeed," then hurried toward the front door as Nettie stepped from the porch.

Dense rain stole Nettie's breath and drenched her with the first step. Feet sliding in rain-filled shoes, she held on to Wade and sloshed forward. It seemed to take forever for them to make it past the barn in the flogging rain. As they moved into the buffeting wind, Andy tightened his grip on Nettie's waistband. When they turned uphill, ground-level, day-bright lightning exploded all around them. Nettie's skin tingled with each sideways flash. Blinking hard, she focused on Win's bobbing, rain-muted fairy fire leading the way through the darkness.

Loud rumbling from higher up the mountain penetrated the storm's roar as the ground began to vibrate. Win and the boys swayed precariously, then tumbled downhill in a growing swath of sliding mud. Inches from the cascade, Andy made a grab for the boys as Nettie dove and snagged Win's shirt. Getting to her knees, she pulled Win back and helped her to her feet. Rolling mounds of mud pushed between them, its thickness making it hard to move. Nettie pushed Win toward Andy. He pulled her out of the flow and reached for Nettie as a large bolus of mud and debris caught her in its downhill surge. She pushed forward, her fingertips brushing his.

Surprise turned to panic as the fast-moving earth swept Nettie down the hill, past Nibi's barn, then her house. Digging into the mud, grabbing everything her hands touched to try to stop, proved fruitless. It all moved with her. An earsplitting crash from some-where below burst through the storm's clamor. She'd be torn up if she went over the rocky ledge at the foot of the mountain. Pushing her arms and legs as deep into the muck as they'd go, Nettie groped for anything solid and still to hold on to. Her feet dragged against something bouncy, a lumpy rope of some kind. She stopped sliding. Forcing her fingers deeper, she found another one. Running cedar. She blessed the vine she'd cursed earlier.

Nettie lifted and turned her head back and forth, trying to take a deep breath as silty runoff splashed in her face and dammed up around her shoulders. The little bit of air she could find smelled of slag and outhouses. Unsure how long the running cedar would hold, she squinted against the downpour, looking for a stable tree or boulder she might be able to reach. What she saw didn't make sense. A raging river thrashed right behind her, melting Nibi's mountain.

"Nettie! Hold on." A hazy Andy stood at the edge of the flow-ing mud, preparing to come for her.

"Don't! Stay there!" she yelled. Sliding her hands and feet along the cedar, she inched toward him.

Dropping to his belly, he reached for Nettie's hand just as the earth beneath her dissolved into the raging water. The intense cold shocked her mouth open; panic closed it as gravelly slush surged in. The hysterical, muddy current thrust her downriver at breakneck speed, splaying her arms and legs and twisting the rest of her in different directions. Wave after angry wave broke on top of her. She fought to find air, to keep from being pulled under. Putrid grit filled her nose and stung her eyes. Hard, unrecognizable things slammed into her, ripping clothes and tearing skin, then spinning off into the darkness.

Dizzy and faint from the relentless, debris-filled assault, she felt the bestial water burying her. Pawing frantically, Nettie felt something jerk her head back and up, keeping it just above the surface. Gasping for air, something hard and sharp hit her cheek. Through pain and panic she knew she'd drown if she couldn't protect her face. An image of the beavers on Bear Mountain sliding through the window in the dam feet first flashed though her mind. "Their legs protect the rest of the body," Chief Brannon had said. Summoning every bit of strength she could, Nettie pulled her legs together, then tucked her thighs to her chest. Forcing her knees almost out of the water, she pushed them straight, her toes pointing downstream. Her feet and legs became buffers against the relentless, murderous debris swirling in front of her. The hard pull on her hair stayed constant as she struggled to keep her legs up and find air in the relentless downpour.

Her strength failing, her lungs burning, Nettie knew it was only a matter of time. Surprisingly calm, she could feel herself letting go. Suddenly the current dipped, sloping her feet and legs downward and slamming her chest into something hard and rough. A tree. Sharp pain ripped from her ribs to her back as she dug her fingernails into the bark. Splinters gouged deep, but the pain did not lessen her panicked grip.

Wild, sludgy floodwater surged around her, but she and the tree weren't going with it. Hooking an arm over the partially submerged trunk, Nettie found a small limb and pulled herself high enough to lift her left leg out of the water. Locating a dent in the bark with her foot, she anchored herself and worked to bring her right leg up. It hurt like hell and didn't move as it should, but she managed to drag it onto the tree. She laid her forehead against the hard, slick wood and found a pocket of air amid the waterfall of rain.

Chapter 17

Minutes dragged into hours as water raged above and below Nettie; the brutal, unrelenting downpour battered her and made each guppy breath precious. Constant waves of gritty slush threatened to push her back into the river. Her tree rocked and bobbed violently as it absorbed blows from whatever the flood tide had captured. The muck filling her ears dampened the roar, but what filled her nose did little to quell the stench. Retching repeatedly, the gravelly sand scratched her gullet on the way out as much as it had on the way in. Despite numbing cold, her ribs hurt whether she breathed or not.

She prayed, over and over, that she'd survive the night, that Andy and Nibi hadn't been pulled into the water, that Win and the boys were safe in the cave, that the people in Oak's Landing would find a way to survive, that Amherst would be spared, and that help would come for them all.

After what seemed an eternity, the deluge lessened enough Nettie could lift her head. Blurry green patches dotted her tree. Turning her face into the rain, she flushed filmy grime out of her eyes and looked again. Fairy fire formed a glowing path along the tree's massive trunk.

As the downpour continued to lessen, a razor-thin ridge of brilliant light cut the jagged blackness over the mountains in the distance. She'd survived the night. Changing to big plops, the cataclysmic rain stopped the same way it had started. Slowly, the massive beehive of ebony clouds lifted in rolls, thinned to gray veils, broke apart, and scurried away, leaving nothing in the sapphire sky but a few vivid stars. Dark water filled the valley like coffee in a cup. Oak's Landing lay somewhere beneath. Scattered wisps of fog escaping the river disappeared upward, as if shadowing ghosts. Nettie laid her face on her arm, the heartache too unbelievable for tears. Something hard pushed into her cheek. Nibi's bracelet. Nettie rubbed the braided metal embedded in her swollen wrist, marveling that the floodwaters hadn't stolen it. "You're braver and stronger than you realize," Nibi'd said when she placed it.

Now that the sun was coming up, Nettie could figure out what was causing the arrhythmic tugging in her hair. It had lessened dramatically once she'd gotten out of the water, but it hadn't stopped. Whatever it was, she didn't need to drag it to shore. Forcing aching muscles to move, she looked over her shoulder. Bouncing on a leafy branch sat her dreamcatcher. Its long strands of sinew held tight to the arrowheads tangled in her hair. Though dirty and filled with river chaff, the web appeared intact. Near the middle, partially covered with mud, spun the spider mother.

Just beyond the dreamcatcher, Nettie met the scarlet eyes of an albino moccasin, its torn and bleeding body wrapped tight around the bobbing branch. Head flat against the bark, mouth closed, it didn't challenge her with its eyes. As she was, it seemed grateful for the respite.

Nettie's cold hands were locked in a claw position, her fingernails split by dirt and bark. She managed to loop her fingers around the dreamcatcher's outer ring, then pull it onto the trunk in front of her. It had helped keep her head above water while she'd been in the river and had kept her awake, gripping the tree, throughout the horrific night. One way or the other, they'd finish this together.

On the riverbank, barely visible in the predawn, stood a

semicircle of boulders, some upright, some pushed over by sliding mud and trees. Despite the carnage, she knew this place. She and Win had hiked up here with Nibi the day they'd found the red willows and grapevines to make their dreamcatchers—the same day Nibi had introduced them to the Gospel Oak and fairy fire. The flood had brought the river halfway up the mountain.

The Gospel Oak's wide trunk and rough bark had saved her. Now, most of its spidery roots were dancing in the air or bobbing erratically with the current, the few still buried in the bank pulled taut. She had to get to shore before they surrendered. Aligning herself with the path of fairy fire, she pulled forward on her elbows. Burning pain seared her right leg. She sucked air as her vision filled with sparks. If she fainted, she'd fall in and die. Pressing her shredded fingers harder into the wet bark, Nettie concentrated on breathing until the worst of the pain subsided. When her vision cleared, she looked over her other shoulder. Most of her clothes were gone. Her battered right leg lay at an odd angle.

Startled by a sharp crack, Nettie tightened her grip as the limb that had held her dreamcatcher splintered and surrendered to the flood, taking the apathetic, red-eyed moccasin with it.

Clenching her teeth, she braced and pulled forward again as someone called her name, the sound muffled but loud enough to slip through the din. Nothing moved on the bank or above the blurry incline of boulders. She called out but made no sound. Hocking and spitting river dreck, she tried once more. She could barely hear her own rasp. She strained but didn't hear the voice again.

Pushing the dreamcatcher farther ahead, Nettie pulled herself after it. Inching only a couple of feet, she trembled as if it had been miles. She laid her head on the bark to rest, then jerked it up. Amid the green glow of fairy fire, tangled in the debris along the shoreline, hung the bulging, distorted body of an old woman. Her clothes were gone. Her elbows and knees straddled branches at odd angles, her head was twisted, her tongue protruded, and sandy grit trailed from her open mouth and eyes. Mrs. Loving.

Nettie vomited the remaining river slush at the horror of the sweet woman's death. Lying in the reek and roughness of her own spew, she forced herself to crawl forward again, determined to reach the bank before the flooding river took her tree, to know who called her name. When she reached the base of the old oak, her heart sank. The only way to cross the six-foot span to the bank would be to hang from one of the remaining roots and drop into the angry river. If by some miracle she managed to hold on and make it across, she wasn't sure she'd be able to climb out with only one leg. Another root snapped as she deliberated what to do. She had to go.

"It's you and me, God."

Pushing her dreamcatcher over the edge, Nettie gripped the closest root with both hands and slid her hips off the tree.

"Nettie! Don't!"

Andy's voice cut through the fear and surging pain as Nettie's legs followed her into the water; the ragged current twisted her back and forth, up and down. She tried to keep him in sight as he ran to the river's edge, dug his heels into the muddy bank, and slid to a lower ledge.Wrapping a snapped root around his arm, Andy leaned over the water as Nettie released her grip enough to slide toward him. Catching movement at her side, she flailed helplessly as another uprooted tree careened toward her oak.

"Grab my hand!"

She made a frantic stretch for Andy as the trees collided. The oak lurched wildly, snapping her root and dropping her into the convulsing current. Gritty darkness pressed against her as a tangled web of submerged roots captured her legs, pulling her down and away. Wild with panic and pain, she struggled to get free. Every hair on her head was suddenly pulled taut. Her descent stopped, and she began moving upward. Kicking free of the rough tentacles, she broke the surface, coughing and gasping for air. Angry water slapped at her as she continued to be pulled toward shore. Feeling the rocky riverbank against her shoulders, she raised her arms, grasping for anything to hold on to.

Grabbing her hand, Andy pulled her halfway onto a narrow, muddy ledge. Letting go of her dreamcatcher, he put both hands under her shoulders and pulled her out of the water.

Unable to speak, Nettie coughed debris and gulped air. She could hear Andy talking, his voice muffled. "We have to get off this ledge before it gives way. Hold on." He pulled Nettie to her feet. She cried out as her right leg dragged in the mud. Throbbing and wobbling, it refused to hold any weight.

Scooping her up, Andy pivoted on the narrow ledge enough to lift and push Nettie to the top of the bank. Using a thin root dangling from the dirt, he scrambled up after her. Kneeling, he brushed hair out of her eyes. "Thank God you're alive."

Blinking to clear the blur, she searched for the details of his face, trying to form words but drifting into nothingness.

Terror fueled Nettie's struggle to get free as a heavy whupping sound pounded in her head. Blinded by light, she couldn't breathe. Her arms and her legs wouldn't work.

"Honey, don't. Don't move."

She squinched her eyes against the burning grit and blurriness, then forced them to stay open.

"It's me, Andy. Don't move. You're hurt."

She quivered, trying to say his name but not knowing if she could.

"Don't talk. You're safe now. I've got you."

Nettie swallowed and cleared her scratchy throat enough to whisper, "Win? Boys?"

Andy shook his head. "I haven't seen them since last night."

She found his hand. "Mrs. Loving. In the brush."

"I found her. She's up on the bank now. I covered her with leaves."

The whupping sound, which had almost disappeared, grew louder.

Andy let go of her hand and ran to the middle of the clearing. "They're coming back!"

Even through her clogged ears, the noise was deafening as an olive-green helicopter topped the trees, beating a path toward them. Andy jumped up and down, waving. Slowing, the aircraft hovered at the edge of the clearing, its blades creating a blizzard of tree rain, leaves, and twigs. The aircraft made a quick dip toward them, then banked and sped away.

Andy skidded to his knees beside her, his bare chest and face sprinkled with bits of green and brown debris. His shirt wrapped her like a cocoon.

"They saw us. There's no place to land, but at least they know we're here. They'll send help. We need to get you to a hospital." Andy's voice softened with worry. "It's going to be dark soon."

"Dark?" Just beyond him, layers of orange and yellow trailed the sun into the deepest draw in the mountains.

"You were out cold most of the day. You didn't even stir when I moved you up here. I know it had to hurt."

The desire for pain-free sleep pulled at her, but she wanted to stay with Andy more.

"I doubt rescuers will get here before morning. But the river's not rising anymore and the mudslides have stopped. We'll be okay until then. Are you warm enough?"

Nettie nodded. "Thirsty."

"The river's a cesspool. Maybe I can find a clean puddle."

She raised her hand enough to point toward the boulders. "There's a spring."

"What?"

She cleared her throat again. "By the rocks. There's a spring."

"How do you know?"

"Nibi."

As Andy rustled among the storm debris near the boulders, Nettie concentrated on breathing more deeply and keeping her right leg still to lessen the pain.

"Found it! Bless that woman."

Dropping beside her, he dribbled the few drops remaining in his cupped hands onto Nettie's parched lips. "This isn't going to work. I need to get you over to the spring." He positioned himself to look into her eyes. "You're all banged up, and your right leg is broken. I splinted it, but I'm afraid to lift it. I'll have to drag you. It's going to hurt."

Nettie nodded. Her pain paled in comparison with the terror Andy had rescued her from.

He stripped a small stick. "If it gets too bad, bite on this." Squatting, he slid his hands under her arms and pulled.

Their backward momentum stopped abruptly as the bottom points on the makeshift splint dug into the ground. Nettie moaned and bit the stick harder.

"Jeez, I'm sorry."

She nodded as he brushed perspiration from her forehead. Seeing nearby trees, Nettie remembered how Nibi got big game back to her house. "Evergreens. Litter."

Andy jumped up. "I'll be right back." Minutes later, he reappeared with thick green branches that smelled of Christmas. "Think you could stand it if I moved you onto these?"

She nodded.

Rolling her gently from side to side, Andy positioned the soft branches under her, using smaller pieces as a makeshift pillow. He dragged the litter next to the bubbling spring. Taking the stick from Nettie's mouth, he wiped bits of bark from her lips. "Okay?"

"Okay."

Cupping his hands, he couriered water for Nettie to rinse the grit and foul taste out of her mouth. After she drank her fill, he drank his.

Nettie's throat still felt scratchy, but she could speak more easily. "Would you rinse my eyes, please?"

Dribbling fresh water over and under her lids until it ran clear, Andy carefully washed her face and flushed the debris from her ears. "Better?"

"Much."

Using the sleeves of his shirt, he dried her off. "I thought I'd lost you. When you went in the water back at Nibi's, I nearly went out of my mind."

"I'm sorry you had to go through that." She took his hand. "How did you find me?"

"Grace of God. I tried to follow you downriver, but it started raining even harder than it had up on the mountain. I couldn't see. I could hardly move. I couldn't even breathe without holding my hands over my nose. I managed to crawl under an evergreen, which broke the downpour enough that I could find a little bit of air."

"Trees saved us both."

"I could hear the landslides—big ones, roaring down the mountains, shaking everything. One after the other, they just kept coming. It was a miracle one didn't take out the tree I was under. I've never been so afraid. For both of us."

"You could have died."

"I couldn't die. I had to find you. I prayed for that all night long. Just before dawn, the rain let up enough that I could get out from under the tree. There was nothing but bedrock and mud on both sides. I worked my way downstream, calling, searching. I'd just reached the edge of this clearing when I spotted the fairy fire and you. I started running and yelling when I realized you were getting ready to go into the water. I would have lost you all over again if it hadn't been for your dreamcatcher and the hold it had on you." He cupped more water and combed it through her hair with his fingers.

"How did you manage to get it untangled? From the arrow-heads, I mean?"

"After you warmed up, there wasn't anything to do but wait, so I started unraveling them. The white one was the worst. It was wrapped in a ball the size of my fist. I was afraid it might have to be cut out, but I kept working at it. By midafternoon, it was free."

"Where is it? My dreamcatcher."

Andy retrieved the webbed ring, washed off the remaining river debris, and laid it next to Nettie. "It followed you all the way into the river. It must have gotten caught when you fell the first time. Damnedest thing."

"It helped keep my head above water until the tree caught me."

"Then it saved you twice."

"It wouldn't have without you." Nettie ran her hand over the web. "Making it was supposed to be a summer project. Nibi knew it was meant to do more. A lot more."

"She knew about the storm?"

"Not at first. She knew a blood moon was coming and that something big was going to happen. She also knew Win and I were involved and that the dreamcatchers were going to play a role, but until last night she didn't know exactly what it was or how bad it was going to be. I pray she's someplace safe."

"Me too." Andy lay on his side, leaning on his elbow. "She was worried about you."

"Me? Why? Wait, how do you know that?"

"Win."

"You talked with Win?"

"A couple of weeks ago. She was worried about you too."

"Let me guess—Danes."

"She didn't trust him."

Nettie tried to move to get more comfortable. "I should have listened to her. I just wanted those damn sessions to be over with so I could get baptized and move on."

Andy sat up and helped her reposition. "I went to see him."

"Danes?"

"Last week. Win told me he'd been pressuring you to talk about us. I told him you didn't have anything to prove about being a Christian and that our relationship was none of his concern."

"What did he say?"

"He danced around it. Said it was all a misunderstanding and that he'd straighten everything out when you all met this week. I was going to talk with Pastor Williams too, but Mrs. Mac beat me to it. Apparently, she was concerned as well. Later, she told me Pastor Williams had agreed that last night would be your final session, and that Mr. Danes would be leaving the church at the end of the month. Apparently, he has a drinking problem."

Nettie stared at the night sky, trying to put the puzzle pieces together. "They fired him? Before he tried to hurt me?"

"From what I understand."

"That's why he had a suitcase and other stuff in his car last night. He wasn't going to wait and leave at the end of the month—he was going to leave after he . . ."

Andy moved closer, putting his arm over her. "He can't hurt you now."

"I don't understand how he could do what he did. Turn into that horrible person."

"I don't either. People live with all kinds of demons. Some you can see; most you can't."

"He was spying on us back in the spring, when we were at River's Rest."

Andy sat up. "What?"

"He was there. Hiding in bushes. Watching."

Andy tensed. "That sick bastard. He had to have followed us there. The night we broke up, I knew something wasn't right. I could feel it. But I blamed it on what was happening between us."

"I wonder if he hurt any of the other girls."

"My guess is, the police are going to ask him the same question."

"If they catch him."

He took her hand. "Don't worry, they will. He can't get but so far."

"Our parents must be worried sick."

"We'll be able to call them soon."

"And Pastor Williams is probably beside himself."

"I would imagine. He won't think twice about baptizing you now."

"I was baptized last night." Nettie looked at the stars. "I believed when I went into the water, and I believe now. The rest is icing."

"A lot of believers died last night."

"They weren't alone. Neither was I."

"What makes you say that?"

"Something Danes said about bad things happening to good people. That physical safety here is not the same as spiritual safety for eternity."

Andy glanced at the mound of leaves covering Mrs. Loving. "I hope you're right. I don't understand it, but maybe we're not meant to."

"Danes said that too."

"Great. So he knows his Bible but got confused about the sinning part?"

"I don't think he was confused at all. I think he's tormented and weak."

A lustrous, cream-colored supermoon rose above the mountains, just as it had for billions of years, oblivious to the death and destruction that lay beneath. As the hours passed, Nettie's pain worsened, ground-in dirt and sand stabbed her skin like needles, her ribs hurt, and her right leg throbbed.

Andy fidgeted, not knowing how to help.

"Talk to me. Maybe it will take my mind off it."

"Maybe this will help too." Beginning with her feet, he drizzled spring water all over her, rinsing grit and bits of debris from her battered body. Rolling her onto her side, he washed her back, massaging unbroken skin as he went. As the water dripped into the boughs of the evergreens beneath her, it carried away some of the discomfort.

Nettie hadn't thought about the fact that she was naked under his shirt until now but couldn't bring herself to blush. It simply didn't matter.

"When I got you out of the water, you were ice cold. I couldn't even start a fire—everything was soaked—so I wrapped you in my shirt and covered you with leaves until you warmed up and got some color back."

"I hurt in places I didn't know I had. Good thing I don't have a mirror."

"It's a good thing your legs took the brunt of it."

"Give me a cast and some aspirin, and I'll be good to go. Just in time for school to start."

"Hard to believe we're seniors."

"I never thought I'd look forward to going back, but I am, even if it is on crutches."

"Speaking of school, I have something to tell you."

"What?"

Andy sat cross-legged, propping his elbows on his knees. "Remember the surprise I wanted to tell you about that day at the lake?"

Nettie nodded.

"These last few weeks, when you couldn't find me, I was at VMI."

"Virginia Military Institute? Why?"

"They have a summer boot camp for those applying for early admission."

"But you wanted to go to West Point."

"No. My dad wanted me to go to West Point, like he did."

"You're not changing your plans because of me, are you?"

"No. I changed them for me. I've had a lot of time to think this summer. I don't want a long military career. Dad was gone for so much of my life. I want to serve my country for a few years, then settle down and build a life. With you."

Above the sound of the engorged river, the night offered nothing familiar. All of Nature's living noisemakers seemed to have vanished. In the silence, Nettie acknowledged the reason for her indecision about Andy. "Forever is a long time when we're barely thinking past tomorrow."

"What?"

"It's what I told you at River's Rest the night we broke up. You were going away to West Point, starting a whole new life—one I couldn't be part of. I thought it would be easier to let you go if I didn't love you."

Andy pushed a stray hair from Nettie's forehead. "I'm so sorry about that night. I should never have pushed you to say something you weren't ready to say. It was unfair. I thought I had my life all figured out, except for one missing piece: you. I knew right away I'd made a mistake, but I was too stubborn to admit it."

"Is that why you asked Anne out?" Nettie teased.

"I didn't ask her. She asked me."

"Figures."

"Going out with someone, anyone, seemed like a good idea at the time. I was hurting. I thought it might make you jealous enough to come back to me. It didn't take long to realize I'd made another big mistake."

"Was she responsible for you two being named May Day king and queen?"

Andy rolled his eyes. "Her grandfather was. He's on the May Day committee and gives them a lot of money. They were glad to give him what she wanted."

"That night at the Tastee Freez, were you all breaking up?"

"We weren't going together, despite what she kept telling people." Andy picked up a twig and spun it. "That night, I apologized if I'd misled her, and I told her the relationship was never going to go where she wanted it to."

"I'm sure she didn't take that well."

"Not at all. When you and Ethan pulled in, she was quick to point out that you'd moved on and that I needed to do the same."

"I hadn't moved on. Ethan just happened to come to town at the right time. We were both going through a lot. He's a nice guy."

"Yes, he is. He's responsible for getting me to Nibi's last night. He was worried about you and Win." Andy stopped spinning the twig. "He said you were in love with me."

"I've known it for a while."

"I've known it for a while too."

"We're so young. What we feel now may not be what we feel a year from now, or five, or ten. Maybe more."

Andy flicked the twig away and kissed her. "Isn't that the way it's supposed to be? Relationships are supposed to evolve. Look how far we've come since the sandbox days. I'm betting the way we feel will change. It will grow stronger. We just need to take it one day at a time."

"I hadn't thought about it like that, but you're right." Nettie carefully pushed herself up onto her elbows. Despite the pain in her leg and ribs, it felt good to stretch. "So many things are still up in the air right now. I still don't know what I want to do, if I want to go to college or where."

"One day at a time, remember. What you decide to do and when and where you do it is up to you. I'll support whatever decisions you make."

The churning hum of an outboard motor interrupted the moment.

Andy jumped to his feet and searched the river. "Lights!" Running to the bank, he yelled and waved until the concentrated beams turned their way.

Flashlights bobbed as the long johnboat motored close to shore. Stopping the engine, two National Guardsmen used paddles to pull the boat into the muck close to the bank. Win sat on the middle seat. Dropping over the sides, the guardsmen pulled the boat far enough into the mud to anchor it. One carried Win to the bank, while the other unloaded supplies.

Win hugged Andy. "Where is she?"

"Over by the spring."

Dodging debris, Win hurried over, dropped to her knees, and gently laid her cheek against Nettie's. No words were necessary.

Nettie lay back down. "Are the boys okay?"

"Yes. They're in Lovingston. Officials have set up an emergency flood command center outside of town."

"Nibi?"

Loss transformed Win's face. "They haven't found her."

The flood had taken so much. Now Nibi. "She could still be alive somewhere. Look at us."

Win sat back on her heels. "She's not."

"How do you know?"

"Just before dawn, she came to me in a vision. She was standing with my grandfather and others." Win brushed away tears. "She was smiling. She hand-signaled me to be strong and live a long and fruitful life. She put her hands over her heart and the vision faded away."

"I'm so sorry."

"I think she knew she was going to die with the blood moon but never said a word. That's why she gave all of her things away. Why she gave us her jewelry."

"I think so too."

"She wasn't concerned about herself, just us and the boys."

"How did you all make it out?"

"When Andy went after you, it was raining so hard I wasn't sure I could get them up the mountain, much less find the cave, but we did. When it quit raining and the sun came up, there was no going back down. The floodwaters were halfway up the mountain. Mudslides were everywhere. Nibi's house, barn, everything was gone."

Nettie tightened her hand around Win's.

"That's when we realized Oak's Landing was gone too. The boys took it hard but knew we had to keep moving. We waded through the mud to the top of the mountain and ran the ridge. We came out of the woods just above Walton's Pass. Sheriff Tanner was there, checking road blocks where Route 56 used to be. He gave us a ride to the flood command center. There's enough asphalt left on Route 29 that the National Guard is using it as a staging area for helicopters bringing in rescue personnel and supplies."

"Have they found other survivors?"

"They hadn't when we left, except for the boys. They're still trying to get to the small towns upriver. Roads and bridges are washed out. Nobody can get in or leave, except by air or boat."

"What about home? Amherst? Our families?"

"Sheriff Tanner said parts of Amherst County had some flooding, but nothing like this. He was going to try to get in touch with our families while I came with the guardsmen to get you and Andy."

Nettie winced as the muscles in her broken leg spasmed.

"Jeez, I almost forgot." Win took Nibi's bag off her shoulder and pulled out two miniature bottles. Uncapping one, she put the rim to Nettie's lips. The contents smelled of oak and tasted medicinal. "This will keep all your cuts and scrapes from getting infected." Putting the first bottle away, she uncapped a cobalt-blue one. "This one is for pain."

The scent filled Nettie's head with a deliciousness that crested and flowed away like an ocean swell. "Angel Water." The thick, sweet-tasting liquid soothed her mouth and throat. "I thought it was supposed to ease heartache."

"The smell does that. The liquid eases physical pain."

"I hope one works as well as the other."

"It will. Give it a few minutes."

"How did you know? Where Andy and I were, I mean?"

"A vision. I saw you, clear as day, by the spring in the shade of the Gospel Oak."

"I should have guessed. You're getting good."

"I told them you and Andy were alive and exactly where you were. They didn't believe me—that is, until Sheriff Tanner told them to get off their asses and get a bird in the air. I flew with them to show the way. Once we confirmed you two were here, they sent the boat."

"It's a wonder they let you onboard, as dangerous as the river is."

"They didn't want to. Sheriff Tanner insisted. He told them I knew my way around these mountains better than anyone, even in the dark."

Andy and the guardsmen unfolded a stretcher next to Nettie. Replacing the makeshift splint with one made of metal and Velcro, the four of them moved her from a soft green bed to a sheet-covered canvas one and tucked a blanket around her. The Angel Water had already begun to blunt the pain as the guardsmen cinched the buckles holding her on the stretcher. She searched for Andy. "My dreamcatcher."

"Don't worry. I have it."

"Win, it saved my life. Nibi knew it would. Where's yours?"

Win hesitated, her voice low. "At the emergency center. The sheriff said he'd keep it for me until I was ready to get it back."

Nettie understood. Losing Nibi meant a major life change for Win. Her dreamcatcher was now that of a Monacan medicine woman.

Lifting the stretcher, the guardsmen carefully made their way toward the riverbank. Nettie raised her hand. "Please, stop. Andy, Mrs. Loving."

"They know about her, honey. They'll come back to get her and the others in the morning."

Others? Nettie didn't ask.

Navigating the muck, the guardsmen straddled Nettie's stretcher between two seats and tied it down. Andy climbed in, settling next to her. After helping Win onboard, the guardsmen paddled the boat into the slurried current, then started the motor.

As they skimmed downriver, the cool breeze, brilliant starry sky, and now lakelike floodwaters seemed surreal compared with the savagery of a few hours ago. Nothing hinted at the horror and devastation beneath them, of the spirits having flown. In the distance, moonbeams shone off the stations of the tilted cross standing atop the water, the only remnant of a world that was.

Nettie closed her eyes to walk in the shade of the grand oaks, roam the familiar streets, trek the path to Nibi's, and say goodbye.

Chapter 18

The johnboat pulled up to the emergency landing on the outskirts of Lovingston. Men with odd black hats and long beards without mustaches worked with the guardsmen to secure the boat and help everyone out. Unhooking the stretcher, they carried Nettie to a first-aid station housed in a large military tent, then gently moved her to a soft cot and gave her a pillow—seemingly little things that lessened her pain on contact. Andy and Win settled on folding chairs beside her.

"Mennonites?" Nettie asked.

Win nodded. "Volunteers from all over Virginia and up and down the East Coast started arriving this morning in droves, especially the Mennonites. They're doing anything and everything to help up and down the valley."

Volunteers and medical people were scattered about. Rows of empty stretchers filled the tent.

"They must have sent a lot of folks to the hospital already."

"I don't think so."

It took a moment for Nettie to realize what Win meant. The helicopters were ferrying bodies.

"Any news on survivors?"

"Nothing. I checked both lists when we got here."

Lists? Survivors. And those who weren't.

Andy accepted a sandwich from a woman in a white bonnet and a long, aproned dress. He offered Nettie the first bite. Before she could take it, a petite blonde in green military khakis with rolled-up sleeves and a stamped name badge that said LINDA HOWE, RN, took the sandwich and handed it back to Andy. "Sorry, young lady. You can't eat yet."

Nettie's mouth had started watering the moment she'd seen the sandwich. She hadn't eaten in two days. "Why not?"

Linda set a small tray with three syringes on the corner of the cot. "From the looks of your right leg, you're going to the operating room as soon as we get you to Lynchburg General. Your stomach needs to be empty."

Linda's blue eyes were kind but not kidding.

"The operating room? Why?" Having had her tonsils out, Nettie knew enough about hospitals and surgery to know she wasn't crazy about doing it again.

Linda tore open an alcohol wipe, then cleaned Nettie's upper arm in a widening circle. "Dirty water, lots of cuts and punctures, and at least one broken, dislocated bone. They'll put you to sleep, reduce the dislocation, and set the fracture. When you wake up, that leg will feel a lot better and you'll be able to eat." Opening a second alcohol wipe, she cleaned the same spot again, then pulled the red rubber cap off one of the syringes. "This is a tetanus booster. It might sting."

Linda quickly and precisely injected the vaccine without drawing a drop of blood.

"It didn't hurt."

"Good." Linda turned to Win and Andy. "Who wants to be next?"

Neither volunteered, but that didn't save them.

Nettie giggled. "Jeez, you two. It's just a needle."

Once their immunizations were done, Linda covered Nettie with a clean sheet and removed Andy's shirt. Gathering a squeeze bottle of antiseptic, a tall stack of gauze pads, and white tape, she cleaned and dressed Nettie's broken skin without significantly increasing the pain and without exposing anything that didn't need to be seen.

Nettie paid close attention to everything Linda did and how she did it. "You're pretty slick with this stuff."

Linda winked. "When you work in a tent filled with people and no walls, you have to be slick."

Putting Nettie in a hospital gown and covering her with a clean sheet, Linda turned to Andy. "You have some cuts that need attention too, young man. You're going to have to let go of her hand long enough for me to get to them."

Within minutes, Linda had everyone cleaned up, patched, and ready to evacuate. "We're going to fly the three of you to Lynchburg as soon as one of the choppers gets back. Your parents have been notified that you're safe. They're going to meet you at the emergency room."

Linda picked up the remnants of her work and disappeared as Sheriff Tanner ducked into the tent. Weariness dragged at his shoulders; sadness circled his eyes. Removing his hat, he nodded to Nettie and Andy. "Mighty glad to see you two."

"Yes, sir. We're relieved to be here."

Andy stood and shook his hand. "Thank you for sending them for us, sir."

"Don't thank me, son—thank Win. Without her, we wouldn't have known where to begin to look, or even that you all were alive."

One of the volunteers set a folding chair beside the Sheriff. He lowered himself slowly, as if unsure his knees would bend. Accepting a steaming cup of black coffee, he slumped back and took a sip.

"Sir," Win asked, "have you had any rest since this started?"

He shook his head. "Rescue effort is just getting under way." He sighed. "I survived the 1936 flood, served in Korea for three years, and have been the law in these parts for more than forty years. I've seen a lot of horrible things, but nothing like this. Ever. I doubt anyone has. Forty plus inches of rain fell in less than eight hours. The whole valley drowned. Folks washed away in their beds."

A deputy entered the tent to hand the sheriff a piece of paper. Tipping his hat to the rest of them, he left as quietly as he'd come.

The sheriff studied the page, then pressed his eyes, as if trying to process the words.

"More survivors?" Nettie needed to know.

He shook his head.

"Please."

Andy squeezed her hand.

"A hundred dead so far, most from Nelson County. Entire families. Bodies are being found from the Tye to the James, some as far away as Richmond. They've lined prisoners from the state penitentiary along the bridges to help spot bodies. The Coast Guard has set up spotters in the mouth of the Chesapeake Bay." He laid the paper in his lap. "We may never find some of these folks."

Sheriff Tanner stared through the page until a volunteer approached. "Sir, would you like more coffee or something to eat?"

He shook his head and thanked the diminutive woman. When she'd moved away, he continued. "So far, the Warren boys are the only survivors from Oak's Landing. And the only reason they survived is because they were on Nibi's mountain with you all."

Win blinked back tears. "They survived because of Nibi. We all survived because of her. She connected dots we didn't even know were there."

Sheriff Tanner handed her a crumpled handkerchief. "Nibi would be very proud of what you did, and even more for what you're going to do, what all of you are going to do."

"Sir?"

"You all are going to recover from this nightmare and live the lives Nibi would want you to live. My friend deserves no less. Neither do you."

The pulsing sound of approaching helicopters grew louder as Sheriff Tanner donned his hat. "You all stay in touch."

As the sheriff exited, Linda appeared in the entrance with Wade and Skip Warren, cleaned up, pale, eyes red-rimmed, hesitant, and holding hands. "These two wouldn't leave until you all got here safely. They want to say goodbye.

Wade spoke as Skip stared. "Miz Win, thank you for getting us here. You, Nettie, Andy, all of you saved us." Wade nodded at each person as he said their name. "And Miz Nibi."

Win gave both boys a hug, then offered them seats. Andy motioned for Skip to sit in his chair. Squatting next to the little boy, Andy put his arm around him and talked in whispers. Wade moved a chair close to Nettie.

"Are you okay? They said your leg is broken."

"It is, but it will be fixed soon."

"You look pretty beat up."

"Nothing a little mercurochrome and Epsom salt won't take care of. Are you all right?"

"Our house is gone. It washed away. Mom and Pop were inside."

"I'm so sorry."

"Our neighbors, our friends, Miz Nibi—they're all gone."

Tears brimmed as Nettie's heart broke for him. "A lot of good people died last night."

Wade stifled a sob, rubbing his sleeve across his eyes.

"It's okay to cry."

"Folks keep telling Skip and me not to, that everything will be okay. Nothing's okay. It will never be okay again." Wade's eyes were swimming in loss.

Nettie pretended to clear her throat to cover the catch in her voice. "Nibi once told me that tears are what moves sadness from the inside to the outside, where the light can reach it. We have lot of sadness to move outside, don't we?"

Wade managed a nod.

The sides of the tent ballooned in and out as a helicopter landed.

"Where are they taking you two?"

"To the high school in Amherst. They turned the football field into a landing zone. Our aunt and uncle are coming from Charlottesville to pick us up."

"I'm glad you and Skip have someone. I think your mom and dad would be glad too."

Wade's voice cracked. "My heart hurts so bad. I don't know what to do."

Nettie wove her fingers through his. "Yes, you do. You go slow. You take one step at a time, just like when we were dancing. Remember? One, two, three. One, two, three. One, two three. One step at a time. That's all you have to remember."

Wade glanced at his little brother. "I guess we can do that."

Linda reappeared at the door. "Boys, it's time to go."

Nettie held on to Wade's hand as he stood. "Do you remember what else I told you that night?"

It took a moment, but a hint of pink returned to Wade's cheeks. "That we have a date for lunch on my birthday."

"That's right. July fifteenth. Twelve noon. Howell's lunch counter in Amherst. Don't stand me up."

Once Nettie, Win, and Andy were secured in the helicopter, Linda buckled herself in and gave the pilot a thumbs-up. As the aircraft lifted, Nettie pushed to her elbow to look out the window. The surreal world below lay in shades of marl and rust. Half-buried houses and upside-down barns torn from their foundations littered the mountains or bobbed in topsy-turvy pieces in the receding, muck-filled river. Mounds of splintered tree trunks and jagged boulders the size of railcars clogged the foothills. Embedded along the edges were mangled trucks, farm equipment, furniture, clothing, and unrecognizable things. The guardsmen used binoculars to watch for bodies, radioing to someone on the ground where they were. On a hill in the distance, the tilted cross, as well as part of the roof of the Baptist church, rose out of the water.

"Win, the church—it's still standing. Maybe they can save it."

Win leaned over to look out the window. "Nibi said for us to go there when this was all over." Her voiced trailed to a whisper.

The helicopter rose over naked mountaintops raked with deep, ugly gashes as far as Nettie could see. Avalanches of ancient earth had stripped everything all the way to the river. The destruction of the mountains, all living things, equaled that in the valley.

Neither Nettie nor Win spoke as the chopper crested the peaks and descended toward Amherst. The view from the window changed from unspeakable tragedy to the vibrant colors of summer. One mountain, two worlds. A few toppled trees and swollen creeks were the only evidence there'd even been a storm.

Cars moved along the roads surrounding Amherst. Folks walked the sidewalks, and the *Weak and Weary* sat idle at the station.

"Look, Mr. Roberts managed to get the train back on this side of the mountain before all hell broke loose." Nettie thought of all the people scurrying to and from the train just before the storm. He had saved half of them.

As they passed over the Amherst County High School football field, another helicopter sat in the middle of a red cross painted on the grass, its rotors turning in slow motion. Somewhere down there, Wade and Skip were starting a new life, an unwanted one. Weariness closed Nettie's eyes. Whatever lay ahead for her paled in comparison with what awaited those little boys. She prayed.

Nights were the worst. Once visiting hours ended, Nettie's back had been rubbed, her sheets had been straightened, and fresh ice packs had been placed around the traction on her right leg, the hospital went quiet and dark, except for the dull glow of an EXIT sign somewhere down the long hall. In the emptiness, nothing held back the memories. Murderous water contorted her arms, legs, and back. Her lungs screamed for air. Searing pain fought with horrifying panic as Mrs. Loving's face circled her like a moon, and Danes hovered in the shadows. Drenched in sweat, heart pounding, she fought sleep, knowing they'd follow her.

"Nettie, are you awake?"

Silhouetted in the doorway stood Pastor Williams, hat in hand, brown suit baggy on his thin, aging frame.

"Yes, sir."

"I know it's late. Do you mind if I come in?"

"No, sir."

Pastor Williams flipped on the small, frosted light behind the bed and laid his hat on the bedside table. "Miss Howe seemed to think this would be a good time to come. I've wanted to talk with you since you were admitted, but every time I stopped by, you had a room full of visitors."

"Yes, sir. Folks just want to know I'm okay."

"Of course." He pulled a straight-backed chair close to the bed and sat, propping one leg on the other. "*Are* you okay?"

Nettie studied his wrinkled, sun-spotted face. He wasn't asking about her broken leg and bruises. "Most of the time. Days are easier to get through."

"I would imagine. From what I understand, you went through hours of hell during that flood."

"Yes, sir." At least he wasn't skirting around what had happened. Most visitors hesitated to bring it up and got uncomfortable if she tried to. They'd use empty words of encouragement and make a quick departure. Andy and Win understood, but they had to leave when visiting hours were over.

"Miss Howe told me you're having some bad dreams."

"It's not like they're a secret. I wake up this end of the hall every night."

"That has to be hard on you."

"And them." Nettie pointed to her leg. "Linda, Miss Howe, says as soon as the swelling is down, they're going to cast my leg and I can go home. I'll sleep better then."

"Sleep takes us to a vulnerable place, doesn't it?"

Nettie glanced at her dreamcatcher leaning in the corner. Since the flood, it hadn't done its job. Maybe the legend was just that, or maybe the blood moon had taken everything it had to offer. Win had cleaned it, replaced missing feathers, and wiped the wood with walnut oil. Except for some gouges and scrapes in the ring, it showed little evidence of their treacherous journey.

"That is quite a piece of art. May I?" Pastor Williams held the ring up to the light to study the sinew webbing and amethyst. "I've heard of these but have never had an opportunity to examine one up close. Tell me about it."

Given their history, offering the good pastor a lesson of any kind made Nettie nervous.

"It's okay. We're never too old to learn about something new, or, in this case, about something old."

"I just need to remember how Nibi explained it."

"Nibi? That name sounds familiar."

"She's Win's grandmother—or was. She's gone. The flood." Nettie couldn't bring herself to use the word "died"; its edges were too sharp and the loss too fresh. "She was the Monacans' medicine woman."

"Did you know her well?"

"Yes, sir. Very well."

"I've heard tell of her. The pastor of the Oak's Landing Baptist Church was a friend of mine. He said she seldom missed a Sunday and that she'd sprinkle tobacco or sage on a large stone that sat at the bottom of their hill every time she came."

"That's her. Nibi's father built that church. The tobacco was to honor him."

"Traditions are important. Was the dreamcatcher a tradition of hers as well?"

"Yes, sir. Win and I made ones just like hers."

"Was it difficult?"

"Very." Step by step, Nettie explained the meaning of the different parts of the dreamcatcher and what she and Win had to do to collect them. "Nibi showed us how to put all the pieces together."

Pastor Williams propped the dreamcatcher on his bent knee. "Sounds as if you two had quite the summer adventure."

"Yes, sir. We learned a lot."

"I understand you had this with you the night of the flood. That it helped save your life."

Pastor Williams waited and watched as Nettie struggled to control a surge of emotions. "So many people died. Good people."

"Tragically, yes." He handed Nettie a tissue and softened his voice to match hers. "People do not live or die in natural disasters because they lived good or bad lives. You know grace can't be earned."

"Yes, sir. I know." The flashing red lights of a silent ambulance passed under her window. "But why me? Why did I survive and they didn't?"

"Survivors have asked that question for thousands of years, and we still don't have an answer. Grace as we know it defies our ability to reason. However, that doesn't make it any less real."

"The guilt is real too."

"Did you cause the flood?"

Nettie's eyes widened. "No."

"Did you fail to save people you could have saved?"

"I don't think so."

"Did you save yourself at the expense of someone else?"

"No."

"Guilt has no place in an innocent heart, Nettie. It's a burden you need not carry."

Footsteps and muffled voices grew louder, then faded, as the nurses completed their rounds. Linda gave Nettie a little wave when she passed.

"I'm glad she's here for you."

"Me too."

"When there is so much sadness to deal with, it's important to have people around whom you can count on." Pastor Williams sounded as if he were talking to himself more than to her; the lines in his face deepened. "I owe you an apology, Nettie. My heart isn't innocent when it comes to the situation with you and Mr. Danes. I'm guilty of holding so tight to the mindset that you were not ready for baptism and that he could accomplish what I hadn't. I failed to see the truth about both of you, even when it was right in front of me. I put you in harm's way, and for that I'm truly sorry. Forgive me?"

"Done." Nettie smoothed the bedspread covering her lap over and over. "Truth is, I learned a lot from Mr. Danes before everything went bad."

"It's not unusual for good and bad to live in the same person."

"Chief Brannon said that bad can't exist without good any more than good can exist without bad."

"Chief Brannon? Is that the Dr. Brannon who runs the clinic on Bear Mountain?"

"Yes, sir."

"I didn't realize he was also chief of the Monacans. He sounds wise." Pastor Williams spun the amethyst. Even in the dim light, it sparkled. "Light is interesting, don't you think?"

"What do you mean?"

"Just as good cannot exist without bad, light cannot exist without darkness."

Nettie leaned forward to touch the white and black feathers covering the dreamcatcher's portal. "That's what these are supposed to symbolize, like opposite sides of the same face. Nibi said they're meant to remind us that we have a choice."

"Another wise person. Life certainly gives us plenty of opportunities to make all the wrong choices, doesn't it?"

Nettie untied one of the owl feathers and handed it to him. "Just in case you ever need some help."

"Thank you." Pastor Williams twirled the feather by its quill. "I regret not having met Nibi, but I'll make a point of seeking out Chief Brannon."

"What's going to happen to Mr. Danes?"

"He's going to be in jail for quite a while, perhaps for the rest of his life, not only for what he tried to do to you, but police discovered that he'd been involved in similar situations in and around New Orleans. When the courts finish with him here, he'll be extradited there to face charges."

"Did you go see him?"

"I did. And I'll go again."

"Good. He needs your kind of help."

"And he needs yours."

Nettie studied her wiggling toes through the pulley lines and traction bars. "Are you saying I need to do more than forgive him?"

"He'd like to talk with you."

"I know what he wants."

"I'd like to think remorse, an apology, and forgiveness have something to do with it, but I don't know for sure. However, my primary concern is you."

"Me?"

"Yes. Things left unspoken can haunt us for a lifetime."

The idea of meeting Danes face-to-face wasn't intimidating, but getting answers to the what-if questions that haunted her nights were. "I need to think about it."

"Good. Talk it over with your parents. It won't be easy for them either, regardless of what you decide. If you all would like to talk with me about it, just say so." He glanced at his watch. "My goodness. It's after midnight." Standing, he steadied himself against the bedside table. "Best you try to get a little sleep."

Nettie had never viewed him as frail before. "Pastor?"

"Yes?"

"You know most of the pranks around the church over the past few years were my idea?"

"I do."

"Forgive me?"

"Done." He held out his hand. "Pray with me?"

Nettie took his hand and bowed her head as familiar words took on new meaning.

"Father God, you see the heavy laden among us and call them

to you. You assume the burden of the willing and offer rest for their bodies and souls. Grant us the wisdom to hear Your call and accept Your gifts, for You are the strength by which a shattered world moves from darkness into light. Amen."

"Amen."

Pastor Williams retrieved his hat, then kissed Nettie's forehead. "Sleep well, child."

As his shadow disappeared down the hall, moonlight hit the amethyst, painting the whitewashed walls violet. Maybe the dreamcatcher had done what Nibi intended it to do all along. Nettie drifted off to sleep as Linda pulled the door closed.

Nettie slid the eraser side of a pencil under the edge of her cast, angling it to reach the spot that wouldn't stop itching.

"How many times do I have to tell you not to do that?" Linda leaned against the door, one hand on her hip, a paper bag in the other.

"It itches."

"Then do what I told you to do: scratch your other leg in the same spot."

"This feels better."

"You've done too well to risk getting an infection under that cast." Linda pocketed the pencil and took Nettie's small suitcase from the wardrobe. "Are you excited about going home?"

"I can't wait. Mom and Dad are letting Andy and Win pick me up."

"I can understand why. They've been here every day. Have you been practicing walking with the crutches?"

"Yes. They're a pain in the ass."

"Quit complaining. You're up and mobile." Linda laid Nettie's dreamcatcher on the table. "Don't forget this."

"Not a chance." Nettie fingered the white arrowhead. "What's the count now?" She dreaded the answer but asked the question every day. Linda didn't hide anything from her like some of the others did. "Healing starts with the truth," she'd said.

Linda kept packing Nettie's things. "Over one hundred seventy so far, most from Nelson County, others from all over central Virginia. Most bodies have been identified, but some not. The coroner thinks some of the unknowns were just traveling through or were migrant workers coming in to harvest apples. Thirty-some are still missing. Officials think they were either buried in the mud or washed downriver. They've found bodies as far away as the Chesapeake Bay."

For a moment, Nettie felt the choking panic of catapulting through the raging water. She nodded at the memory, then packed it away. It served no purpose to give that nightmare more of her life than it had already taken. "Have they settled on exactly how much rain fell?"

"The number changes almost daily, depending on which expert is weighing in. Most sources are saying the hardest-hit areas of Nelson County got over forty inches in six hours. The Weather Bureau said it was the highest amount of rainfall considered theoretically possible. Areas west of there, like Glasgow, Buena Vista, and Waynesboro, got up to twenty or so. All told, it was almost a billion tons of water, remnants of Hurricane Camille no one saw coming."

"Camille? Wasn't that the hurricane that hit the Gulf coast?"

"Uh-huh. Apparently, the massive clouds held together all the way up to Virginia, then let loose. Observers said the clouds were so black, they looked green."

"The storm came out of the Gulf of Mexico."

Linda stopped packing. "That's right."

Nettie continued, as if talking to herself. "The water in the gulf isn't blue; it's green. That's why they call it the Emerald Coast." She'd grown up spending summer vacations in the southern Wiregrass and swimming in those beautiful waters.

Linda waited and watched.

Nibi had known the darkness had an emerald aura but hadn't realized the danger was coming from a thousand miles away, nor that it would appear in the form of an inland hurricane. No wonder she hadn't been able to identify it.

"Are you okay?" Linda asked.

Coming back to the here and now, Nettie nodded. "Just putting the last pieces of a puzzle together."

Linda closed Nettie's suitcase and set it by the door. Retrieving the brown bag, she handed it to Nettie. "I have a little going-home present for you."

Nettie pulled out a book with worn edges; a picture of a young nurse covered the front. *"Cherry Ames."*

"A few days ago, you asked me why I decided to become a nurse. When I was growing up, this was one of my favorite books."

"This helped you decide?"

"It raised the possibility. What made me decide were the nurses and doctors in the MASH unit that saved my brother's life in Vietnam."

"What's a MASH unit?"

"Mobile army surgical hospital. The nurses and doctors work close to the fighting so they can treat the wounded faster. I've worked with the National Guard for the past year but move to regular Army next month. I ship out on the first."

"Where are you going?"

"Vietnam. Third Surgical Hospital."

Nettie knew very little about war, except that her uncle Jack had died in World War II and several young men from Amherst had been killed in Southeast Asia. "Be careful."

"I will. You too."

"Thank you. Not just for the book, but for everything. I don't know what I would have done without you."

Linda gave Nettie a long hug. "Here's my forwarding address. Keep in touch. Let me know what you decide about college."

"I will."

"Linda?"

"Yes."

"Keep your head down."

Ethan helped Nettie onto the orange swivel stool at Howell's lunch counter, then propped her crutches in the corner.

"How much longer do you have to use them?"

"I get a walking cast next week, just in time to start school. Two weeks after that, they'll cut it off and I'll be free."

"If I didn't know what you'd been through, I would never have guessed. You look great."

"Thanks. Outside work is done. The inside stuff is coming along pretty well too."

"Sleeping?"

"No more nightmares, if that's what you're asking."

"It was."

The waitress placed small glasses of water and utensils in front of them, then took their orders.

Nettie gave Ethan a surprise hug. "I want to thank you again for what you did that night. If you hadn't told Andy what was going on, I don't think I'd be here."

"You never know. Fate has a big toolbox. If one thing doesn't work, I'm pretty sure it will try something else."

"Since when did you become such a philosopher?"

"Since I came here. This summer changed a lot of things for me."

"Your mom and dad?"

Ethan nodded. "They called last night. They didn't tell us, in case it didn't work out, but they've been back together for the past few weeks."

"That's wonderful."

"I think it was Grams who pulled them back from the edge. They even talk differently now, like they did when Cal and I were younger. It's as if they forgot how for a while."

"I'm sure your grandmother is happy."

"Ecstatic. It's not been an easy summer for her either."

"Did you know she came to see me in the hospital?"

"No, but I'm not surprised. What did she have to say?"

"That she was glad you and I were friends. That sometimes friends keep each other from falling down without getting in the way."

"That old gal is one smart lady."

"You did the same for me." Nettie sipped her water. "She also gave me a present."

"What?"

"A plaque she used to have on her desk when I was in elementary school. It says SEE THE INVISIBLE, BELIEVE THE UNBELIEVABLE, AND RECEIVE THE IMPOSSIBLE."

Ethan laughed. "Cal and I have the same plaque in our rooms at home."

Nettie laughed. "And here I thought she gave it to me because I was special."

"She did. And you are. She gives it to people she cares about. Always has."

"I bet she's going to miss you and Cal terribly."

"That goes both ways. We want her to come back to California with us, but she thinks we need time together as a family. My folks asked her to consider moving there, but she said no."

"Why?"

"Because Amherst is her home. Her memories of my grandfather are here. They were childhood sweethearts. They raised my dad in that house and celebrated their fiftieth wedding anniversary there the summer before he died."

"Forever love."

"What?"

"Something I've spent the better part of the summer trying to figure out."

"And?"

"Still working on it."

"Andy's a lucky guy."

"I'm the lucky one. It just took me a while to realize it. You have a friend there too, you know."

"I know. He stopped by the house after the flood. He wanted to thank me again for helping with the Danes thing and for letting him know you and Win might be in trouble."

"He told me."

"Did he tell you the rest of it?"

Nettie shook her head.

"He also said if he weren't around, he'd want you to be with someone like me—but in the meantime, I'd do well to remember he *was* around."

Nettie sputtered the water she'd just sipped.

"He has it you know."

"Has what?"

"Grit. Remember the movie we saw this summer, the one about finding a man with grit?"

Nettie nodded.

"You asked if you could find someone with grit if you didn't have it?"

"I remember."

"Andy has it. So do you."

The waitress set their milkshakes on the counter.

"What it took for you and Win to build those dreamcatchers and help Nibi save those boys took courage. What it took for you to stay alive and for Andy to find and rescue you that night required a lot more.'

"Faith and luck."

"Yes, and grit. It's what makes the two of you different."

"Thanks, I think."

Ethan laughed. "Different in a good way."

The waitress returned with their cheeseburgers and French fries.

"When are you and Cal leaving?"

"We fly out of Dulles tomorrow."

"So soon?"

"Mom and Dad want a few days with us before school starts."

"I'm happy for you but sad you're leaving."

"Me too."

"Will you be back next summer?"

"Too early to say."

They both made a grab for the check as the waitress laid it on the counter. Nettie won. "I want to buy your lunch."

"Why?"

"Because that's what friends do. Next time, you buy."

"Friends also write."

"I have your address, and you have mine. Win and Cal are writing to each other too."

Ethan took a big bite of his burger, catching a glob of ketchup as it escaped the bottom of the bun. "Who knows, we might just get the two of you out to California." With that, he leaned in and gave her a kiss on the cheek, leaving smeared ketchup in his wake.

"Dammit, Ethan."

He laughed as his sticky hands went up in the air. "Just saying."

Chapter 19

Nettie had never seen the inside of a jail, but the starkness of the outside wasn't misleading. The waiting room's flat green walls, metal folding chairs, and uncovered fluorescent lights were just as unwelcoming. Two squat windows near the ceiling were so small, she wondered why they'd bothered to put them in at all, much less cover them with bars. Andy sat to her right, her parents to her left. As a state policeman, her father didn't want her here. Her mother knew she had to be.

A balding guard came through the heavy metal door, his gun holster snug under his plump belly. He nodded as her father stood. "Gene."

"Max."

"Don't worry. We'll be with her." He motioned to Nettie. "You can come back now."

Andy walked her to the door, then squeezed her hand. "You've got this."

She followed the guard down a long, painted-gray cinder-block-and-concrete hall with few doors and no windows. Their footsteps created an unbalanced echo that led and followed but could not leave. The tunnel to nowhere unsettled Nettie worse than the rows of cells she'd imagined.

"Wait here, please." The guard unlocked a narrow door that melded into a room the same color as the hall. Through a skinny vertical window, she watched another guard escort Danes to a small table. A day-old shadow and wrinkled beige scrubs had replaced his usual clean-shaven, crisp appearance. Wrists cuffed and ankles chained, he teetered, then slumped into the chair.

Nettie's jitters dissolved on sight, replaced by indignation, as her guard guided her to the opposite end of the table, staying between her and Danes until she was seated. Both guards went to stand by their doors.

Danes's gaze had locked on Nettie the moment she'd entered the room. "I heard what happened in the flood. How are you?"

"That depends. Which one of you is asking?"

"What?"

"You heard me. The good guy or the bad guy?"

Danes smirked. "Still haven't lost that smart mouth, have you?"

Nettie leaned back, crossed her arms, and waited.

"The better one. Maybe. Anymore, I can't separate the two."

"Can't or don't want to? Seems to me you're pretty good at using one to serve the other."

Danes's gray eyes sparked. "So much for forgiveness."

"Are you asking or telling?"

"Same difference."

"Even you don't believe that."

"Who are you to tell me what I believe and what I don't?"

Nettie sat straight. "Because you're the one who told me evil doesn't ask—it tells."

"You think I'm lying? That I don't want to be forgiven?"

"I think your dark side is looking for company, and you'll not get that from me. If your good side is asking, that's another matter."

"Why are you here?"

"Why did you want me to come?"

"I didn't."

"Pastor Williams doesn't lie. You do."

The inside guard chuckled.

Danes stared at the man until he looked away. "I thought I wanted to see you. Now, I'm not so sure."

"Again, which one wanted to see me: the teacher or the rapist?"

"Will you stop? You can't see one without the other."

"Not true. You can't know one without the other, but you don't have to live both. That's a choice."

"You think I chose to be like this?" Danes's voice rose to the point of raspiness.

"Yes. You knew what you were doing. You knew it was wrong and did nothing to stop it."

Danes rubbed his neck.

Nettie steadied herself, preparing to ask the questions that wouldn't leave her alone. "All summer, you were setting me up, weren't you? From the first day we met. You planned it, didn't you?"

Danes turned away.

"The least you can do is look at me."

Danes met her gaze and locked his jaws.

"You planned it."

"Yes."

"Why?"

His voice lowered. "Planning is part of the excitement."

"While we were working together, this is what you were thinking about?"

"Not all the time."

"Just when you were drinking."

"Drinking made it easier."

"How was it all supposed to end? An affair? Rape? Something worse?"

Danes stuttered, before finding words. "I'm not a murderer. It was just about sex. That's all. It's always about sex."

"So, if you hadn't been fired, or if Ethan and the others hadn't shown up when they did, what would you have done with me?"

"I don't know."

"Of course you do. What did you do with the others when you were finished with them?"

The last bit of color drained from Danes's face. "Guard, I'm done."

"No, you're not," Nettie said. "Answer me."

Danes turned from one guard to the other. Neither moved.

"You left them, right? Isn't that how it works? You got what your twisted brain and body wanted, then just left them to pick up the pieces, to try and put their lives back together."

Danes stood. Both guards stepped forward. "Sit down," one said.

He hesitated, then eased onto the edge of his chair.

"How does your Christian side reconcile what you did to them? What you tried to do to me?"

Red-faced, Danes slammed his palms on the table. "The same way any sinner does. Convince yourself that next time will be different. And the next time. And the next."

"Then do something about it."

"Don't you think I've tried?"

"Then try something else. I have a friend who's a nurse. She said there are professionals who help people like you. Pastor Williams said the same thing. You just have to be willing to own what you did and accept the help."

"So, now you're an expert?"

"No. You're the one who said evil seldom survives the light of day."

"It's not that simple."

"Yes, it is. Unless you're just blowing smoke about wanting to change."

"Do you see where I am? It doesn't matter what I want."

"Really? You're going to wallow in self-pity after what you've done? Give me a break. Yes, your twisted double life is over. But if you mean what you say, here's your chance."

"For what? There are no second chances in a place like this."

"That depends on which direction you're looking. Regardless of your motives, you helped me find my way through some tough questions about faith. Maybe it's because you've seen things from both sides. Who knows? Get yourself righted, and maybe you can help someone else, even in a place like this."

Danes swallowed as if it hurt.

Nettie stood, her chair protesting its slide along the concrete floor. Her guard moved quickly to the table, but she slipped past him to look Danes in the eye. "Back in the summer, you said my job was to forgive, forget, and move on. I forgive you. Both of you. And after today, I refuse to let your darkness steal one more minute of my life."

The guard tried to leverage Nettie away from the table, but she leaned closer to Danes instead. "It's your job too. Forgive it, fix it, and move on. Your good side has a lifeline. Don't waste it."

With his hand tight on her elbow, the guard steered her toward the exit as Mr. Danes stood and called out. "Nettie, wait."

Shaking free, Nettie turned back.

"Have a good life."

October colors blanketed the Amherst side of the mountain as Nettie, Andy, and Win drove toward the top of the mountain. They hadn't been back to Rockfish Valley since the flood. Not only had Nettie not been ready, but Sheriff Tanner wasn't allowing anyone in except road construction crews and officials still looking for remains. Once a rudimentary new road system was in place, he'd given them permission to return on this peaceful Sunday afternoon.

Nettie braced herself as they crested Walton's Pass and descended into the valley. She'd heard the biblical storm had caused more than two thousand years' worth of erosion in one night. Anticipating darkness and destruction, she found a colorful view instead. Ringing the top third of the mountains were the expected jagged gray scars, but mixed among them were islands of green, red, yellow, and orange leaves. Even the area around Lookout Point seemed to be returning to life. The mountain's midsection had the same bursts of color but still hosted countless dislodged boulders, some the size of houses, and downed trees traumatically stripped of limbs and bark.

"At least things are growing again," Win said. "Nibi would like that."

Andy whistled and stopped the car. "Would you look at that?"

For as far as they could see, the valley floor resembled an earthen bowl, scraped clean except for buttes of dirt three stories tall, fifty feet wide, and spiked with trees and debris. Zigzagging across the Tye, the buttes went upriver until they were little more than specks. Burial mounds. Nibi and more than thirty others were still missing.

Lines of yellow bulldozers, earthmovers, and other construction equipment snaked around a dozen work trailers tagged with VIRGINIA DEPARTMENT OF TRANSPORTATION and US ARMY CORPS OF ENGINEERS signs.

Andy drove cautiously down the compacted gravel road, then crossed a clattering temporary metal bridge. He stopped on the edge of a wide strip of scraped-flat land that had once been Oak's Landing. "Let's walk."

With little to absorb the sound, the car doors closed with serial thuds. The earthy scent of sunbaked soil seemed almost pleasant compared to the stench Nettie remembered. Nearby, the lazy waters of the Tye glinted against a dramatically reshaped shoreline, the river's long, lazy turn now straight. Long patches of groundcover intermixed with straw protected newly graded banks. The lush great oaks, picturesque park, and lazy river walk were gone. The once thriving train station had disappeared without a trace, except for a small section of tracks still dangling on the side of the mountain. Upriver, the memory of the pulp mill sat on a stripped-bare knoll. As in the days preceding the flood, nothing moved, not even the normally incessant bugs.

Win turned with slow steps. "This used to be Main Street. Mrs. Loving's Candy Store should be right here, Huffman's General Store there, the Post Office over there, and Carter's Drugstore around the corner. It's as if the town and its people never existed." The memory of Wade and Skip's bicycle chain clanged as they made their way along the invisible street.

Win ran ahead as they approached the hill at the edge of town. "Oh my gosh. Look. It's still there."

Andy helped Nettie gimp along faster on her recovering right leg.

There, in its original position, sat the preaching stone. It didn't take much to understand how it had survived. Now that the topsoil had washed away, an isthmus-like connection between the preaching stone and the granite mantel anchoring the foundation of the church was visible, extending into the heart of the mountain.

Win ran her hands over the top of the stone as if it were sacred. "I'm so grateful it's still here." She opened a small pouch and sprinkled tobacco over the stone. "For Nibi and all those who came before."

Nettie pulled a similar pouch from her pocket and drizzled sweet-smelling sage from one end of the stone to the other. "And this is in honor of the Monacans' new medicine woman."

Surprise and doubt lowered Win's voice to a whisper. "I don't even know where to begin."

"You'll figure it out, one step at a time."

Leaving a wobbling path of footprints in the reconstructed hillside, they climbed to the stone shell of the church. A few reinforced trusses and a small remaining section of roof kept the cracked steeple and tilted cross upright.

Nettie sat on the stone threshold to rest her leg. "It's a miracle this place is still standing."

Andy eased down beside her. "A miracle of inspired design. It sits on a hill, and the windows and doors were kept open, which allowed the floodwaters to flow through. Are they going to rebuild?"

"Some of the surviving church members want to, but it may depend on whether the town decides to rebuild." Win drifted along the perimeter of the gutted sanctuary, skimming her hand across the stone wall.

Andy gathered river pebbles off the floor and rolled them in his hand "Two towns and seven villages got washed away. There might not be enough people left to do it."

"They're rebuilding the road. That's a good sign."

Win stopped at what was left of the stone altar, then motioned to Nettie and Andy. "Come look."

Scratched on the center stone in a perfect ring were six words: Faith. Wisdom. Courage. Hope. Strength. Commitment. The same qualities Nibi had said they'd need to develop if they were going to be able to build the dreamcatchers—and survive.

In the center of the ring was a slightly tilted cross with a partially hidden inscription.

Nettie brushed off the dried dirt. "He marks the horizon on the face of the waters as a boundary between light and darkness. Job 26:10." She stepped back. "That's incredible."

Win traced the letters. "All the times I've been in this church, I never knew this was here."

"Nibi knew. I bet that's why she told us to come here."

"If this is any indication, they'll rebuild, and they'll do it around this stone."

When they reached Indian Mission Road, Nettie and Win stopped for a breather.

"Leg okay? Still think you can handle the hike up the mountain?"

"I think so. It feels stable."

They'd arranged to meet Chief Brannon at the schoolhouse. Unlike last time, the door stood open.

"Good morning, girls. Welcome." The chief unstacked the last of a dozen boxes scattered around the room.

"Good morning, sir."

The smell in the room had changed from the sharpness of the forest to a familiar amenity of herbs and dried flowers.

As they moved farther inside, Win's eyes widened and her jaw dropped. Nibi's kitchen surrounded them. Her table and chairs stood in the middle of the room, topped with her mortar and pestle, teapot, cup, colorful baskets and jars, and palm-size otter-skin bags full of this and that. In the far corner sat her inside and outside rocking chairs. Her favorite shawl draped the back of one; her leather apron dangled from the corner of the other. Weathered wind chimes hung from rafters all around the room.

Nettie stayed one step behind as Win slowly wove from box to box, trembling as more remnants of Nibi's world were revealed. Chief Brannon waited patiently. When Win had opened and closed the last box, he spoke. "Nibi knew from the beginning she wasn't going to survive the darkness. She wanted you to have these things."

Motioning them to sit, the chief handed them each a paper bag. Inside were beautiful hand-sewn moccasins, the stitches small, tight, and close. Beading made of colorful river glass adorned the top and sides. The leather had been rubbed until it felt buttery soft. "Nibi said she promised to make these for you two earlier in the summer." Reaching into his jacket, he laid Nibi's leather journal on the table in front of Win. Full of medicinal recipes, the journal had been passed down through generations.

"Nibi said most of the answers you'll need are in here. What you don't find, we'll figure out together."

Win wiped her eyes. "Isn't this just like her? Always a dozen steps ahead. Trying to make it easier for everyone else."

"That was her way, her legacy, as well as that of generations of medicine women who preceded her."

"I miss her so much."

"Understandably. Nibi loved you and knew you were capable of continuing her work."

Win looked around the room. "I don't know what to do."

"Neither did Nibi at first. She wasn't much older than you when she took over for her mother. Give it time."

"I need to figure out where to keep all of this."

"You may keep it here if you wish. The tribal elders voted to allow you free use of the schoolhouse. It sits empty except for tribal meetings, and those can be moved next door to the church. You're free to set up this place as you see fit, and there's no rush. After you finish school, you can decide what you want to do, and when, and how. Until then, here's the key. Come and go as you please. I'm right across the road should you need anything."

"I don't know what to say."

Nettie nudged her and grinned. "Maybe 'thank you.'"

Win hugged the chief. "Thank you so much."

The chief hand-signaled, "Welcome home."

For two hours, Nettie, Win, and Chief Brannon followed Tyree's Creek up the back of Bear Mountain. They stopped at the base of the mudslide where Nettie had found the white arrowhead and the Indian brave's skull. Grass, vines, seedlings, and weeds had already begun to reclaim the displaced soil.

Squatting to get a drink from the creek, the chief studied the edges of the washout. "We didn't get the deluge of rain Rockfish Valley did, but we got enough to cause more slides. Thankfully, they were small and didn't hit important areas, especially this one."

"The burial mound made it through?"

The chief nodded. "Thanks to the tribe. We started working on it the day after you two were here." He cleaned off a small branch and gave it to Nettie to use as a walking stick as they headed up the soft edge of the washout.

Near the top, above the burial mound, rose a thick, semicircular berm of sticks, logs, and mud.

"It looks like a beaver dam," Nettie said.

"Who knows how to manipulate water better than beavers?" the Chief asked, chuckling. He pointed to long strands of running cedar crisscrossing the base of the mound. "These vines have strong roots. They'll help stop erosion as well."

Nettie ran her fingers across the spidery boughs scattered along the ropey vine. She could attest to its strength but stayed quiet. Some memories didn't need to be shared.

Leading the way to the far side of the mound, Chief Brannon found the stone marking the spot where they'd reburied the Indian brave's skull. Moving it aside, he dug a small, deep hole.

Nettie rubbed her thumb over the smooth surface of the white arrowhead that had helped save her life. Part of her wanted to keep it, but she knew where and to whom it belonged. He'd simply loaned it to her.

"Point up." Chief Brannon motioned for her to place the stone.

Once they had returned and repacked the dirt, Win sprinkled sweetgrass over the mound as the chief chanted a beautiful, melodic prayer. After replacing the marker, they made their way back to the creek, then down the mountain. Win and the chief stayed deep in conversation most of the way. Nettie said a quick prayer of thanks, grateful her friend had such a friend.

Back at the schoolhouse, Chief Brannon said he'd give them a ride home. He stayed unusually quiet until they reached Allen's Hill. Pulling over, he studied the sunset-tinted slope. "Nibi lived a full and meaningful life, but she bore a sadness that time couldn't heal. Part of the reason lives in that house. Nibi wanted you all to do what she couldn't." From his shirt pocket, the chief pulled a faded photograph of two girls with long, dark hair, oval faces, and happy smiles. One of the girls looked like a young Nibi; the other, Nettie didn't recognize. Two young men stood behind them. The face of one had blurred with time; the other was no one she knew. On the back of the picture were the words "I love you."

"Nibi asked that you two return this photo to the woman who lives in the mansion."

Nettie gasped and studied the picture again. "That's Alise Allen? And Nibi?"

The chief nodded.

"Who are the men with them?" Win asked. "Who loved who?"

"That's not for me to say. Let the story unfold as Nibi wanted. When you return the picture, she asked that you take Piccolo with you."

Now that he had only the Amherst train station to care for and the *Weak and Weary* was limited to twice-a-day passenger runs to Richmond, it wasn't hard to find Pic. The last train for the day left as Nettie and Win settled on a shaded bench to share penny candy with him. He'd struggled when Nibi passed, but lately seemed to be bouncing back.

"What can I do for you girlies today?"

"We want you to go with us to see someone."

"Me? Who?"

"Alise Allen."

Pic stopped chewing. "Why?"

"We have something to give her. From Nibi."

He swallowed hard.

"Nibi wanted you to go with us."

"May I ask what it is?"

"A picture."

"May I see it?"

As he studied the photo, Pic's wrinkled face went smooth, as if transported back in time. Turning it over, he looked away quickly. "I don't know about all this. Some things are best left in the past."

"At the police station, the night of the flood, when Nibi was in trouble and Win and I were heading to Oak's Landing, you hurried off, saying you had to tell Alise. You know her."

He whispered, "I know her. That doesn't mean . . ."

Nettie's voice softened. "You're the night visitor we've seen climbing Allen's Hill, aren't you?"

Pic's hand shook as he straightened his shoulders. "Yes."

Win covered his hand with hers. "You and Nibi were friends for a long time. You know she wouldn't have wanted us to do this if it wasn't important."

"You don't realize what you're asking."

"No. But Nibi did."

Pic wiped his sleeve across his eyes and looked at the railroad tracks, then stared at the picture for a long time. He finally took a deep breath and returned it to Win. Reaching into his worn leather bindle, he dug to the bottom, searching for something. "Maybe Nibi's right. Maybe it *is* time." In his hand lay a beautiful raw amethyst.

Chimes resonated through the mansion as Nettie, Win, and Pic waited in front of double doors of frosted, carved glass with a matching transom and heavy brass knobs. Large coach lanterns and planters with miniature trees stood on each side.

"This porch is beautiful. It's a shame not many people get to see it."

Cool air rushed out as a brown woman with salt-and-pepper hair answered the door. Recognition flashed across her face. "Good evening."

"Good evening, Marianna," Pic said. "Please tell Alise I'm here with friends."

She hesitated.

"It's all right, Marianna."

"Of course." She backed up and allowed them to enter.

The raised-paneled foyer had mirror circular staircases, a marble floor, an oval center table with a vase of fresh flowers, and a chandelier so bright it hurt Nettie's eyes.

Marianna ushered them into a room full of sofas, chairs, inlaid tables, and hardwood floors covered partially with Oriental rugs. "Please have a seat."

Pic settled into a wingback chair in one of three separate sitting areas in the large room while Nettie and Win explored. Hurricane sconces gave a rich glow to beautifully papered walls, heavy drapes, shelves full of books and intricate fancies, and paintings of distant places and unknown people. There wasn't a speck of dust anywhere.

"Pic, did you know any of these folks?"

He nodded.

Marianna reappeared at the door. "Mrs. Allen is not receiving visitors today. She asked if you could come back another time."

Nettie and Win moved toward the door, but Pic raised his hand to stop them. "Please tell Alise I said it's time to end this. We're not leaving until we talk with her."

"But, sir."

"Please, Marianna."

Nettie had never heard Pic speak this way. Quiet. Resolved.

Marianna left the room, moving more quickly than when she'd entered.

Pic rubbed the stump where his right hand should have been, lost in a time and place only he could see.

Nettie and Win sat on the edge of a velvet sofa, glancing around the room, at each other, and at Pic. Somewhere a clock ticked, but no doors opened or closed, no air conditioners hummed, no voices chatted, no dogs barked. Nothing gave the mansion the semblance of being anything more than a home for ghosts.

Nettie and Win rose as an elegant version of Nibi appeared in the doorway, in black trousers and a gray silk blouse, her silver hair in a soft bun. The woman's pale, oval face showed few wrinkles. Marianna stood by her side.

"Good evening."

Pic stood. "Hello, Alise."

The two stared at each other, deep in a silent conversation.

"Pic, may I speak with you privately for a moment?"

Nettie and Win could hear their muffled voices down the hall, sometimes raised, sometimes barely there. They talked for a long time.

When they reappeared, Pic had his arm around Alise's waist. She appeared shaken, her eyes red. "Girls, I'd like for you to meet Alise Allen, Nibi's sister and Win's great-aunt."

Win wobbled, as Nettie stammered, "S-s-sister?"

Alise nodded. "We should talk on the veranda. Fresh air might help all of us."

Pic took Alise's elbow and escorted her toward the back of the mansion. They walked comfortably, practiced. Nettie and Win followed, speechless.

They exited the house through oversize French doors onto a sandstone patio bordered by a low wall that opened into a garden of boxwoods and flowering shrubs. Nettie caught the faint scent of Angel Water. In the center of the garden stood a trilevel fountain; the soothing glissade of water reflected the flickering light of lanterns mounted along the wall.

Alise led them to a lanai and invited them to have a seat. She and Pic settled on one sofa while Nettie and Win sat across from them on a matching one, the cushions soft as down. A spotless glass-topped table sat between them.

"Marianna, would you please bring our guests some lemonade and cookies?"

"Certainly."

Pic turned to Alise. "The girls have something to show you."

Win handed her the picture. Alise studied it closely.

"Turn it over," Pic whispered.

Alise Allen slumped as she read the words. Pulling a lace-trimmed handkerchief from her pocket, she murmured, "I can't do this."

Pic put his arm around her. "Yes, you can. Nibi paved the way. You've punished yourself long enough."

"Enough? It will never be enough."

"Then stop punishing me. I'm an old man, Alise. My happiness rests with you. I want to step out of the shadows."

"If Carlton finds out—"

"If he finds out, he finds out. Forty years of living under his threats is enough. I'm done. Nibi loved these girls. She wouldn't have sent them to you if she didn't want them to know our story."

"I wouldn't know where to begin."

"I do." Interlacing his fingers with Alise's, Pic took a deep breath and smiled at Nettie and Win. "Do you remember that day on the train I told you about coming to Oak's Landing from South Carolina during the Depression? That Nibi's father had given my brother and me jobs at the pulp mill and let us sleep in his barn?"

Nettie and Win nodded.

"My brother's name was Dell."

Another piece of the puzzle fell into place.

"That summer, Dell and I met his daughters, Nibi and Alise, beauties then and now. Nibi and Dell fell for each other almost overnight, spending every minute they could together. In three months, they were engaged. Three months after that, they were married and living on Buffalo Ridge Mountain." Pic kissed Alise's hand. "That's when we fell in love too."

In the distance, the *Weak and Weary*'s whistle blew, interrupting their moment.

"When we met, Alise was engaged to a man named Carlton Wilkes, son of the man who owned dozens of pulp-and-paper mills up and down the East Coast, including the one in Oak's Landing."

Alise spoke so softly, Nettie had to strain to hear. "I met Carlton when he came to Oak's Landing from New York to oversee the retooling of the pulp mill. He was charming and attentive. And rich." The last word fell from her lips as if it burned. "He worked for his father and had to travel a great deal. He sent me flowers every day he was gone and brought expensive gifts when he returned. Early on, it was easy to convince myself that I was in love with him."

Crickets in the surrounding flower beds began chirping, forcing Alise to speak more loudly. "After we became engaged, Carlton changed. He started criticizing my family and friends, most of whom didn't like him either, especially Nibi. He became suspicious and controlling. He wanted to decide when and where we went as a couple and didn't want me going out at all if he wasn't in town. I told him I felt like a prisoner and wasn't going to live like that. He apologized and blamed his behavior on prewedding jitters. Afterward, he returned to his normal, charming self. Nibi didn't believe the change would last. Foolishly, I did."

Marianna came out of the house with a tinkling tray. After handing out cloth napkins, she placed lemonade in crystal glasses on coasters in front of everyone and passed a plate of homemade cookies.

"Thank you, Marianna," Pic said.

"You're most welcome."

Alise continued, "Not long after Carlton and I had that conversation, he left on an extended trip to retool another pulp mill in the South. While he was away, my father hired Pic and Dell to work at the mill here and to help out around the farm. That's how Nibi and I met them. Pic was so handsome and fun-loving. He made me feel more lighthearted than I had in quite a while. Over time, I realized he was also the most kind and caring man I'd ever met. Still is." Alise leaned against Pic's shoulder.

"Alise and I would sit by the river and talk for hours or go for long hikes in the mountains. Sometimes we'd go with Nibi to gather plants."

Alise nodded. "Those were special days."

"We even went with Nibi and Dell to the amethyst mine. Nibi needed a stone for her dreamcatcher, so Alise and I decided to go along and mine one too."

Alise took a slow sip of lemonade. "That was the day I knew I was in love with Pic. I asked him to keep our amethyst until I could break my engagement. I planned to tell Carlton as soon as he returned from his business trip, but before that could happen, someone wired him that Pic and I were spending time together. Carlton came back to town right away and went to see Pic."

Pic frowned. "He said he knew about me and Alise and offered me a thousand dollars to leave town. I said no. He kept offering more money, until I told him he was wasting his time, that he didn't have enough money to make me leave. He got angry, called me railroad trash, and said he'd kill me if I ever came near Alise again—and if that wasn't enough to stop me, he'd kill Alise."

Nettie moved to the edge of her seat. "That's crazy. Did you go to the police?"

"Yes, I went right away. Back then, Sheriff Tanner was a deputy and a friend of ours. He went to see Carlton and told him that threatening to kill anyone was against the law and would land him in jail. Carlton lied, said it was all a misunderstanding and that he'd smooth things over with Alise and me. He knew Tanner would be keeping an eye on him, so Carlton hired a thug named Monroe to watch Alise. Dell and I knew Monroe because he used to hang around the hobo camp near the train station. He was mean as a snake. I knew if Carlton decided to make good on his threat to hurt Alise, Monroe wouldn't hesitate to do it, so I stayed away from her until I could figure out what to do."

Alise fingered the lace edges of her handkerchief. "Carlton came to see me later that day. He didn't let on that he'd seen Pic until I told him I was breaking the engagement and tried to give his ring back. He slapped it out of my hand and pushed me against the wall. He said he knew all about my pauper boyfriend and that if I broke the engagement, Pic would disappear permanently. Then he said if I told anyone, Nibi would disappear too."

Nettie and Win were hanging on every word.

"I was terrified he'd hurt the people I loved, so I stayed quiet. Nibi tried her best to talk me out of marrying him. She knew he was blackmailing me and said she'd help me find a way out. But I knew Carlton would make good on his threats." Alise paused to take a deep breath. "After we were married, he moved us to Amherst, to this big house, and hired Marianna and Albert, the gardener. By then, Carlton wasn't even trying to be nice. Not to me, Nibi, or anyone else I was close to. He became physically abusive as well. Every night he'd badger me with questions, demanding to know where I'd been, whom I'd seen and talked with. If my answers didn't match what Monroe told him, he'd hit me." Alise shuddered. "Always below the neck, so no one could see."

Pic took her hand.

"We'd been married a couple of months when Carlton found out Marianna and Albert were actually friends of Nibi's. When he got home that night, he was livid, and drunk. He beat me so badly I couldn't stand up. Marianna and Albert heard my screams and kept banging on the bedroom door until he stopped. Carlton pushed past them and stormed out of the house. Marianna and Albert helped me up and said Nibi, Dell, and Pic were on their way. Nibi had had a vision and knew I was in trouble." Alise paused and shook her head. "She'd just had a baby a few days before, but there she was, coming to rescue me."

"That sounds just like Nibi," Win said.

"As soon as Pic and the others arrived, we headed for the train station, while Marianna and Albert went to tell Tanner what was going on."

Alise paused as the repeated *hoos* of an owl floated toward them from beyond the fountain. Nettie couldn't help but wonder what color its feathers were.

"Apparently, Monroe saw us leave the house and went to tell Carlton. The train station seemed almost deserted when we got there, except for a couple of people at the far end. Dell went ahead to buy tickets while Pic helped Nibi and the baby and me out of the car. We were climbing the steps to the platform when Monroe ran up and grabbed Pic from behind, dragged him into the gravel, and started beating him."

"He had brass knuckles and kept hitting me in the face," Pic said, rubbing his jaw. "All I could see were stars."

"I tried to pull Monroe off Pic, but he pushed me down," Alise said. "Dell came flying down the steps and tackled Monroe, knocking him off Pic. It was a terrible fight. They were so close to the tracks, and the train was coming. The engineer kept sounding the whistle. Dell finally got the upper hand and pinned Monroe on the ground. Monroe struggled but couldn't get free. He finally quit fighting, put his hands in the air, and yelled, 'Enough!' Dell let go of him and got to his feet. He told Monroe he couldn't beat one brother, much less two, and that Monroe had best keep his distance from me. Dell was walking away when . . ." Alise paused, unable to continue.

"Monroe charged at Dell while his back was turned," Pic said. "He pushed him onto the tracks in front of the train."

Nettie and Win gasped in unison.

"I tried to save him, to pull him off the rails, but I was too late. The train hit and killed Dell and took my hand." Pic rubbed his stump, his face reliving incredible pain. "For years after, I dreamed about that night. In the dream, I was able to pull harder, faster."

Alise rocked back and forth, clutching her stomach. "It's a night terror I never wake from. The man I loved lay on the ground, bleeding and writhing in pain; Dell was somewhere under the train; and my sister was on her knees, clinging to her baby, moaning."

The lanai went quiet as they all steadied themselves.

Win used her napkin to dry her eyes. "Did Monroe get away?"

"No," Pic said. "As soon as Marianna and Albert told Tanner what was going on, he rushed to help. He got to the train station in time to see Monroe push Dell onto the tracks. Tanner shot and killed him as he tried to run away."

"What about Carlton?" Nettie asked.

"When Tanner left to rush Pic to the hospital, Carlton came out of the shadows. He'd been there watching the whole time. He said if I ever tried to leave him again, I'd be the next one in front of the train. Nibi heard him and got up. She handed me the baby and calmly walked toward Carlton, chanting. The look on her face was not of this world. The closer she got, the farther he backed up. Nibi stopped, raised her hands to the heavens, and ended the chant with a hand signal. Carlton turned deathly white and ran away."

"What was the chant about?" Win asked.

"Loss."

"And the hand signal?"

"Forgiveness. Even in the midst of overwhelming sadness, she knew it was the only way she'd find her way out."

"Did the police arrest Carlton?" Nettie asked.

"Tanner and others questioned him but couldn't bring charges," Alise said. "Other than his being Monroe's boss, there was no way to prove he played a part in Dell's murder."

"Couldn't they get him for beating you?"

"Yes, and they did. Tanner charged Carlton with assault and battery and put him in jail. By the next day, his family's New York lawyer was down here, bailing him out. The lawyer said if I'd agree to drop all charges and not file for divorce, the house and a generous monthly allowance for its upkeep would be put in my name." Alise's hands shook as she set her glass on the table. "I had no money and no place to go. I signed the papers."

"Couldn't you have gone back to your family?" Nettie asked.

"That night, I cost my beloved sister the husband she loved, my newborn niece her father, and Pic his hand. There was no going home."

"Is that why you never leave this house?"

"It's only right that I serve the same life sentence I gave them." She studied the back of the ornate mansion. "This is a just prison. I'm surrounded by everything Carlton Allen loves."

Win went to sit next to Alise, placing a hand on her arm. "I don't believe what happened was your fault, and I don't believe our Nibi would either."

"None of us believe it," Pic added.

"But I do," Alise said.

Nettie thought of what Pastor Williams said the night he visited her in the hospital—words that lifted her guilt about surviving when so many others hadn't. She turned to Alise. "You married Carlton to keep Pic and Nibi safe, correct?"

"Yes."

"Did you know what Monroe was going to do that night at the station?"

Alisa's eyes widened. "No."

"Could you have stopped him?"

"I don't think so."

"Guilt has no place in an innocent heart."

Pic put his arm around Alise. "Nettie's right. It's time for you to lay down that burden."

Alise's voice sounded hesitant. "I don't know how."

"Sure you do," Pic said. "One step at a time. You took the first one tonight. We'll figure out the next one tomorrow, and we'll take it together."

"Pic, if Carlton is back in New York, why did you have to sneak in here at night?" Win asked.

Alise answered before Pic could. "Because of me. Before he left town, Carlton said he was having the house watched and threatened to kill Pic if I continued a relationship with him. For decades, I've lived in fear that someone like Monroe would make good on that threat. I kept telling Pic to stay away, but he refused."

"There was no way I was going to stay away from the woman I love. So I kept my job, helped Nibi and her daughter and her grand-daughter, like I knew Dell would want me to do, and came to Alise as often as I could."

"We've seen you sometimes. There's a spot on the hill where you can see the path to the back of the house."

Alise smiled. "We knew you were there, at least most of the time. We'd turn off the lights and watch from the window. It was good to see someone enjoying the hill."

"Pic, didn't you ever want to get a better job? A better place to live?"

"Alise used to ask me the same thing, but I loved my job, still do. I'm good at it, even with one hand. It doesn't pay much, but I don't need much, and I've saved a lot. I was able to travel to Oak's Landing for free whenever I wanted. My room is plenty big, with a comfortable bed and bathroom. It's warm in the winter and cool in the summer. I have friends who care about me that I get to see most every day. It's close to Alise. And I feel close to Dell there." Pic took Alise's hand. "And tonight, for the first time in decades, I'm holding hands with my sweetheart for everyone to see. What more do I need?"

Marianna opened the French doors and stepped outside with an empty tray. Alise stood and embraced her. "It's over."

"Pardon?"

"We're not hiding and worrying about Carlton's threats anymore."

Marianna looked at Pic, then back at Alise. "Is he dead?"

Pic laughed. "Probably not, but it doesn't matter. We've chosen to step out of the shadows. Whatever comes comes."

Marianna smiled and put her arm around Alise. "I've waited a long time for this day. My friend Nibi would be very happy."

Anne Johnson's yard looked as polished as she did: finely trimmed grass, manicured flower beds, sculpted shrubs, and symmetrically pruned trees. The sidewalk had been swept clean, as had the steps and small, gable-covered porch. The glass storm door sparkled as if it had never known clingy dust or fingerprints.

Nettie took a deep breath and pushed the bell. Behind the front door, high- and low-pitched tones alternated until they disappeared into the recesses of the house.

Mrs. Johnson opened the front door. She wore a pearl choker and a starched shirtwaist dress cinched with a wide belt that matched her pumps. Unlocking the storm door, she pushed it open. "Why, Nettie. What a nice surprise."

"Hi, Mrs. Johnson. Is Anne around?"

"She is. Come in." Mrs. Johnson led Nettie across a spotless foyer, through a living room that could have been in a home-decorating magazine, and into a sunroom with bamboo furniture covered with green cushions and yellow throw pillows. She motioned to one of the chairs. "Please have a seat. Would you like some lemonade or tea?"

"No, thank you, ma'am. I'm fine."

"You seem to be doing well since that horrible flood."

"Yes, ma'am. I am." Nettie looked around the room, avoiding Mrs. Johnson's prying eyes. She wanted details Nettie wasn't willing to give.

"Well, I'm so glad. I'll go get Anne."

Scattered around the room were plants with colorful flowers of all shapes and sizes and not a dead leaf to be found anywhere. Two potted fig trees stood guard beside sliding glass doors at the back of the room. Beyond the glass, smooth turquoise water glinted in a rectangular pool with rounded edges. On one side stood a brick bathhouse, and on the other were scattered lounge chairs and a large wrought-iron table with matching seats covered with a big red umbrella.

"What do you want?" Anne stood in the front entrance, arms crossed, scowling. Her polo shirt, tennis skirt, socks, and shoes matched.

"I'd like to talk."

"Make it quick. I have a match in thirty minutes."

A shadow crossed the floor near Anne and stopped at the threshold. Sighing, Anne crossed the room, pushed past Nettie, and opened the sliding door. "Come on." She headed for the poolside table. Selecting a chair facing the back of the house, she crossed her arms and legs. "What do you want?"

Nettie sat across from her. "I don't care if your mother hears."

"I do. Now, for the last time, what do you want?"

"I want to apologize." Nettie had stirred the words around so much, they came more easily than she'd thought they would.

Anne's eyes narrowed to suspicious slits. "For what?"

"Never giving you a chance."

"A chance for what?"

"That day at the lake. You said I'd never given us a chance to be friends, even when we were little. I never thought about it like that. I knew we didn't like each other, but I never realized that I'd played a role in starting it. Anyway, I'm sorry. For all of it. I hope you'll forgive me."

Anne stared, eyes wide and unblinking. "And that's supposed to make everything okay?"

"It's a start."

"Why should I believe you after all the mean things you've done to me?"

Nettie's mouth flew open. "Mean things I've done to you?"

"You heard me."

Nettie checked the anger surging in her chest, remembering Mr. Danes's words. God loved Anne just as much as he loved her. Not her acts, her. Nettie swallowed hard. "I guess we just remember things differently."

Anne's expression turned darker. "You're just trying to be a goody-two-shoes and make me look bad."

"How does my apologizing make you look bad?"

"Because I'm not apologizing to you."

"I came to give one, not get one. Maybe one day you'll accept it." Nettie stood.

Anne scraped her chair getting to her feet. "How does Andy feel about you almost getting him killed?"

"I forgive you for that too." Nettie turned to leave.

"Wait." Anne came around the table. "Let him go, Nettie."

"I didn't come here to talk about Andy. I came to talk about you and me. Hopefully, one day you'll be able to separate the two." She started walking. "Until then, the ball's in your court."

Chapter 20

Nettie's ponytail swayed, her crisp white dress crinkled, and her hands sweated in their white kid gloves as she went up the steps to the altar, then turned to face the congregation. In the front row were Andy, Win, her parents, her brother, and her sister. Andy blew her a kiss. Win winked. Behind them sat Mrs. Smith, Mrs. Mac, most of the GAs, and all of the regular faces she'd watched from the choir loft on Sunday mornings.

Pastor Williams dabbed his forehead with his handkerchief as he closed the big podium Bible. "Baptisms are special events, not only in the life of an individual, but in the life of the church. It's especially meaningful when we baptize someone we've had the privilege of watching grow up."

Joining Nettie on the steps, he escorted her up to the baptismal pool, then turned toward the congregation. "Our lifelong journey as Christians seldom follows the same path. We attend church, we read and study the lessons of the Bible and thousands of years of biblical scholars, we follow the faith traditions of our families, yet we often hesitate when it comes to accepting that which we cannot fully understand. The Holy Spirit is our bridge across doubt. It says, 'Come to me. Believe. Follow. I will show you how to see the invisible, believe the unbelievable, and receive the impossible.' The act of baptism says to the world that we have accepted this gift and marks us as one of Christ's own. From that point forward, our life has new direction, serving those Christ serves."

The baptismal pool sparkled as Pastor Williams stepped in, causing little waves to splash against the sides. Slipping out of her shoes, Nettie accepted his hand and followed. As she descended the steps, the little weights her mother had sewn into the hem of her dress made it float down around her like petals.

Pastor Williams placed one hand on her back and wrapped the other around her left hand. "Ready?" he whispered.

She nodded.

"Nettie, do you accept Jesus Christ as your Lord and Savior?"

"I do."

"Then I hereby baptize you in the name of the Father." With confident hands, he lowered her into the water. The moment it flowed over Nettie's face, she had a fleeting surge of panic, as if she were back in the savage, muddy river that had almost drowned her. But then, as quickly as it had come, the fear disappeared, replaced by an overwhelming sense of peace. She said a silent prayer as he raised her up. "The Son." The water felt lighter as he lowered and lifted her again. "And the Holy Spirit." The third time, she barely noticed the silky water but could tell Pastor Williams's arms were quivering. Nettie helped right herself.

As the organist and congregation broke into a heart-felt rendition of *Amazing Grace*, Pastor Williams gave Nettie a big hug. "Welcome to the community of believers."

"Thank you, sir. It's been quite a journey."

"Yes, it has, for both of us. Today is a happy day."

The last hymn followed Nettie as she made her way into the hall, where Win waited with towels and a change of clothes.

Nettie blotted her face. "Nibi was right."

"About what?"

"About choices and journeys never leaving our lives in the same place."

"Amen."

After the service, Nettie met Pastor Williams in his office. The papers, the books, the dust were all as they'd been every time she visited. But this time he sat in the old wing chair next to her.

He returned the white Bible her parents had given her as a baptism gift. "Today's date and your witnesses have been recorded in here. The information will also be recorded in the minutes and other records of the church. You are now an official member of the congregation."

"Thank you, sir. For everything."

"You are most welcome."

Nettie handed him a piece of paper.

"What's this?"

"Things I still have questions about."

Pastor Williams chuckled. "I should have known." He unfolded the list. "Free will?"

"Mr. Danes said free will isn't free at all."

"Predestination?"

"Can't talk about free will without talking about that, can you? It's confusing."

"It can be. Baptism by sprinkle?"

"The Presbyterians, the Methodists, and the Lutherans all baptize by sprinkle."

"Yes."

"And the Bible says it's okay to do it different ways, doesn't it?"

"Yes."

Nettie pushed her still-drippy ponytail off her soaked shoulder. "Maybe the Baptists should consider making a change."

Pastor Williams winked. "As I'm sure you realize after this morning, the Baptists consider immersion a life-changing experience, especially when performed in such an artistically scratched pool."

Nettie lay in the shorn grass of Allen's Hill. Waves of thin, silver-rimmed clouds trekked across the moon as she waited for Win. Light radiated from a dozen windows in the mansion.

Win slid into the grass next to her. "Hey."

"What kept you?"

"I had to drop off my mom's broken watch at the jewelry store. Guess who was there?"

"Who?"

"Pic. You should have seen him. He was dressed in new trousers and a white shirt and had just been to the barbershop for a shave and a haircut. He said he wanted to surprise Alise. He looked spiffy."

"Spiffy, huh?"

"He told me Carlton Allen was dead. Not a week after we were at Alise's house. A stroke. How's that for timing?"

"Sounds bad to be glad someone is dead, but I am."

"Pic was at the jewelry store picking up a ring he had made for Alise—a gold one with the amethyst stone he carried in his bindle all these years. The one they mined with Nibi and Dell."

"An engagement ring?"

Win nodded. "I think so."

"That's great. The town's already buzzing about them. This will really stir things up."

"Guess what else Pic was carrying in that sack?"

"What?"

"Money. A heck of a lot of money. He paid for that ring with hundred-dollar bills. He wasn't kidding when he told us he'd saved a lot. That bindle was his bank."

"Wonder why he never spent any of it until now."

"I asked him. He thought he and Alise might need it one day."

"Where do you think they'll live?"

"I don't know, but I bet he keeps his job."

"I hope they stay on the hill. New owners might not want us around."

"If they do, I'll bet they'll remodel. Just to make it theirs." Win stretched out in the grass. "How did your talk with Anne Johnson go?"

"Not well. She wasn't interested in accepting my apology."

"Does that surprise you?"

"No. Still, it was the right thing to do. I hope her better angels are whispering in her ear as hard as mine were whispering to me. If she listens, who knows what will happen?"

"You know she's going to Sweet Briar."

"Everybody in the world knows she's going to Sweet Briar."

"Have you told your parents what you decided?"

"Last night. Once I explained that I wanted to go to nursing school and that Sweet Briar didn't have a program, they were okay with it. They were especially glad when I told them you were doing the same thing and that we were going to apply to Virginia schools. In-state tuition is a lot less. Even with a tuition break, I'll have to get a part-time job."

"We both will. We also have to get our driver's licenses and buy cars before college starts."

"It's mind-boggling, isn't it? So much has happened, yet things are still changing."

"I agree. All we can do is deal with it as it comes."

The fading yellow-orange layers of sunset allowed them to see without headlights as Andy turned onto the dirt road and wound his way through honey-colored sheaves of hand-raked hay. Stopping the car, he turned to Nettie. "You're sure you want to do this?"

"Positive."

"You're not worried?"

"Worried? No. Afraid? Yes. That's why I had to come."

"If you're sure." Andy put the car in drive, then inched into the darkening, knotty woods bordering the river.

Nettie closed her eyes and leaned against his shoulder. Rocking with the ruts and turns in the dirt road, she concentrated on the crisp air, the sound of the river lapping the shoreline, and the back-and-forth song of whip-poor-wills. In the distance, low-pitched, repetitive croaks of bullfrogs trying to find a mate competed with a few remaining chirping crickets attempting to do the same. They'd all be gone soon; the first frost couldn't be far off.

She opened her eyes as Andy stopped and turned off the motor. In front of them lay River's Rest. The view had evolved as if in a kaleidoscope. From the new greens of spring to the lush colors of summer to the dark, lurking shadows of that night, it now overflowed with rich golds, rusts, browns, and corals. Its beauty settled in before anything less had a chance to.

"Okay?"

Nettie nodded.

Opening his door, Andy helped her slide from behind the wheel. Doing a slow turn, she took a deep breath. Summer's perfume had given way to the sharp, mind-clearing scent of fall, with a hint of ripe apples. The low canopy swayed in the evening breeze, causing a myriad of colorful leaves to drift and spin down around them. Nettie kicked off her shoes and tunneled her feet under the leafy carpet to the lush moss below. Andy did the same.

"It still feels like velvet. Like it did when we were here last time."

"We'll give it some time before we take that step again."

"I agree."

Andy pulled her to him. "There's no reason to rush. As long as you're close, I'm good."

Choosing to ignore her remaining qualms about being so near a river, Nettie took his hand and kicked a path through the leaves toward the tangled roots of the old riverbank trees. Reaching their favorite sitting spot, she eased herself down onto the smooth bark.

Andy settled behind her, cocooning his arms around her as she leaned back.

"I'm glad we came," she said.

"Me too," Andy said. "It's like we never left. Almost."

"We came so close to losing this—us."

"Too close. At least we know how not to get to that point again."

"Do you suppose we'll still be coming here fifty years from now?"

"I don't know." Andy rubbed her arms as the evening chill moved in. "Fate brought us this far; I don't imagine it's going to let go of us now."

As evening turned to night, the benevolent face of a new full moon appeared on the seemingly still river.

"The water's like a mirror," Andy said.

Nettie remembered the night of the dance in Oak's Landing. "Nibi called it *manosa mani*, moon water. It means the light and dark energies of the earth are in balance."

"Maybe they'll stay that way for a while."

"Maybe."

Nettie lay awake for hours, watching her dreamcatcher lilt in the breeze, shadow-dancing with moonbeams. The amethyst spider mother glinted as she went busily about her work. Nibi had guided them through such an incredible journey. One missed step, one wrong turn, one missed cue, and she, Andy, and Win wouldn't be here. More important, they wouldn't have been able to help save Wade and Skip, the legacy of an ordinary people in an extraordinary place now lost in time. Then again, maybe it hadn't been Nibi at all. Maybe everything unfolded the way it did by chance, fate rolling the dice at every turn. Nettie wasn't sure, but if fate was responsible, it seemed to work best when someone had eyes willing to see and ears willing to listen to what it had to say. Nibi's soft laugh followed her to sleep.

Acknowledgments

Historical novels are seldom written in isolation. To accurately capture the time, place, people, and events requires learning from those who lived it, as well as those who were left behind. It also requires immersing yourself in the records of the historians. To that end, I would like to acknowledge the contributions of the following people and organizations:

Victoria Last Walker Ferguson (Monacan), Monacan Life Interpreter and Exhibit Manager for the Living Exhibit at Natural Bridge in Natural Bridge, Virginia. I am indebted and grateful to my friend, and Virginia treasure, Vicky Ferguson. This extraordinary Native American embodies the wisdom of the Monacans. She did her very best to help me understand Monacan history, lifestyle, traditions, and their relationship with the natural world. If anything in *Moon Water* misrepresents the Monacans, rest assured the responsibility lies with me; either I misunderstood or needed creative license in crafting the story.

The Virginians who died in the flood and those who were left behind. On the night of August 19, 1969, remnants of Hurricane Camille drowned the Rockfish Valley of Virginia. The moisture-laden clouds traveling north from the Gulf of Mexico dropped an unprecedented 630 million tons of waterfall-like rain on a sleeping valley in about six hours. Reported rainfall amounts varied between 26 and 46 inches, depending upon location. The resulting flood caused massive landslides that scarred the Blue Ridge Mountains, washed away towns, villages, roads, and bridges, and killed 176 people who never saw it coming. Many of the physical and emotional scars are still visible today.

I was a freshman at Amherst County High School when this biblical flooding hit. I remember little about the storm; however, Amherst, which is less than twenty miles from Rockfish Valley, saw only a fraction of the rain Nelson County did. A friend who lived across the street lost twenty-two members of her extended family that horrific night.

My father, Gene Bayliss, was a Virginia State Trooper stationed in Amherst County at the time. He played a supporting role in the recovery effort. His friend and colleague, Trooper Ed Tinsley, was stationed in Nelson County and played an essential role in the rescue and recovery effort. I recently had the privilege of reconnecting with Trooper Tinsley. His vivid recollection of the event and the days following are documented in a personal diary titled *Portrait of a Disaster: The Flood of 1969*. He graciously shared memories, thoughts, and a copy of his diary with me.

Nelson County Historical Society and Oakland Museum, Nelson County, Virginia. This museum's exhibit on the impact of Hurricane Camille is powerful and humbling. Their dedicated volunteers helped access records, photographs, and maps describing the environmental cost of the historic flood. However, the museum's collection of personal accounts of survivors, their families, and those charged with rescue and recovery proved to be invaluable and unforgettable.

While *Moon Water* is a work of fiction, inspiration was drawn from numerous, and at times conflicting, accounts of the event. Two books about Hurricane Camille and its catastrophic impact on Nelson County and other regions of Central Virginia were particularly valuable:

- *Torn Land* by Paige and Jerry Simpson (1970). Printed by J. P Bell Company, Lynchburg, Virginia. This book, which was commissioned by the Nelson County Chamber of Commerce to record the events surrounding the flood, provided firsthand accounts of survivors, rescuers, and others who were on the front lines of recovery.

- *Roar of the Heavens* by Stefan Bechtel (2006), Citadel Press/Kensington Publishing Corporation. This book provided a more scientific, meteorological look at the unprecedented rain event the Weather Service calculated as being on the upper end of what was considered theoretically possible.

Additional, heartfelt thanks to:

- My wonderful husband and best friend, Jeff. His unwavering love and support helped make writing possible.
- David R., Jeff B., Lisa M., and Jim D. We made each other better and laughed a lot along the way.
- The readers who wanted more.

Also by Pam Webber:

The Wiregrass

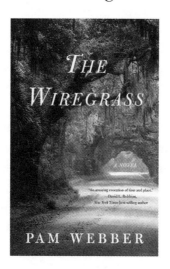

Order *The Wiregrass* (soft cover, e-copy, or audio version) at any of
the following:

Amazon: http://amzn.to/2cKd7Co
Barnes and Noble: http://bit.ly/2cytIXp
Books A Million: http://bit.ly/2cZ5cjM
Winchester Book Gallery: http://bit.ly/2cKdvR6

Book Group Discussion Questions

1. Nettie's journey toward adulthood has many twists and turns. Do any of them resemble your young adulthood? If so, how?
2. Nibi and Win can see the unseen and know the unknown. How is this gift double-edged?
3. How did your perception of Nibi evolve over the course of the narrative?
4. How do the events surrounding Ethan and Cal's family situation parallel the storyline?
5. In what ways does Alise Allen's self-imposed isolation parallel Piccolo's life?
6. Nettie and Anne's antagonistic relationship begins long before their interest in Andy. Have you experienced similar relationships? Would you have done what Nettie does? If yes, why? If no, why not?
7. Nettie pays a price for being honest regarding her doubts about faith. Have you ever voiced similar doubts? If so, what was the reaction of those you told?
8. Nettie's gritty behavior and language challenge her relationship with Pastor Williams. What is unique about how both react to these challenges over time?

9. Mr. Danes reflects the duality of good and evil in the same person. What about Nettie makes her an easy target for his evil side? His good side?

10. In what ways has Nibi prepared Win and Nettie for what they ultimately have to face?

11. Andy is not a typical teenager. In what ways is he different? How do these differences influence the storyline?

12. How does Chief Brannon help bridge the gap between Native American traditions and contemporary Christianity? In what ways do his views influence the storyline?

13. Describe the symbolic parallels between the dreamcatchers, the engraving found in the church, and Christianity.

14. Take a few minutes to read about the history of the Monacan Indians of Virginia at www.monacannation.com. What about their history makes Nettie and Win's friendship special?

15. In the end, what has Nettie discovered about love, hate, life, faith, and reconciliation? What did her journey help you discover about yourself?

Selected Titles from She Writes Press

She Writes Press is an independent publishing company founded to serve women writers everywhere. Visit us at www.shewritespress.com.

The Wiregrass by Pam Webber. $16.95, 978-1-63152-943-6. A story about a summer of discontent, change, and dangerous mysteries in a small Southern Wiregrass town.

I Like You Like This by Heather Cumiskey. $16.95, 978-1631522925. When social outcast Hannah captures the attention of a handsome and mysterious boy who also happens to be her school's resident drug dealer, her life takes an unexpected detour into a dangerous and seductive world—and she is forced to reexamine what she believes about herself and the people she trusts the most.

How to Grow an Addict by J.A. Wright. $16.95, 978-1-63152-991-7. Raised by an abusive father, a detached mother, and a loving aunt and uncle, Randall Grange is built for addiction. By twenty-three, she knows that together, pills and booze have the power to cure just about any problem she could possibly have . . . right?

Arboria Park by Kate Tyler Wall. $16.95, 978-1631521676. Stacy Halloran's life has always been centered around her beloved neighborhood, a 1950s-era housing development called Arboria Park—so when a massive highway project threaten the Park in the 2000s, she steps up to the task of trying to save it.

Fire & Water by Betsy Graziani Fasbinder. $16.95, 978-1-938314-14-8. Kate Murphy has always played by the rules—but when she meets charismatic artist Jake Bloom, she's forced to navigate the treacherous territory of passionate love, friendship, and family devotion.

Bridge of the Gods by Diane Rios. $16.95, 978-1-63152-244-4. An evil is rising in the land. The country is under attack, and all creatures, man and beast, must hide. As twelve-year-old Chloe struggles to survive, she discovers an ancient magic that still exists deep within the forests—and learns that friendship doesn't always come in human form.